THE BRAVE BULLS

The Brave Bulls

A Novel by **TOM LEA**

With drawings by the author

LITTLE, BROWN AND COMPANY

BOSTON • TORONTO

Published simultaneously
in Canada by McClelland and Stewart Limited

PRINTED IN THE UNITED STATES OF AMERICA

TO THEE

SARAH

J DEDICATE THIS

BOOK

PLAZA DE TOROS
CUENCA

N° 54

SOMBRA
Primera Fila

PREFACE

THE CITY OF Cuenca is rimmed around three sides by blue mountains. It sits down in a valley cup, mellow in the sunshine of Mexican December. The wind blew this morning and a lot of us were worried, when we went by to get our tickets at the Plaza Club, for fear the wind might last and spoil the fight, but it died down a while ago and left just a touch of breeze and perfect weather for the men with the capes.

During the week the curved wall of the bullring is dead and lonesome, a big cement circle around nothing at all, with only the wind to rattle the red gate under the sun-bleached letters that say PLAZA DE TOROS CUENCA 1889. But on Sunday afternoons during the season the curve of the wall comes to life. It reaches around in a big sweep like a magnet and pulls into itself something alive, full of juice and strong feeling.

The day of a bullfight there are pennants alternating red and yellow around the top of the wall so you'll know there's a corrida even if you can't read, and on a pole over the main gate that day they hoist a yellow flag lettered with one red word — TOROS. That's alive too when the breeze lifts it and it moves in the sunlight.

It's a quarter to four when you come down the street to the ring. The minute you get out of the cab you can feel something in the air, with the crowd milling toward the entrance there in the bright sun, and the hubbub of all the voices.

You walk past the lines at the ticket windows into the crowd with the hawkers all yelling; smoke from the frying tacos on the push wagons by the gate and smoke from corn-husk cigarros put the real Mexican twist to the flavor of the air.

The souvenir banderillas the vendors carry above their heads make gaudy clusters of color bobbing through the crowd. You notice the yellow card hooked on the barbed end of each banderilla. A matador's face is printed on the card and under the face there's the name LUIS BELLO. That's who you came to see this afternoon. Luis Bello.

A brass band perched on the outside balcony above the main gate strikes up the "March of Zacatecas." It fits your feeling of being glad you're there with the noise and the color and the expectation moving all over you as you pass from the sunlight into the blue shade cast on the big wall. For a moment you're guilty about feeling so good when the kid with skimmed milk eyeballs holds out his hand at the moving crowd, and you pass the man who can't move because he hasn't got any legs, and even with the brass band going hear the old lady with the sores whining for pennies.

At the bottleneck entrance to the stairs leading up to your section of the stands you lose the beat of the band and get past all the beggars, and then the ticket takers, and scuff up the concrete steps pinned in the crowd to the top where the bottleneck opens out suddenly and there you are high up in the curve of seats that look down on the circle of sand.

You rent a cushion for fifty centavos and carry it under your arm, following the man who has your ticket stub down the aisle and through the gate in the rail that marks off general admission from ringside, to where you climb over the pipe-iron back of your first-row seat and settle down on your cushion.

The life of Cuenca, high and low, has poured with you into the plaza, filling it to the brim. As you take your seat, the crowd is in the last moments of savoring the flavor of itself and its rich expectation before impatience sets in.

On the shady side where seats are more expensive the crowd is genial, but more genteel than on the sunny side where people have louder fun cracking peanuts and drinking beer. Over there a raucous gang of regulars high in the stands gives each flashy babe it spots entering the plaza a chant of *Ole-Ole-Ole!* timed with every step she takes in getting to her seat. If her skirt is tight going up steps, and she smiles, the Oles are deafening, followed by applause.

Some joker over there brought an old sock half full of dry calcimine powder, and you see him wing it into the next section for a laugh. A thick puff of green dust flowers up over the hit; the outraged target, marked with **green,** grabs the sock and slams it back into the crowd. It flies back and forth, ending each flight with a green explosion while the crowd roars, until somebody hides the thing where it falls.

The management sends out one of its handy men carrying a tall sign. It says that throwing bottles or cushions into the ring is punishable by a fine of ninety-nine pesos and ninety-nine centavos by order of the police, and it brings a great hoot of applause while it wobbles solemnly all around the ring. During its exit the rooster imitators — there are hundreds at a bullfight — begin crowing until the stands are one big barnyard.

Out of this rooster medley grows the first impatient round of applause and shouting for the show to begin. It dies down with people looking at their watches and shifting in their seats. The wags who stay awake nights thinking up cracks to yell in the plaza on Sunday warm up with a few bellowing openers about what they paid their money to see this afternoon.

In front of you a concrete parapet bumps your knees; its other side drops straight down eight feet to the level of the ring. An armspread out from the wall is the barrera, the red wooden fence built all around the plaza. Inside the shoulder-high barrera is the bullring proper. The passageway between it and the wall of the stands is the callejon, the alley, just below you, where all the extra personnel serving the corrida will keep out of the way, and where now they are making certain final preparations for the show.

You notice the four narrow openings in the barrera. In front of each one is a wooden shield built parallel to the fence and out from it about the thickness of your body, so that a man can squeeze around it, but not a bull. These shielded openings are called burladeros, and each one is in a different quadrant of the ring. As you look over the parapet you're almost directly above the important one where the matadors will stand when they're not working with the bulls, and where they'll exchange their fighting capes for muletas and swords before they go in to kill.

Swordhandlers and their assistants carrying fancy leather sword cases, wicker baskets full of folded capes and muletas, towels and clay water jugs, come walking around the callejon and put down their loads behind the burladero below. Carefully folded lengthwise, the stiff rose-colored capes with their bright yellow linings are hung over the barrera. The heart-shaped pieces of scarlet woolen serge are shaken out. You watch the experts fold each cloth over the notched stick that forms the muleta handle, fastening it by impaling the serge on a metal point at one end of the stick, then pulling the cloth tight to the other end of the handle where a thumbscrew is set in to hold it. Folded around their handles the ready muletas are laid back into the baskets, and the swords are taken from their tooled cases. The handlers pull them by their red hilts from their limp leather scabbards, give them a final check, push them back into the thin sheathes, and set them against the back side of the barrera, ready.

These servants of the matadors are taking no chances on being unready if the wind comes up again: they're filling their mouths from the water jugs and spewing the lower parts of some of the capes, to make them heavier and less likely to swing the wrong way in a breeze. And so that the cloth will pick up some sand and a little extra stiffness and weight, the handlers use their feet to scuff the lower margins of the capes upon the ground.

A bullring official has tied a string along the back of the barrera farther to your right, and over the string he's hooking the barbs of the approved pairs of matched banderillas for the afternoon's performance. They're bright against the blood-red planking, each pair colored with a different combination of gaudy tissue-paper frills.

New faces are showing above the barrera all around the callejon. Soldiers with rifles slung over their shoulders and policemen wearing big badges and pistols are taking their posts behind the fence, to keep enthusiasm or protest within certain bounds this afternoon. Two photographers have their loaded cameras propped on the top plank of the barrera. Behind one of the shields built in the callejon radio technicians with headphones are setting up equipment for a broadcast. There are a lot of drifting observers, too, mostly in snappy sport suits and sunglasses, who for reasons known or unknown to the management have been allowed into the callejon to rub shoulders with the workings of the corrida. These ground-floor show-offs, waving to their friends in the stands, will be moving much less calmly later if a bull jumps the barrera and gets into the callejon with them. Then they'll be crowding the cops right out of the burladeros.

In the sun over on the opposite side of the ring there are some sections of the barrera that are really gates when they're pushed open on their hinges at certain times during the corrida. They're all in front of passageways leading under the stands to the patios and corrals attached to the ring. The largest is lettered CUADRILLAS on the arch over its entrance, where the matadors and their cuadrillas, their troupes of assistant toreros, form up for the parade at the beginning of the corrida and enter the ring. One of the double gates under the archway is partly open now, and for the first time you catch a glimpse of the bull-fighters in their silks gathered in the shady passageway, waiting.

Over to the left there's a big-bolted red door marked TORILES. Bullfighters call it the Gate of the Fright. It's where the bulls come out. A man is hanging a handful of green and gold ribbons high on the wall by the side of the door; another is tacking a paper sign on the door itself. Those ribbons are divisas, silk streamers fitted on a barb the man will jab into each bull's shoulder, from above, as it comes out of the toril. Every breeder has his own colors to show off proudly, as racing stables have silks. Green and gold are the ribbons of old Don Tiburcio Balbuena of Las Astas. When the man with the tack hammer moves away, the sign on the door says 74 TRAMILLERO. That's the number and the name of the first Las Astas bull that will come tearing out of the toril in a few minutes now.

There are two more openings into the ring. The one marked PICADORES is for the mounted men with their lances; the other is the ARRASTRE where the dead bulls leave the plaza. The picadors' lances are propped against the wall by their gate now, steel points shining in the sun. Between them and the arrastre the callejon is crowded with monos sabios, bullring servants in red shirts and caps, waiting for their chores when the corrida begins.

All these details of the bullring of Cuenca, this sunlit and shaded stage for a drama no one can foretell, are touched now with a kind of magic color and hum from the crowd.

A wave of applause rises up, and you turn to see the President of the Plaza, with his two technical advisers and his bugler, taking his place in the central box marked AUTORIDAD high in the stands at your back. The crowd is not applauding the officials for their popularity: it's cheering because now the referees have come and the show can start.

"O say Mister Judge where have you been?" a fan bawls from the sunny side.

"He overslept," squawks an enthusiast waving a tequila bottle.

And then the band comes in from the balcony, the sun shining on its big brass horns high up there on the rim of the plaza, and it starts to play, play "La Virgen de la Macarena," paso doble of the ancient bull festivals of Sevilla, the old Andaluz song of bravado in the minor key that brings a roar from the throats of the crowd and sinks into the hearts of bullfighters.

The cuadrilla gate is wide open now and there are the three matadors in their silks and gold, lined up in front of their men, three abreast, ready to march out into the ring. The embroidered capes draped over their left shoulders are all gathered about their waists and held tight with their left hands and they stand very still now listening to what the Macarena says with the sun in their eyes.

The first bars are like the strides of a proud man stepping out to accept a challenge. As he walks the music weaves a hollow echo into his steps and doubt takes hold of his heart hearing that echo mock him as he goes. The

drumbeats measure his footfalls then on some darkening
lonesome road where the music casts a black shape against
the sky, and he is afraid. In the silence a trumpet speaks
out all alone.

The trumpet player tilts the horn high over the rim of
the plaza up there in the sun and the notes he makes come
from far beyond a humble trumpeter of Cuenca. They
arch out into the air like hope, clear and sweet, to climb
and turn and fall at last into the quietness encircled by
the big curved wall.

You do not escape the portent says the trumpet. There is
no way I know of walking past the end of the road or singing past the final silence. There's only the way to walk
while the light lasts and the road lasts and the song lasts.
Walking bravely is the glory. The black shape itself may
be a glory when a man is not afraid and can let his heart
reach up and up with the trumpet until it reaches the last
highest and clearest long note, clean and perfect above
the bullring of Cuenca, above the rim of the sierras.

And the trumpet having spoken, the music takes up the
steps of the man walking out to meet a challenge straight
and proud on the road still lit with sunlight, the challenge
yet unmet, the footfalls unfinished in the final measures of
the song of "La Virgen de la Macarena."

Half heard in the applause, the president's bugler blows
the five fanfare notes that signal the corrida to begin. Red-
shirted monos run pushing open the hinged barrera in
front of the cuadrilla gate, the band strikes up a march,
and here come the toreros in step with the music, left arms
wrapped in the capes they hold about their waists with
their left hands, right arms swinging out in time to their

easy level-eyed swagger, stepping as if they were reaching out with their toes to find and feel the smooth sand through the soft soles of their slippers.

The three matadors come first in line, cuadrillas following in file after their masters. Three picadors on their padded nags ride abreast behind the twelve men marching, and bringing up the rear are gaily harnessed mules, their driver afoot with the reins and a whip. Against the sunlit sand and red barrera the color of the parade sings out in gold and sky blue, lilac and silver, crimson, green, orange, pink and purple. The scarlet pompons on the wide beaver hats of the picadors ride like high notes over the brilliance and even the black mules have fluttering flags set in the tops of their polished collars.

That's Luis Bello to the right there in front, and the welcome he gets is louder than the music. With waves of sound pounding down on him, Bello looks up from his level-eyed march, and smiles. The crowd stands and roars.

Out of the sunlight into the shadow they cross the ring straight toward you. A step from the barrera the matadors stop, the parade halts. The bullfighters make their bows to the Judge, inclining their heads forward gravely, touching their hats before they straighten up, setting the black monteras firmly over their brows again. The mules swing out to the left to leave the plaza by the arrastre and the picadors spur the nags for their gate.

The embroidered capes are handed over the barrera to swordhandlers who toss them up for friends in the first row seats to spread for display on the parapet wall above the callejon. Toreros take up the plain fighting capes from the barrera, swinging them open going to their places.

Two men from the cuadrillas walk with capes across their arms to their stations in the burladeros at the sides of the ring.

When the matadors have taken a bow, acknowledging the applause that encircles them, and stepped back behind the barrera, they wet their mouths from the water jugs, take up their capes, and stand together in the burladero just below. You try to read their faces by the lines of their glittering backs as they wait, peering across the ring toward the red door of the toril.

The men with the smoothers finish erasing the last mark of the parade from the sand of the ring, leaving the tan circle empty and untracked. The only noise in the plaza is a hushed hum. The man by the toril is ready with the divisa. There's sweat in the palms of your hands. Then the bugle blows and they unbolt the red door.

THE BRAVE BULLS

ONE

At every bullfight in Cuenca, Eladio Gomez stood behind a plank shield built by the toril door where the bulls came out. He always wore a brown fedora hat and a brown leather jacket and he always stood there in the same place, a solemn brown fixture unnoticed in the

drama that surged around him. Leaning against the planks
with his hat brim pulled down over his eyes, Eladio Gomez
looked considerably less than an implement of fate. Yet
he was. He owned the bullring.

As its sole impresario Eladio Gomez built all the bull-
fights there out of his own brain and cashbox. In so doing
he was a weaver of destinies, a promoter of triumphs, an
agent of calamities, a contractor in the blood of bulls and
men. Yet Gomez certainly did not think of himself in a
dramatic role. His thoughts were usually practical.

He enjoyed certain other features of living, especially
in his earlier years, but now in middle age he had only
two real passions, money and the bulls. If asked, he would
surely say he loved the bulls the best, but that would
hardly be true. In Gomez the two passions had merged so
that they were intermixed and blended for him into a calling. He devoted himself to keeping the blend of his two
passions balanced; whatever he accomplished as a promoter of brave spectacles, he did at the lowest possible
cash cost to Eladio Gomez, in hope of the highest profit.
The figures old Lara totted up in the account book at the
box office on Monday were as stirring to Gomez as the
figures he had watched in his plaza the day before. A happy
man in his calling, Eladio Gomez liked to complain of its
difficulties, its risks, the hardships it worked upon his
health and his state of mind. The frightful specter of losing
money was of course the hardship; the rest of it he loved.

The elements that go into an afternoon of bullfighting
share many of the complicated and mystical elements of
a work of art. Such an afternoon may be anything from a
riotous fiasco to a poignant drama of great symbolic

portent. There's no predicting. There are, however, simple safeguards that reduce the chances of a fiasco: as with any art form, the materials that go into a bullfight have much to do with the shaping of its final quality.

In the gathering of materials for the dramas of which he was proprietor, Eladio Gomez partook of the attributes of an artist himself. Into his bullring he mixed certain ingredients, brought together certain men and certain bulls, and a crowd of a certain attitude and spirit which he tried to shape, and from these ingredients he created the atmosphere out of which the success or failure of his dramas grew. The motives of Eladio Gomez as an artist were passionately commercial. But the end result of his creative efforts at times passionately transcended commercialism; it was this that fascinated Eladio Gomez with the bulls.

The chain of events that led him to the creation of the corrida of December Fourth had their beginnings on Hidalgo Street in Cuenca on a hazy November morning. Upon that morning, finding the bottle in his desk drawer empty, Gomez left his office and walked a block to the Plaza Club for his ten o'clock tequila. It is in such completely ordinary and explainable actions that the weavers of destiny begin their unseen patterns.

Gomez's walk to the Plaza Club that morning was a mystic occurrence. At the precise moment he stepped up to the Plaza bar, Luis Bello, a matador with a hangover, took two aspirin tablets before he went to his uncle's funeral in Guerreras four hundred and thirty kilometers from Cuenca; and a black bull with the tassel missing from his tail licked up the last grain of cracked corn in his stone trough, tossed his head to dislodge a blackbird sitting on his shoulder, and moved to the shade of a giant nopal cactus in a stone-fenced pasture almost seven hundred kilometers from the Plaza Club. It is remarkable that such an unremarkable man as Eladio Gomez should, in going after a drink of tequila, begin to assume the role of an implement of fate for a famous man and a black bull utterly unaware of each other's existence.

Rufino Vega and old Alberto Iriarte were standing at the bar when Gomez walked up and put his foot on the rail.

"Good morning, Eladio. We were speaking of you."

"Good morning, gentlemen. What were you saying?"

"Naturally we were wondering what you are confecting for us these coming Sundays."

"The situation is difficult," said Gomez, shaking his head. He turned to Carlos behind the bar and ordered a tequila. The first swallow burned a sharp trail down his throat, and the heat spread down through his middle, right out to the silver buckle on his belt. "It is hard to get bulls, gentlemen. And a number of toreros are not eager to sign this early for any appearance in Cuenca until their richer contracts are scheduled. It is our misfortune here in Cuenca to take what is left."

"We have misfortune in the matter of the bulls, all right," boomed old Alberto. "It is painful to remember recent scandals. I may tell you it is the general feeling that our friend Eladio Gomez might improve his cards."

Gomez's stiff face gave no indication that the Spaniard's words were as hot to his insides as the tequila.

"Just how do you propose this improvement, Don Alberto?"

"Our city of Cuenca should be enabled to witness, occasionally, a real corrida of bulls. The truth is that when we have good bulls we watch cowards and incompetents kill them; and when we have a brave man in Cuenca he finds himself waving his cloth across the face of a cart ox. It is the ancient complaint. You must complain to yourself about it."

"May I ask, Don Alberto, if you believe it possible to put a clause in a contract that will make a man brave? That will give him style? And may I also ask if you believe it possible for me, owner of one of the modest rings out in the states of the Republic, to compete in price with the immense plazas that pay criminal sums to get all the first class bulls?"

In his heat Eladio Gomez asked Carlos for another tequila.

"My friend," said Iriarte, "it is unjust to blame an impresario for everything. But he gets the blame. As a penalty of his position, his financial interest in the brave festival. Now, it is no personal criticism against you when I say I hope to see a real man against a real bull when I attend your plaza."

"My effort is to provide that spectacle. Bookings are going forward. They promise well."

"Who will lead off on the Day of Santa Barbara?" asked Rufino Vega.

It had worried Eladio Gomez for some time. He did not know. The date of the opening of the real season in Cuenca was still blank, December Fourth, just twenty days ahead.

"I'm working on it. It will be good." The impresario finished his second tequila with a gulp, and wiped his mouth.

"But who?"

For no reason at all, then, when his mind reached out for a name, any good name, Eladio Gomez said, "I'm trying to sign Luis Bello."

"Good for you!" snorted old Iriarte. "Can you get him?"

"I don't know yet," said Gomez, truthfully. He hadn't tried.

"Get him. And what bulls?" pursued the rich old Spaniard.

"Maybe Tierra Negra, or Buenpaso," said Gomez, again truthfully. He had contracted for such bulls.

"Bello deserves better than that," declared the fat Rufino.

Gomez scowled. "It's not all settled yet."

Iriarte put his hand on Gomez's shoulder. "We remember Bello killing his second bull here last February, eh, Eladio? That was one of Bello's afternoons!"

"May I mention it was also one of ours?" Gomez asked.

"Ai, Eladio. Of course we give you thanks!" He showed his false teeth under his white mustaches. "Have another drink."

Gomez touched his empty glass. "I seldom take even a second, before noon. Thank you. I have to get back to the office."

He paid Carlos for his own two tequilas and walked out into Hidalgo Street where the sun had burned away the morning haze, and he stepped through strips of cool shade and warm light along the sidewalk back to the sign that read EMPRESA DE TOROS CUENCA.

He opened the door and walked past blurred rotogravure portraits of smiling matadors into the dimness of the big room. Behind a railing and a box office window sat old Lara on his high stool at his high desk, his bald head and spectacles shining in the light of one unshaded bulb hanging on a thin wire from the ceiling over him. He was sorting books of tickets. Gomez went through a swinging gate in the railing and walked over to his desk where a man in overalls stood waiting.

"Listen Sanchez, the ring needs paint. I am offering you the work because you will go easy on the price. Here is a list of what is necessary. You got a man for sign lettering?"

"Yes senor."

"The box offices need lettering and the signs on the cuadrillas and so forth look bad. But nothing doing unless you give me your best consideration. It may be too expensive to paint in front of the ringside rail. Anyway bring me your figures. We got to start."

"Yes senor," said Sanchez. He left.

Gomez sat down at his desk and turned on the lamp. It threw a queer light into the dusty glass eyes of the stuffed bull's head that loomed out from the wall over the desk, the bull that killed Cayetano Chavez in '36. Gomez looked like a gnome sitting there with his brown hat on in the dim light under the bull's head. He leaned back in his chair, nursing his feelings against fools like Iriarte and that fat Vega. A belch from the two tequilas broke the silence.

"Anybody want me, Lara?"

"The bills of lading for the Buenpaso bulls are here. And Santana was on the phone. Said he would call later."

That Santana coyote that gobbles money, thought Eladio Gomez. He eats my money and makes my propaganda but he eats better than he makes. He better make some propaganda soon. To be just, there was something to what that rich old Spanish son of —

The battered nickel-plated French phone on his desk jangled, and he picked it up.

"Yes, Senor Colonel! Clearly. I am always attentive. Exactly. Exactly as you wish. Your co-operation is magnificent. Of course I will send them. It is a pleasure, an honor. Until I see you, Senor Colonel."

And that army coyote that eats my tickets, thought Gomez. Eats my tickets and makes my "military protection" — such protection — at the plaza. That coyote with the big bite.

"Lara, fix up twelve front-row season passes for Colonel Villalobos and put them in an envelope with his name on it."

Gomez leaned back in his chair again, clasped his hands on the back of his neck under his hat brim, and sighed.

Why this morning did I happen to say Luis Bello, that high-priced bastard, thought Gomez. They reached for it like candy, those two grandstand Senecas that know so much sitting up there where there are no horns but the kind that grow on cuckolds' heads.

That Bello was something the last time he was here, all right. He lays that sword in like he was killing the Antichrist. But too expensive. Too goddamned expensive.

He sat silent for several minutes, while money and the bulls fought a battle. Maybe the double ten o'clock tequila upset the balance, and carried the field of battle. Some unaccustomed element that morning brought up reinforcements for the bulls. With his face solemnly set as if nothing had happened, Eladio Gomez reached for the phone, reluctantly.

"Young lady, get me long distance. Mexico City."

TWO

LUIS BELLO WOKE UP in the dark. He had awakened in so many unfamiliar rooms that always when sleep left him now his first thought was to place himself and remember. It took him a moment to decide where he was, in his mother's house, in the house he had bought for her, in his home town.

His leg hurt. He put his hand on his right thigh and touched the place. That's just sore from the healing where they took the drain out, Bello said to himself. There's no more infection. There can't be any more infection. He looked up into the dark and thought hard, holding the thought until he was tense thinking to himself, There's no infection now. It hurts because it's getting well.

His feet began to sweat, and he kicked them over to a new cool place under the covers. He could feel his mind swinging off at a tangent too fast to fit his body that ached all over asking for sleep. He fumbled through his pockets on the chair by the bed until he found his matches and he struck a light. It flamed orange and violent in his face while he squinted, reading his watch. The hands pointed to thirty-four minutes after four.

Jesus and Mary I've only slept a couple of hours. I'm all right now, I'm well, I'm ready, why can't I sleep? He put his hand inside the leg of his underwear and laid it on the welt where his thigh hurt, and he ran his hand all over the scarred flesh of the thigh feeling the hollows, the twisted wrinkles, the bumps from old stitches that no longer hurt like the welt.

The bulls have horns, said Luis Bello to himself there in the dark. They got horns all right. It brought a kind of comfort because it was certainly true. There wouldn't be anything to it if the bulls didn't have horns. But they did. There in the dark there was something mysterious about the horns.

Luis Bello did not like making mysteries inside of his head. But he was making them now. Here they came, crowding in on him while his ears burned and his eyeballs felt dry looking up into the dark.

I'm off my stride. Seven days home in Guerreras and I'm way goddamned off.

That corrida Sunday and then the old man dying in his chair. My leg. My brother Pepe: I wish it had been a triumph for him Sunday, us fighting together for the first time. It was certainly no triumph. But old Uncle Pedro, that's the worst. He was a father.

He used to get me up, a long time ago. He used to get me up about this time in the night when I was a kid without shoes. We milked the cows. We poured the milk in the pans and then broke the eggs in the milk. I remember how we'd bring up the horses when it was getting light. Those horses were giants with big long yellow teeth arching down over me while they sucked loud on the milk and eggs.

Some of that stuff never got to the horses. The uncle tried to feed us, he tried, and I helped him, us Bellos without a father, living in the three rooms with all those yelping cousins, fifteen people always hungry. While the horses had the milk and eggs. And those big high mountains of oats I sifted with my fingers bleeding. All for the pretty horses to run nice for Don Angel Pedrazo. I ran nice myself when that son of a filth swung his whip at me.

The bulls have brought us along, thought Luis Bello. He ran his hand over the deep scar in his left armpit. The bulls have done some good things. All the old uncle ever had to do after I got in the money was sit on a chair. He got a damn good rest before he died. He got a damn nice coffin. Some of the others that hang around here being related to Luis Bello, Jesus in His Sacred Name I'm tired of them.

I wish it was light. He heard a rooster crow outside far away and another answered. I wish I was out of Guerreras. I wish I was with Linda. He turned on his side and as he lay looking wide-eyed into the darkness, for the first time he heard the deep regular breathing of his brother Pepe in bed on the other side of the room. I used to sleep like that, Luis Bello lay thinking.

His mind drifted slowly away from namable things, out into the dark, into the blackness which was the color of the bulls, the color of the old man's coffin. He drifted out so far into the blackness he fell asleep.

A knock on the door brought him suddenly awake; he opened his eyes and the room was light.

"Luis! It's Chona. I've got a message!"

"Come in, chicken. What do you want?"

A brown-faced little girl with her hair braided in pig-tails opened the door. "Luis, a man from Aguilar's store is here and says the long distance is calling you on the telephone over there." Her eyes were round with her importance.

Pepe Bello raised his head from the other rumpled bed in the room. "What's all this?"

"Long distance for me, she says. It must be Raul. Look, Chonita, tell the man I'm coming as soon as I get dressed."

The door closed and Luis got out of bed.

"Raul's the only one that knows how to call me at Aguilar's. This is early in the morning for Raul. I wonder what he wants."

"Hope it's good," said Pepe. "Find out what he's doing for me too, will you, Mano?"

Luis pulled on his pleated pants and yellow sport shirt. "Sure Pepillo, we'll fix you up." He straightened the long tabs of the sporty collar, and combed his hair, slicking it back from the careful part. When he had buttoned his tweed jacket, he took a handkerchief from its pocket and wiped the corners of his mouth. Then he cleared his throat and spit in the corner.

"I wish we could get a phone installed in this house. Aguilar's is a nuisance. Get up, Pepe. We'll have some coffee after I talk to Raul."

Luis stepped across the patio, unbolted the door to the street, and walked out into the sun. His eyes flinched from the glare of the whitewashed walls as he walked along the empty street under the plumes of the tamarisk trees. He came around the corner of the Good Faith Grocery Store and walked in past the smell of roasting coffee, then strong meat, then moth balls, and beyond, to the open door of the office where he smelled the smoke of Aguilar's morning cigar.

"Ah, Luis!" beamed Aguilar, jumping up from his desk under the big calendar on the wall. "How are you?" The calendar was lithographed with a gaudy painting of Luis Bello in a veronica with a black bull.

"Well, many thanks," said Luis, looking at the calendar. It advertised a laxative.

"And your mother, and all the family?"

"Also well. I would like to get long distance again."

"Ah, Luis, be seated please. Allow me to get the connection. Have a cigar."

Luis lit the cigar while Aguilar stood at the wall telephone.

"Senorita? Casimiro Aguilar speaking. I now have Luis Bello at my phone ready to speak to Mexico. Yes of course Luis Bello himself, the matador. I await the connection." Aguilar adjusted a frown over his iron-rimmed spectacles and brushed his mustaches.

"Eh?" said Aguilar finally. "One moment."

Luis took the receiver. "Bueno. Luis Bello. That you, Raul?"

"This is Raul. What do you say, boy?"

"How did you crawl out of bed at this hour?"

"I didn't yet. Listen Luis, how'd you like to be on the card in the Plaza Mexico this Sunday?"

"Huh? What's that?"

"Velazquez got gored yesterday in Puebla and can't fight Sunday."

"Gored bad?"

"They say bad."

"God damn the bulls!"

"Wait a minute, Luis. This is a break for you. They called me from the bullring office last night and offered to put you on in Velazquez's place. I tried to get you on the phone last night, but nobody answered. This will be an extra appearance for you in the Big One. Same deal as your regular scheduled contracts there. How about that?"

"Okay Raul. Good. What are the bulls?"

"They say they were hand-picked at La Punta. You better get over to Monterrey today and catch the plane. Say, how's your leg?"

"All right. I'm coming. Did the cuadrilla get there all right after our fight here?"

"Well, they got here. Somebody stole one of the sword cases on the train. Tacho is losing hair over it. Monkey Garcia got thrown in jail Tuesday. Two hundred pesos fine. I got him out. Your Jackdaw the Picador is having wife trouble again. But I'll get them all in line today when I tell them they're in the Big One Sunday. They were thinking they could be shameless for another week until they leave for the Guadalajara booking. They weren't expecting this."

"Neither was I," said the matador.

"Say Luis, I had to spend some money on Pepe's propaganda. I got him the center spread double truck in *Taurino* for this week, like you wanted. The photo is the one you and Pepe liked. It says under the picture — here, I'll read it — 'Jose Antonio PEPE BELLO, young brother of the Grand Killer of Guerreras, receiving the Sword and Cloth at the hands of Fermin Espinosa, ARMILLITA, when Pepe took his Doctorate of Bulls in the Plaza of Guerreras last Sunday. The brilliant young Bello alternated with his brother and the Master from Saltillo, dispatching bulls from Buenpaso in an afternoon of valor and triumph.'"

"Hm. They hit us very hard for that?"

"Tell you when I see you."

"Raul, what else you doing for that kid?"

"That's another thing I called about. It's hard to sign him now until he does some more as a full matador — frankly, even if he is your brother. You know that."

"Listen. Pepe had no luck Sunday at his debut because he had to fight goats, not bulls. Otherwise — "

"I know. I know. Pepe's a sweetheart when he's got a real bug to play with. I have an idea. Yesterday Eladio Gomez phoned me. Wanted to sign you as First Sword on a special what he called extra-fine corrida at Cuenca two weeks from Sunday, the week after the Guadalajara trip."

"I know those extra-fine corridas at Cuenca. I know them well."

"As I was saying, Luis, I had an idea. They really like you at Cuenca. Why don't I tell Gomez you will appear in his plaza if he will take Pepe on the card with you?"

"I will tell you why you don't tell Gomez that. I am goddamned tired of the goats and oxen people like him put in the ring for us to slaughter while the crowd throws cushions." Bello was abruptly conscious of Aguilar listening, and he did not go on.

"Fix yourself, man," said Raul on the phone. "Suppose Gomez got some real bulls for you, four-year-olds with the ancestry in them?"

"He won't spend the money. I know him."

"But if Gomez really got bulls, would you and Pepe sign for his corrida two weeks from Sunday?"

"Why not? But you're blowing smoke."

"You might be wrong. Remember all the corners in this business. What bulls would you like at Cuenca?"

"Agent mine, nothing but the finest. Coming around the corners you mention like miracles in the church. You tell Gomez when he encloses in his plaza pens six Number One bulls from Las Astas, I will come to Cuenca with Pepe for what is called the most beautiful festival of all. That is a laugh. But you tell Gomez if he gets no Astas he will get no Bellos."

Raul whistled. "Las Astas at Cuenca? Okay Luis, I'll tell him. I really want to put Pepe on some cards."

"Good. I'll be on the plane from Monterrey tomorrow afternoon. Meet me in the car, will you? And listen, tell Linda I'm coming. How is she?"

"Linda's fine. I'll tell her."

"Okay, Raul. Until tomorrow." He hung up the receiver. "Many thanks, Don Casimiro."

Aguilar arose from his desk and the papers he had been pretending to read. "My great pleasure, Luis," he said, looking hesitant as if he had something to ask.

"Oh," said Bello, "that was my manager, Raul Fuentes. Antonio Velazquez has been gored and I'm taking his place in the Plaza Mexico Sunday."

"Ah, splendid," said Aguilar as if he had not heard. He hesitated a moment longer, touched his spectacles, and then blurted what he had to say:

"I feel deeply, bothering you with a detail at this time, my admired friend Luis, but there is a matter of a grocery bill that has doubtless escaped your attention. A bill for several months of goods I have sold to your mother's house. It now amounts to some four thousand-odd pesos, and I am sure you would like to liquidate it to aid me in my affairs."

"Christ and Mary, Aguilar. Hasn't my brother Alfredo been taking care of the bill? I send him money for all such things."

"He has not paid anything here since May."

"Damn him. I didn't know it. Give me that statement, Aguilar. I'll send you a check from Mexico. Thanks for treating my mother with consideration."

"Ah, Luis. I am your attentive servant. Discussing this matter has given me pain."

Bello took the statement from Aguilar's hand. "It pains me too. It's a pain in the ass."

His anger grew with every step homeward. Grinding his jaws he raveled out the end of the cigar clenched in his front teeth. It tasted sour. His head pounded, and his stomach felt empty.

I don't have any worries. Nothing to think about. Nothing but little things. Like those two black bulls from La Punta waiting for me with their horns on Sunday and me waiting for them so I can keep my brother Alfredo in fancy whores.

He threw away the cigar and spit. When he jerked open the door, his mother stood in the patio waiting for him.

"Good morning, son. What did the telephone say?" She saw his anger. "What troubles you?"

"Where's Alfredo?"

"Help me God, something has happened now! He's not in the house this morning. Tell me, Luis, what the telephone said!"

"The telephone said nothing about Alfredo. Nothing has happened yet. It's about to. He's been using the money again. This time more than four thousand pesos owed Aguilar since May."

He held out the statement, forgetting his mother could not read.

"He's no brother of mine. Not any more, he isn't."

Senora Bello began to weep silently, a thin figure dressed in black mourning for her brother Pedro. She wept now for more than Pedro, for more than anything she could name, standing before her oldest son, Luis, who was a stranger to her from another world. Weeping silently, she blamed Alfredo, but she understood him. She understood her children Carmela, Rosa, Eulalia, the sainted Juan and little Maria who were in Heaven, and even her baby boy Pepe. But not this Luis.

She did not grasp the undreamable life he bought her in a house of her own, matron of a family, mother of a famous man. It confused her. She was not prepared to meet it as she met the old accustomed and familiar anguishes she had always known before Luis went away. So she wept, standing in front of her stranger son, who was disowning one of his brothers now, and who had carried away another, her baby Pepe, away from her forever into a world she did not understand.

She began to listen to what Luis was saying. " — I'll kick them out. I'll sell this place and take you to Mexico with me and these good-for-nothings around here can all start scratching for themselves." Terrified with the threat of being carried away into Luis's alien world, she sobbed.

Her daughter Rosa heard, and came out the kitchen door. "What in God's name is wrong now?" she asked, looking at her brother.

"I'm tired of moochers living in this house without shame."

"Meaning who?"

"At this moment meaning Alfredo. It should be easy for you to name others." He shot a glance at the kitchen door, where Rosa's husband immediately retired from view.

Eulalia and Aunt Teresa entered the patio just as Pepe

came out of his room. Three men and another aunt followed them.

"What passes?" quavered the fat Aunt Teresa, rolling her eyes, while Eulalia put her arms around her mother. Cousin Lupe carrying a baby, and little Chona with the pigtails, hurried out to join the muster.

Luis felt foolish in the middle of this gathering. His eldest sister, Carmela, appeared and walked up to his side. "What happened, Luis?"

Alfredo Bello chose this unfortunate moment to burst into the patio from the street door. Red-eyed and grinning, he sidled unsteadily up to his mother.

"Were you worrying about me?" he asked, looking around. "It was a fortunate accident. Thanks to God I can tell you that I am unhurt."

He barely lifted his eyes toward Luis in the silence. "But I'm afraid the car is damaged."

All the old rages gathered into one and rose up in Luis Bello's throat. He grabbed his brother Alfredo by the collar, yanked him away from his mother, and with all the power of his sword arm and thick bullfighter's wrist he slapped Alfredo in the face, holding him up and pulling him close.

"Listen — you — you. Get out! I've had enough of you. Don't say you're sorry! You're through."

"Open that door, Pepe. Open it!"

"Now Alfredo Bello, you professional brother of a bullfighter and disgrace to a name, you're finished. You're leaving. So help me Christ if you enter this house again I'll take the puntilla my peon uses to cut the ears off my bulls and I'll carve the guts out of your belly — "

He kicked his brother into the street, slammed the door shut with a crash, and whirled around with his fists clenched, facing his family. They gazed at him paralyzed.

"I'm glad you were all here! You saw it. It's about time. It shows what I got to think about. Everybody asking for money. You ask me for money in my sleep! I pay for this house, I pay for everything, with my flesh. My flesh, you understand? The flesh I expose to the bulls while you get rotten with fat!"

The Bello family stood there like oxen, looking at him, the stranger from another world. Then Luis Bello was ashamed. He was ashamed not of his rage, but of the way his own family stood there like oxen. Cart oxen by God, the kind that always gave you trouble. For a moment he was silent, then he turned to his mother.

"Well. I'm sorry. None of this was for you." He glanced around. "Nor for Pepe. He knows. Nor for Carmela." Finally he almost smiled. "Nor for anyone here. I'm sorry."

He put his arm around his mother's shoulders and spoke to her. "The telephone call was from Raul Fuentes. Sunday I will fight in the Plaza Mexico, taking the place of a man who has been gored. So my visit with you is ending now. This afternoon I go on the train to Monterrey. Let's have some breakfast together, and finish our visit."

At two-thirty that afternoon Rosa's husband went out and found a taxi. Every man in the Bello household tried to help Luis put a handsome pigskin traveling case, initialed LB, in the front seat by the driver. While all the family, and some of the neighbors, stood on the sidewalk around them, Luis kissed his mother good-by. Pepe got in the cab too, and everybody waved to them as they drove away.

Luis sat back and lit a cigar. He felt better. He always felt better leaving that house.

"I think I'll leave tonight, myself," said Pepe, sensing his brother's relief.

"Where you going, kid?"

"Don Julian's. We're both invited, remember? Loco Ruiz has been after me all week, now he's got that car, to go over with a few of the boys and ask Don Julian if they can take part in testing the heifers, and practice their capes."

"You think that tin tragedy of Ruiz's would make it all the way to Hacienda del Sauz from here?"

"Oh, if the gang goes there's lots of muscle. We could carry it to El Sauz. I feel like going, now that you're leaving — and I haven't got a booking. I'll unwind my muleta and remind some people down there that I'm still around."

"Good idea," said Luis. "Don Julian's a great one. Wish I was going too," he added, not entirely with truth. He was thinking about Linda tomorrow.

"Tell Raul where I'll be," said Pepe, "in case he wants me."

"Sure, Pepe. You coming back to Guerreras after the tientas?"

"I guess so."

"No. Come on down to the house in Mexico. Raul will have you booked by then."

"He better," said Pepe. "I'm a matador without bulls. I got nothing to kill but time."

"Don't worry. Raul's got irons in the fire. So have I. If you get a chance, Manito, work with your sword. You're fine with the left, but I don't think you are keeping your right wrist quite straight. When you kill you should not have a right wrist. I know you know it, but watch it — says the old man." He grinned and puffed the cigar.

The taxi drew up by the platform in front of the station, and a dozen cargadores crowded up to take Luis's baggage from the front seat.

"Hey, Number 34," called Pepe.

Number 34 tipped his cap, lifted out the case, and then noticed who had called his number.

"Ole! Los Bellos! Gentlemen!" he cried. "At your orders!"

"The train for Monterrey," said Luis. "We want to buy a ticket, and then a drink."

The Bello brothers sat in the crowded station cafe, waiting for the train, which was late, and drinking beer.

"I guess Alfredo will be back in the house by morning," said Luis Bello. "He will come back sober, with tears in his eyes, and they will let him in. What a nigger-supper that was this morning!

"One thing, we will try Carmela with the money. She says she can handle it. From now on our checks to the family are payable only to Carmela Bello. She's pretty tough."

"Thanks for saying 'our' checks, Mano. I'm a big help."

"Hell, man, you're our insurance policy!"

They both laughed, Luis thinking of the horns on the bulls, and Pepe just thinking of the bulls.

When the train came in, Number 34 put Luis's case in the Pullman and got his pay.

"One thing you forgot to tell me, Luis. Are we going to wear black on our sleeves when we go into the ring, for Uncle Pedro?"

"I thought about that. I think we should. We ought to do it, Pepe. We'll wear the black band."

"Have luck Sunday," said Pepe to his brother, standing by the Pullman steps.

"Go with God, Pepillo. You'll have plenty of chances soon. See you next week in Mexico. Need any money?"

"Eehoh! After this morning?" Pepe grinned. "I'm in good condition."

They gave each other the abrazo, the formal hug, patting each other on the back.

"I'll find Loco and the bunch," said Pepe. "They'll be rabid about El Sauz. I wish Alfredo hadn't wrecked our car."

He waved, and Luis climbed on the train.

THREE

THE TRAIN WHISTLED and slowly started chuffing down the track, carrying Luis toward Mexico, toward the center of the world. Pepe Bello walked alone along the street from the station, uncomfortable in his mind. The achievement of his new rank as matador seemed empty now. Luis had paved the way too easily. Pepe knew his luck in having such a brother. He could never be blind to that. But he felt he could only be grateful for it, not proud, and it made him ill at ease. It seemed to Pepe Bello that the world judged him unjustly, making him a mere by-product of his older brother's fame. He nursed a fiery ambition of his own within himself, and in this he suffered the misfortune, as much as he enjoyed the advantage, of being the kid brother of the Swordsman of Guerreras. Naturally he loved his brother. And was grateful. Naturally he envied him, too.

He envied him, for instance, for the chance Luis would have in Mexico on Sunday afternoon. As he walked along his envy flowed into a daydream. Vividly he felt himself bowing with bared head in the huge plaza, as some great veteran of the ring ceded him, Pepe Bello, his first bull there. He could feel the flannel-wrapped hilt of the sword in his hand, and the handle of the muleta, notched under the scarlet serge, firmly in his grasp. Fifty thousand people watched him, in the center of the world. Pepe Bello was motioning his peons away, was walking out alone to that huge bull, was proving something in a glorious whirl of red and gold, when a battered old car skidded and stopped by the curb at his side.

The car door swung open for him and he saw his two pals, Loco Ruiz and Ramon Delgado, grinning. Ruiz had campaigned with him as an aspirant matador in many bullrings of Mexico. Delgado had renounced his ambitions as a matador to become a member of Pepe's new cuadrilla.

"I was on my way to find you," said Pepe, climbing in the car. "Shall we go to El Sauz?"

Loco rapped the steering wheel with pleasure. "I didn't think you could go. What happened?"

"Luis left on the train just now. Velazquez is gored and Luis is taking his place Sunday in the Mexico."

Delgado whistled. "When do we do that, matador? That is the real peluco."

"Give me time, peon. How about this car, Loco?"

"It will go. Chato can look it over when we buy gasoline."

"You forget I am the expert of engines," said Delgado. "I will keep this thing running like I did the jeeps of Africa."

"People all left Africa tired of your jeeps or your something, Big Gringo. I don't blame them. Jank is a good name for you, Jank," said Loco Ruiz.

"Jank Delgado, the man with the big pistol."

"Listen, Big Pistol, are you going to the tientas with us? Or do you want some money to go to Mexico and wait for me there with the rest of the cuadrilla?"

"I want some money, Don Jose Bello, but I would rather go to the tientas. I am growing so fond of the great Ruiz here. I'd like to see the cows rip his drawers. Who else is going?"

"Carlos of course. Pepote Vera. How about Piki Arenas? He's good for a laugh."

"We're forgetting Abundio," said Pepe. Abundio de la O was Pepe's swordhandler and the owner of the shortest last name in Mexico. "I want to take care of him. Drive me by his house now, Loco."

"He's not there," said the Jank. He had been staying at Abundio's house. "He's out with the boys."

All the novilleros, the aspirant young bullfighters of the

town, made La Azteca their hangout. Yet none of them were there when Delgado got out of Loco's car and went in the bar to find them. So Loco headed his car out the tree-lined Paseo, and drove to the ball field on the edge of town.

In front of the entrance gate, instead of turning off the ignition with the key, Loco reached down under the dashboard and pulled loose a wire about a foot long. He put it in his pocket. "That thieving brother of mine had a key made so he could steal this bug in the evenings," said Loco. "Now the key does him no good." He patted his pocket. "This is a great gringo invention from the war."

"From the jeeps," said the Jank.

They walked through the gate in the billboard fence and onto the field. It was empty and desolate except for a few familiar figures in front of home plate. A faded muleta moved solemnly in the sunlight there as Carlos Bandera, with his feet firmly planted, executed the final passes of a grand faena while his friend Pepote Vera bent over and charged him running, holding a sharp pair of horns in front of his head like a bull. Pepote lunged for a last charge and Carlos passed him by his belly with a spinning end figure called a molinete. He finished with style, looking arrogantly over his shoulder, the red cloth wrapped neatly around his thighs, and he held the pose. Pepote jabbed him in the rump with a horn.

"Ai, the wasp stung Lupe!" sang out the Jank.

"Pack up the rags, boys. Pepe is taking us to El Sauz. Tonight."

"I'm sorry you can't all go," Pepe said as they gathered in a knot around him. "Just six. People who have fought

in a real plaza. Delgado here, and Loco and me. Carlos
and Pepote. And Piki. Say, where is Piki?"

"That cow jumper had a date. He's gone."

"To hell with Piki. Anyway, he'd rather be doing veron·
icas with a bed sheet."

"No," said the Jank, "de frente por detras." They all
howled like wolves.

"What about taking me to El Sauz?" asked Abundio
de la O.

"Don't you want to go to Mexico and wait for me
there?"

"It would be better for me to go to El Sauz. I can serve
you, Pepe."

"Okay, Little O. You can start by going to my house
and packing my stuff. We're going to Mexico from the
tientas, so we'll have to take everything — the case with
my trajes for the ring, the swords, and the bag with my
regular clothes. Loco's cockroach will look like a troop
train."

"Before we go," said Pepote Vera, "dirty the milk, but
Carlos has got to run the horns for me. He owes me. Come
on, man."

"Only a short one," Carlos grunted. Nobody liked to
run the horns.

"Huh, Toro!" said Pepote as Carlos charged. "A nat·
ural with the left. Hah! Another. Huh! Another so beautiful. Huhh! See the forced return of the cloth across the
chest. Classic, my friends. Ai, Toro! Don't cut in like that,
you bull of one ball. Huh huh! Keep that nose bathed in
the cloth. *Huh!* Now watch. I'll break his back. I'll twist
him like a string. Take it, bull. Huhhh!"

He swung the muleta in a sharp flamboyant afarolado, a red whirl of cloth up and around his head, and saun- tered away with his back to the bull. "How's that?"

"It will put the musicians to work," said Loco. "If they're blind. Let's go!"

It was dark when he finally came back to the Bello house to pick up Pepe, Abundio de la O, and the baggage. Over at the garage Chato had worked on the engine for a couple of hours while Loco and the boys, their capes and muletas bundled and ready, sat drinking on credit and waiting at La Azteca.

Their wait was better than Pepe's, who got very anxious, waiting for Loco to come. While Abundio packed his gear, and stacked it by the street door, Pepe found himself sur- rounded with family. Nobody wanted him to leave. Car- mela wanted advice about the new purse strings, Rosa's husband wanted to talk about the towing bill, and the repairs, on the car Alfredo had wrecked. The undertaker came by, with a tombstone carver for Uncle Pedro. Pepe wanted to walk out easy, but he had to run a long gantlet of farewells, dutifully, to his sisters, his in-laws, his aunts and uncles, his cousins. And of course he had to see his mother and tell her he was going away.

After three seasons as a novillero, and many leave- takings from Guerreras, there were still scenes. His mother always wept and asked, asked him why he fought bulls, why he could not stay home and enter some nice business, her baby who had been to school, who had been the object of her hopes, who was so promising, whom she loved so much, prayed for so much.

It was always awkward and he never knew what to do

about it. So he would always stand there until she had no more words, and then he would put his hand on her shoulder and kiss her on the forehead and tell her everything was fine, not to cry.

He couldn't explain it to his mother, why he fought bulls. He couldn't explain it to anybody. Besides, an explanation wouldn't do anybody any good. It was a fever, and he had it. It was not namable, thought Pepe Bello. The fame didn't explain it; neither did the money. It came from deep down. It made men want to fight bulls the way other men had to climb high mountains or shoot bears or paint naked women. But he would not say that to his mother. In the first place, she would not believe it. So he kissed her good-by saying everything was fine; when he climbed in Loco's car at last, he felt better. He felt just like Luis lighting a cigar.

"Let's go," he said.

"Listen to it purr," said Loco, racing the engine with the clutch in, as they turned the corner on the main square of Guerreras. He drove around the bandstand twice, racing the engine, hoping to see his girl, but she wasn't there.

Four blocks down a side street they pulled up in front of La Azteca. The lights were warm and bright inside. Behind the bar the Indio stood, a dirty white apron spread tight over his vast belly. His gold teeth gleamed as he laughed when Pepe walked in.

"Ai, matador," called the Indio, "take these goats out of here. They are drying up the place and paying nothing."

"What goes, Indio? Little O and I want aguardiente. Then this evil meeting travels toward El Sauz."

The Indio came to the swinging door and watched the boys pack themselves and their gear into the car.

"Make the little cows work," he called. "The four-footed kind."

Loco attached his wire, stepped on the starter, and nothing happened. He checked the wire and tried again. The engine was dead.

"Try the lights," said Jank Delgado.

Loco flipped the switch and the lights did not come on.

The Jank crawled out. "It's a chort," he said. "Pile out, lice. Push. Maybe it will run on the generator."

They pushed a block and the engine stayed dead. "Dirt of the apostles!" said Loco Ruiz, working the choke. Sweating, the calves of their legs aching, they pushed Loco's bug all the way to Chato's garage.

Back at La Azteca they waited for Chato to fix the car. A cold November wind came down from the mountains, sighing through the emptying streets of Guerreras, but the lights stayed bright in the bar. The phonograph wailed songs of rancheros bereft of love and the golden smile of the Indio floated above the liquor that poured from the bottles into the glasses on his bar.

He was a touch for toreros. Indalecio Narbona had tried once in his youth to be a torero himself. He knew all about it. He had entered a ring once. He had cited a bull, saying "Huh, huh" just right, down in his throat, holding the cloth just so. But the bull charged with the sound of a rocket, and the future proprietor of La Azteca forgot what the cape was for. He ran. Safe behind a burladero, his face the color of ashes, he found that his fever to fight bulls had all drained away. It returned slowly, like the color in his face, but changed, sublimated from a desire to fight bulls himself into a worshipful joy in these heroes who really did. Since then he had devoted his life to the bulls a step or two removed from their horns, a step behind the barrera, a step behind his bar. In this devotion he gave food and drink to toreros on credit because he loved them, because they fought the bulls for him, always so bravely and well, there in the arena he built in his own simple mind over the well-wiped varnish of his bar.

"You would not believe the triumph I had on the third of August in the Plaza of San Marcos, Indio, my friend," said Carlos Bandera. "It was an apotheosis, like the critics use the big words in *La Lidia*. I was rabid. You should have seen the way I killed my second bull. One enormous thrust. Like this, profiling, going in, in, right in the highest crest, right in the eye of the needle. *Zaz!* The bull rolled over like a sack, his four feet in the air, and I just stood there smiling, limp, while the crowd armed a scandal of applause. Smoke came from the palms of their hands. Handkerchiefs waved. The handkerchiefs were a big white cloud covering the stands while the crowd roared. It was a moment, Indio, when they handed me that bull's ears. I held them up like this, making circuits of the ring. There were tears in the eyes of beautiful women. Hats and cigars pelted down like rain."

The door from the street swung open hard and Piki Arenas came in, uncertain on his feet, blinking in the light.

"Look at that thing! Look at it!" yelled Pepote Vera. "He's been working inside the horns all right. Look how the points pushed him around!"

"Hola," said Piki Arenas.

"He got tossed — off the bed!"

"He got disarmed."

"How's your sword, torero?"

"What do the doctors say?"

"Wound of fourteen centimeters in the seam of the breeches. Prognosis at the plaza infirmary: Very grave. Thirty days in jail with a syringe or in bed alone!"

"Frill yourselves, oxen," said Piki Arenas. "Ole for the fathers of purity!"

"Mule collar man," said Loco Ruiz, "come over and have a drink. Hear how you might have gone to El Sauz with us if you had saved enough of yourself to travel."

"A drink did you say?" asked Piki Arenas. "Maybe a little taco to eat if the Indio can spare it?"

"Indio," said Pepe Bello, "this man with the filthy wound does not talk so crazy. Can the kitchen stir up tacos and a few beans for this meeting? Cash is in my pocket."

"A feast, Matador, a feast."

Not all the patrons of La Azteca were preparing for a journey to El Sauz. Down at the end of the bar a tall brown customer did not like the noise. He finished off a bottle of beer and turned to his companion.

"This Pepe Bello is quite a matador. He lives well on the grease from his brother's collar."

Standing nearest, only Abundio de la O heard it. His right hand went into his pocket, and he stepped, unnoticed, to the end of the bar.

"Listen," he said very quietly, looking up into the tall customer's face, "Pepe Bello fights bulls, not big mouths. It takes no torero to send a mouth to the arrastre. I am no torero but I am a friend of Pepe Bello's. Now you son of a whore, are you getting out of here or what?"

Little O looked up and saw it coming. He dodged, throwing up his left arm as he swung around, and the beer bottle grazed his shoulder and crashed to the floor. Before anyone could move, Little O lashed out with his right. Pepe and the Jank sprang as they heard the ripping sound of the tall customer's sleeve. Delgado grabbed him as he groaned; Pepe had his swordhandler's right wrist in his two hands before it could swing again.

"Put that thing away! What the hell is the matter?" Pepe snarled.

"I'm going to kill this big mouth. I don't like him."

"Leave it! Do you want to put us in a jam?"

The Indio came around from in back of the bar, worried. "Are you hurt, man? Let me see your arm."

"This is something for the police," said the tall customer, watching his arm bleed. His mouth twitched with a kind of silent crying.

"Police my ass," said Jank Delgado, holding him up. "You tried to kill him before he touched you. I'm turning loose of you now and you are going out that door. Your friend here will take you. He's going too, by God. Now get out!"

"Abundio," said Pepe Bello when the door swung shut, "what in the name of Jesus Christ is this?"

"He made a remark."

"Goddammit, what did he say?"

"He made a remark," said the swordhandler. "Pepe, where is my glass?"

"I want to know what remark."

The Little O looked at his matador with Indian eyes as opaque and unreadable as two black buttons. "It was just a dirty remark. About me. He was feeling big, and I had to show him."

"Watch it, Abundio. I don't want you in jail."

"He's sorry," said the Jank, whose instincts were sharp and fast. "Come on, it's all right now. Where's the Indio? Hey man, get the sand smoother and clean up the ring out here. Then we might have a drink to go with the tacos."

La Azteca gradually came loose from the moorings that fastened it to a street corner of Guerreras. The plank floor tilted, and spun around. The bar became unstable. The lights increased in number and swam tangling overhead in splendid loops of sound that shot from the rubbery horn of the floating phonograph.

"Eeeeyai!" howled Piki Arenas. "I am going to El Sauz."

"Woooo!" howled Loco Ruiz. "And to think our Little O wanted to peel a big tall peach with his San Antonio!"

"Indio," Jank Delgado was saying confidentially in the noise, "I will tell you. My life is a tragedy. Completely a tragedy. Three seasons as a novillero, starting in my home town Ciudad Juarez on the border, where Don Roberto Gonzalez first presented me in his ring. Everywhere triumphs. I was 'pointing.' I was a prime figure. Be sure of that.

"But then in 1942 I got discouraged. The bulls discouraged me. Their shoulders that season were made of solid bone. They did not die well. They looked at me in a certain way. I got discouraged. A blonde of my home town Ciudad Juarez also discouraged me in 1942, Indio, she married a druggist.

"One day I went across the gringo bridge of the Rio Bravo very discouraged and speaking English. On the other side of that bridge I had an insanity. I joined their god-damned army.

"Three and a half years, Indio my friend. I fought. I am a veteran of battles you would not believe. You damn right. And what am I, as I risk my fleshes in the army of the North? Ramon? Delgado? No. I am not that.

"I will tell you what I am. An officer asks me my profession to write down on a paper. I tell him I am torero and he says 'What is torero?' and then I say 'Bullfighter' and he says 'I'll be damn. *Toreador!*' You see, Indio? I am of tragic fame. I am the only torero in the United States Army. Named *Toreador*. You should see me one time, citing a bull of Italy, a dairy bull, with a raincoat. Jesus Christ!

"And then it's all over and I am discharged. I take my pay. It's in dollars and what a package of pesos! I go home to my Mexico as I have promised myself. I enter again the atmosphere of the bulls. But I have lost something in that goddamned army, Indio. After the machine gun a sword don't seem so good. I don't know.

"I meet Pepe Bello who is really 'pointing.' He likes a sword. He likes an atmosphere of the bulls. He likes me; so I go with him. I hook the sticks for him, I throw my cape for him, I learn much from old Pancho Perez who is a grand old torero about how to be a good peon for Pepe. The worries go from my mind. But what has happened?

"Am I Ramon? Am I Delgado, name of my dear Mexican father? No, Indio. I am the Jank, the goddamned Jank.

The only gringo soldier in the atmosphere of the bulls!
My life — "

"Come on!" yelled Pepe Bello. "The car's fixed! Indio,
give me the cuenta. I want to pay."

"Diestro," said the Indio, when he had figured the bill
and made the change, "my thanks. My immense thanks."

"Hola the cockroach!" yelled Pepote Vera, holding open
the swinging door. "Now we twist the backs of the cows!"

"Arenas, son of a filth, you got to walk," said Carlos
Bandera. "There is no room, and you can't go anyway.
You got no peluco."

"Yai!" said Piki Arenas, climbing in. "I got more cash
than a bull can drop in ten grand droppings. Fifty frilling
centavos. Besides that, I'm thin. Move over, garbage! Indio,
if you see my brother tell him I have gone to give lessons
to matadors at El Sauz."

"Of course I can drive," said Loco Ruiz, insulted. He
focused his eyes. "Is everybody in?"

The Indio stood on the curb, shivering in his shirt
sleeves. His apron flapped in the wind as he watched the
red glow of the taillight turn the corner down the street
and disappear. He could still hear them singing "The
Blunt-Horned Steer."

"Juanito," sighed the Indio to his dishwasher as they
were turning out the lights of La Azteca, "there are many
ordinary bullfighters, but ordinary people do not fight
bulls."

FOUR

THE FOUR ENGINES droned in the high Mexican sky. Luis Bello, wearing sunglasses, pretended to doze in his airliner chair; he was hoping the lieutenant of cavalry sitting next to him would take the hint and quit talking. The air was not smooth. Luis Bello wished he had not taken so much aguardiente with Don Felipe Torres in Monterrey. The last drinks were now up to his collar and tasting too strong.

Riding a burro is the best way to travel, he said to himself, about to be sick. It's the best if you got no place to go. But I'm going to fight bulls in the Capital Sunday afternoon.

It was strange to be traveling without the cuadrilla. He was sorry now that he had sent everyone, even Tacho, to Mexico while he stayed alone for the funeral and family affairs in Guerreras. His peons were always with him as he went from plaza to plaza; they made traveling hardly noticeable to Luis Bello, who felt somehow naked now without them. He had not traveled alone since he was a kid riding the freight trains, fly style as they called it, hanging on the rods going from town to town and ranch to ranch, looking for bulls to fight. That was fifteen years ago. In those days nobody wanted him to fight any bulls.

It was a different fly style now, for sure.

I wouldn't have to be listening to this lieutenant if I had my peons. They handle people like they handle bulls for me, they take them out of my hair. I know the trouble with bulls all right, and I know the trouble with people.

People talk too much; they talk about themselves. This lieutenant, telling me how he loves the festival that is brave, how he has worked a cape at some kind of tienta — he's the public, the type that wants to tell toreros all about the bulls. He'll brag to his friends that he knows me intimately, then Sunday in a plaza he'll yell son of a whore at me, and throw things, when I have a bad bull. He's the public; I got to be nice.

Of course, thought Luis Bello as the blonde stewardess walked down the aisle with a pillow, being nice would be so easy — with some of the public. But she has a smile like Andres Prieto when he's scared of his bull and chopping at the horns. A public smile. To her I'm the public myself.

"Some of it comes in a nice package, eh diestro?" remarked the lieutenant, touching the little hairs of his mustache.

"It takes a million pesos and then a can opener," said Luis.

He stuffed the cold stub of his cigar into the ash tray at his side, and leaned back, the aguardiente riding up in his throat. With his eyes closed he wondered if Linda would be at the airport to meet him.

He let his mind dwell on how she looked at him, trying to remember exactly how she smiled and what she said when he met her at the party with Raul, the night before leaving for Guerreras. He could not remember exactly, but trying to remember, it gave him a feeling. It was there all right, and it wasn't for sale at the butchers'. None of that stuff. It was the casta, the true ancestry, it stuck out all over that girl. It stuck out pretty, like her name Linda, and it impressed Luis Bello. Like the first time he saw Spanish fighting cows with the glossy curls between their horns. Something for a torero — Ai! He wished he could remember, exactly. Maybe she would be at the airport. She might.

The engines droned on. The minutes and the miles unwound themselves, and the lieutenant talked. The sun went lower than the starboard wing slowly, coloring the windswept clouds over the mountains in the west while long shadows patterned the map of earth below. When the no smoking and seat belt sign flashed on, the map of earth came closer.

Then the Valley of Mexico spread out beneath them, mountain-rimmed and magical in the twilight. The familiar dark peak of Ajusco brooding over Luis's house somewhere down there in San Angel loomed against the sun's last glow. Across the valley in the southeast far above the dark space of the Pedregal and the dim mass of trees that marked Xochimilco, the white crests of the two volcanoes caught the glow from the west and stood light and ghostly, incredibly high over the gathering dusk in the valley where twinkling city lights awakened. The salty shores of Texcoco below were pale like snow in the twilight and the waters were black.

"Magnificent," said the lieutenant.

Looking down, Luis nodded that it was. It was like a dream. The lieutenant was right about something.

Bemused in the blue dusk, Luis's eyes followed a line of lights until the line was lost out in the twisting hills. It was the road to Puebla, his mind told him. He remembered that familiar road when it was not enchanted as it was from the unfamiliar heights of the sky. Like the trip with Uncle Pedro in the dark along that road, the time they drove the herd of Spanish horses. He remembered everything.

He could see the drunk colonel long ago, there in the automobile headlights, waving his pistol and cursing the old man who stood by the mare with the broken leg. He remembered how the colonel shoved the gun in the old man's belly and said he'd teach him how to drive horses under an automobile after dark. He remembered how the colonel said he wished he had run over a peon instead of a horse. He could still see that colonel putting the pistol to the mare's head and blowing out her brains, and how the old man cried, and the other horses ran away in the dark.

It must have been the uncle in the coffin and the uniform in the next seat, made me think of that. All the lieutenant needs is tequila and rank. He'll be a colonel someday. Well, at least I fight bulls.

He felt the plane's flaps and wheels come down, and his heart beat faster with an excitement he would not have admitted. While the pilot banked to shoot the approach, and while the lights below got closer, Luis swallowed, and ran a pocket comb carefully through his hair. When the wheels touched and rolled along the ground slowing, he thanked Mary Mother of God.

"I certainly hope I will be able to attend plaza Sunday," said the lieutenant as the plane taxied across the field to the terminal. "It has been a pleasure to hear you talk of bulls. May you have luck."

"Thank you," said Luis, unlatching the seat belt. "Many thanks."

When the plane swung around and came to a stop they got up and shook hands. Luis stood in the aisle and threw his topcoat over his shoulders like a cloak, turning up the collar. He still wore the big sunglasses; they marked his profession outside the ring almost as much as a pigtail in the old days before Belmonte.

At the plane door Luis was surprised. The blonde stewardess spoke to him, holding out her fountain pen and a paper.

"Senor Bello, may I have your autograph?" she asked in English.

Luis grinned at her. Now she's the public, instead of me.

"Why didn't you ask me sooner?" he said in Spanish. Her eyes were very blue.

He signed his name slowly, with his rubric jutting down from the final *o* like a sword thrust. "Thank you for the voyage and the smile."

"I hope to see you in the ring someday." She had been rehearsing the words in Spanish, and they came out rather well.

"Come Sunday, God favoring," said Luis, looking at her, laughing. "Your Spanish is fine." He said "Good-by" in English, and went down the steps.

Raul Fuentes, handsome and smoothly tailored, was waiting for him inside the railing by the Immigration desk in the terminal.

Linda wasn't there.

The inspector spoke to Luis Bello and waved him by, while the passengers from the States lined up to present their papers.

"Hi, traveler," said Raul in his familiar hoarse voice. "Welcome!"

They gave each other a quick, easy abrazo.

"What goes, Big Agent?"

In the Customs room Tacho the swordhandler was waiting, with his tweed cap in his hand.

"Tachito! What passes?"

"Only buttocks," said the swordhandler, grinning. "There's your suitcase. Give me the claim ticket."

Luis and Raul started through the terminal while Tacho waited for the baggage. Luis could feel people in the crowd looking his way and nudging each other saying, "That's Luis Bello." One of them sang out, "Hola, Luis!" and the matador held up his right hand and smiled as he walked, with his coat over his shoulders like a cape.

"You had a good trip?" Raul was asking. "Everything all right in Guerreras?"

"As usual. How's it here? All lined up?"

"Going good, pal. This'll be your season."

In front of the terminal the electric lights were getting bright in the blue twilight. A newsboy, thinking fast, ran up to Luis, and held one of his papers in front of the matador's face.

"*El Bello!*" the newsboy sang, as if it were part of a song. He pointed to a picture of Luis on the page, holding it up.

Luis took it and gave him fifty centavos. He roughed the kid's hair into his eyes.

"Don't stand in the toril door, Stubby," said the famous matador.

"*El Bello!*" the kid went off baying.

"Your car's over here," said Raul.

The Buick convertible was sleek and shining in the light. It had cost Luis Bello thirty thousand pesos, a whole corrida, to buy that car. It was bright blue, and beautiful to him, and he smiled to see it again.

The boy standing as watchman by the bumper held out his hand; a coin went into one of his pockets and a dirty rag came out of another, with a flourish. Whistling through his teeth, the boy started to polish a fender.

"Never mind," said Luis. "It don't need polishing."

"Keep that rag off this coach!" yelled Tacho, coming up from behind and breathing hard, carrying the heavy pig-skin traveling case initialed LB.

Luis and Raul got in the back seat. When Tacho had stowed the luggage, he took his place as chauffeur, and headed the big Buick for town, smoothly.

The aguardiente was all settled now, far below Luis's collar. He and Raul lit cigars.

But the dirt of it was that Linda hadn't come. While Raul talked, and the car purred into the smoky edge of town where the poor were cooking their suppers and the street lights cut dim yellow holes in the darkness, Luis sat and wondered how to be casual at inquiring from Raul about Linda. Raul usually knew the score a little too uncomfortably well.

Jesus and Mary, I guess I dreamed it all up. I probably misunderstood; she probably forgot all about it. And I forgot she's flower and cream. The bon ton elite. Fly style myself, by God. Born on a dirt floor. I ought to know better. Luis Bello, the sucking calf!

"I've got you signed for Merida on New Year's," said Raul, "and Potosi after that. Antonio is mad of course because you're all tied up with Valles, but he's cooling off and I think we can work you in at El Toreo later in the season.

"Say Luis, I talked to Gomez again about Cuenca on December Fourth. You know, about Pepe and you. You should have heard him when I said you wouldn't come unless he had bulls of Las Astas. He bawled like he had just been castrated.

"I found out it's a festival at Cuenca, on the town's Saint's Day, Santa Barbara. I told him he ought to celebrate it right; that as far as our fees were concerned, we would be reasonable.

"Maybe you feel something about Santa Barbara's Day, Luis?"

Luis Bello wore a medal of Santa Barbara when he went into the ring; he was silent for a moment, thinking the things he would not say. "It's just to give Pepe a chance," he said finally. "Besides, we fight for money, Raul. Not Saints. Did Eladio Gomez call it all off?"

"He finally said he was going to get in touch with old Don Tiburcio and see what the bulls would cost. I stirred his sporting blood. He could have some real propaganda for a change: The Two Bellos! Bulls of Las Astas! Gala Corrida of the Day of Santa Barbara! He'll sell every seat."

"Cow chips! He won't even start by buying any Astas. They cost too much. And he has to have another alternate to appear with Pepe and me."

"He hasn't got to that yet; neither have we. Anyway, he said he'd call me the first of the week."

"Well, you can kiss that good-by."

"Luis, that filth of a Hector really put it to us for the double truck in the magazine, like I said on the phone. One thousand pesos for Pepe's 'triumph' last Sunday."

"What? — Son of the Mother, for a thousand it should be a trip to Heaven. On a purple cloud! Raul, I have fought actual triumphs with my flesh for a hundred pesos. And that coyote gets a thousand for one on paper. Listen, we better get another magazine!"

"I don't want Hector's bunch mad. If we quit them now, they print damaging remarks. Free."

"The dirty coyotes. They get fat on bullfighters' blood. And we got to be nice while they drink it. Some business we're in! Besides the bulls, there's everything else."

They came up to Insurgentes on a cross street, and Tacho stopped the car until he could turn left and nose into the stream of traffic headed out toward San Angel.

"Did you tell Linda I was coming tonight?" Luis finally blurted.

"Sure I told her, Luis. She already read it in the paper. I asked her if she wanted to come out to the airport, but she said she had an engagement and was sorry."

"Oh," said Luis. "I just thought I'd ask about her. She seemed like a very nice girl."

The boulevard took them suddenly by the Plaza Mexico. Over beyond the unfinished underground parking lot and past the Sports Stadium, Luis saw again the vast silhouette of the plaza curving into the darkness. A lighted billboard at the corner, by the biggest bullring in the world, announced Sunday's cartel:

JUAN SALAZAR
LUIS BELLO
CHATO PALACIOS

It looked lonely and mysterious with only the three names lighted and alive there at the corner. The only sound was the hum of the big Buick as they went by.

"Old Skinny Salazar, and that young punk, Palacios," Luis said.

"I forgot to tell you who was alternating Sunday," said Raul. "I knew you'd like Skinny, even if his joints do creak. Don Tomas wanted him to confirm Chato's alternativa Sunday, and cede the kid the first bull."

"That Palacios can do just one thing," said Luis, "a high pass with the muleta, using both hands. It has some emotion, but I don't know what a Doctorate of Bulls means now, when they give it for that."

"He's one of the stable, you know. Special promotion. How's Pepe, Luis? We got to promote him. He ought to be in there Sunday instead of Chato."

"Haven't I been telling you? Pepe went to a tienta, to practice on the cows at Don Julian's. He said to phone him there if you signed him. I felt sorry for the kid. He went to El Sauz with a bunch of his bullring bums from Guerreras. Julian Llaguno will probably throw them off his place. At that, things are sure nicer than when I used to drift around hungry in my shirttail, looking for anything with horns to wave a cloth at."

"That's one reason you know so much more than these kids."

"Well. A lot of that's luck. You take Goyo Salinas, my peon of confidence, he knows more about bulls than ten matadors today put together. What has it got him? Horn scars, and just five hundred pesos a Sunday, when he's working. Of course I give him a bonus — "

"That's a part of the festival. Goyo is like old Pancho Perez."

"Pancho Perez, the same. I'm glad I got him for Pepe. He'll teach the boy."

"What do you think now of Pepe's peon Delgado?"

"He's a kind of clown, and he's been around gringos too much. But you know, Raul, that boy is smart?"

"No tragedy there. I get tired of the barnyard boobs we see trying to make a living throwing a cape at the wrong time."

"If you mean barnyard, Raul, you mean picador. They were a fright last Sunday! Most pics should never have left the farm. They don't know the difference between a bull's eye and a bull's ass. I often wonder just which place they will shove that long pole they carry."

"The pics get knocked off their nags too often. It shakes up their brains."

"In that case it don't hurt a bit. Say, how are the Jackdaw and the Little White, my own noble cavalry?"

"You'll see. They're probably waiting for you now."

Beyond the Obregon Monument, Tacho turned the car up the slope into San Angel. They drove past the familiar domes of the convent and the empty plaza where the street lamps cast a chalky light on the undersides of the trees. Beyond the Church of San Jacinto the car climbed a steeper, darker way where the smell of pine drifted and the street became a lane flanked by the walls of old houses and gardens hung with bougainvillaea. Slowing to a stop before a big barred double gate, Tacho shattered the evening quiet of the walled lane with a violent blast of the Buick's horn. The gates swung open and the car went in and stopped by the lighted entrance of the two-storied house in the high-walled garden. Tacho cut the engine.

"Back in the bull pen," said Luis.

The watchman who had opened the gate and closed it came up smiling in the half light, with his hat in his hand. His wife, the fat cook, came trotting around the corner of the house.

"Don Luis! It pleased God to bring you back!" Four of her children followed her, big-eyed and bashful.

While Luis was shaking hands, the whole cuadrilla filed out of the house toward him.

"Goyo! What do you bring that's good? Pancho Perez, himself! And Monkey, how do you carry what's bad? Ah, Jackdaw. And here's the Little White. What goes, Enrique?"

They all shook hands with the boss.

Luis looked around and laughed. He was pleased. "What kind of an evil meeting is this? Let's go in and taste a small cup with a cigar."

The cook brought glasses and Tacho opened a new bottle in the parlor, on the table amidst the cards of the game of brisca the cuadrilla had been playing, under the big hand-tinted photo of Luis dedicating a bull in the Plaza of Madrid.

"Luck," said Luis. "It's good to be back. Are you ready for Sunday?"

Sipping the manzanilla, they eased down into the modernistic chairs of their matador's garish parlor. Luis Bello was their master in the plazas; outside, they depended upon him in a peculiar way. When he was in form, his cuadrilla was a team, and felt like one. When he was not, the team fell apart into single morbid pieces. Each piece was a man without confidence. Even Enrique, the new one, had come quickly into this emotional dependency upon Luis Bello. It was built upon their relationship as master and workman in an uncertain and dangerous pursuit, a pursuit that made them sensitive to omens because they were all so professionally subject to tragedy; and it was made complicated by the intimate knowledge they had of each other, living, traveling, working together. The cuadrilla had come out to San Angel to gauge Luis Bello's spirit, and they each sampled it carefully, like the manzanilla.

"How's your leg?" asked Goyo Salinas, the senior banderillero.

"It's okay," said Luis. "Getting well. Any of you boys ailing?"

"No," answered Goyo. "Except maybe the Jackdaw. He got a little trouble of the heart again."

The seams of the Jackdaw's brown leather face moved into a grin and he scuffed his big feet on the shining tile in front of his chair. The wineglass looked like a little tubular crystal that might melt any moment in his horny paw. "Eeehoh!" he said.

"The man has had enough of that heart trouble to have a remedy by now," said Luis. "Haven't you, Jackdaw?"

"The remedy is hard to get at," said Monkey Garcia.

"It's usually hard," said Rafael Blanco, the Little White.

"Love will find a way," said Luis. "The harder the better."

"Eeehoh," said the Jackdaw. "To keep me in trouble."

"These bullfighters," said Raul, winking at Tacho, "they only think of two things."

"Mostly one," said Tacho. "They don't have much time to think of bulls."

"What a business," said Goyo. "We got to go, Luis. We are due at a meeting."

"I never saw more of a meeting than this," said Luis. "Where you going?"

"The union. It will be a *mitin* all right. The Rabbit says he wants us peons to protest the management of the plaza at Merida. Maybe close the joint with a strike."

"Listen, Goyo," said Raul, "I told you we had a booking there on New Year's. The hell with a strike."

"They won't do it. It's just wind."

"Luis," Pancho Perez spoke up, "I came by with your people, to ask about Pepe. Where's my diestro? Is he booked?"

"He's at the tientas at El Sauz. Raul's working on some bookings for him. You know how it is. Stay here in Mexico with your family, Pancho, and Pepe will be here soon, and call you. He sent his regards. You'll be working in all the plazas with him before long. You need any money?"

"Well, my niece — "

"Here, Pancho. This ought to help until you get busy with Pepe. How's that picador of his, the Soup?"

"He's waiting around."

"It won't be long. You hold everything."

"Luis," said Raul, "I have an engagement too. I have to go back to the Ritz. Sure glad you're home. You want to see Valles tomorrow? I'll call you in the morning and we'll meet."

"I'm sorry everybody is leaving. Sure, call me in the morning, Raul. I'll take a little supper now, and then make myself some sleep. Tacho, drive Raul home to the Ritz."

They all shook hands with Luis again, puffing cigars, and left him in his parlor.

He heard them talking in the garden, and asking the watchman to open the gate. The starter on Goyo Salinas's old car ground noisily and the engine took hold, and when they had gone there was silence.

The lonely anticlimax of his arrival bore down upon Luis Bello suddenly. Irritated, he walked over to the radio, flipped it on, and tuned it to music, loud. Standing by a window he looked out into the darkness, drawing on his cold cigar, absently watching the tiny toy lights of traffic moving along the slope of the highway over the mountain to Cuernavaca. The cook set his table, and brought in his supper.

He ate without relish, alone. The light over the table seemed too strong to him, now that his sunglasses were put away. The radio moaned that a girl had sinned and regretted; Luis Bello thought he could still hear aircraft engines, droning in tango time. He was tired, but he wished everybody hadn't gone away.

It's no use to call her, thought Luis Bello. She wouldn't be home; she told Raul she had an engagement. The hell with her. She's probably drinking champagne with some Embassy pimp. Besides, I got to face bulls, Sunday.

When Tacho returned with the car, he saw the light was out upstairs in his matador's room.

Luis Bello's leg hurt again when he awoke in the night, and he had disquieting dreams.

FIVE

IT WAS ALMOST NOON when Lala brought chocolate and put it on the table by Linda's bed.

"Senora," said the maid.

Her Cuban eyes enjoyed the rich image of her mistress curled asleep in the canopied bed.

"Senora, shall I open the curtains and let the morning come in?"

Linda straightened her legs under the ruffled counterpane. Without opening her eyes, she nestled her jaw in the hollow of her bare shoulder. "Ai, Lala. I was having a dream." She sighed. "What day is this?"

"A lovely day," said Lala at the tall French door, pulling the heavy damask curtains slowly, so that sunlight filtered in, warming the soft blues and grays and golds in the room. The mockingbirds in the yellow cages on the balcony outside were whistling two notes, over and over.

"I mean what day, Lala."

"This is Friday morning, the eighteenth of November. It's almost noon. Shall I bring in the papers?"

"No, no papers. I'll have my chocolate when I'm awake. The champagne last night — "

Linda finally opened her eyes, carefully. The foamy hot chocolate was fragrant; she turned toward the table at her side. Beyond the edge of the ruffled satin canopy cascading from above her head, the crystal table top bore its accustomed burden, the silver clock and cigarette box, the silver tray and chocolate pot, the fragile blue china — and something that brought a puzzled wrinkle across the smooth roundness of Linda's forehead. By the satin with the silver and china she saw three massive books stacked on her bed table. Their blunt titles were burned like brands upon their raw leather backs: *LOS TOROS*.

"The bulls?" she breathed, half awake. "My God." Then she remembered.

Luis Bello. I was going to read about toreros and know

all about the bulls. Those are the books Raul Fuentes
brought last night. They tell everything, he said. What a
lot! They look like dictionaries of all the tongues.

"They have beautiful pictures," said Lala, pouring the
chocolate.

When Linda had bathed and powdered she sat on a blue
divan to read while she awaited lunch. Her honey-colored
hair, drawn up high and smooth from the nape and fixed
with a golden-headed comb, looked well with the pale blue
negligee she wore. Relaxed and languid, she could feel
the warm inner sides of her naked legs pressing together
under the chiffon. Her chin touched the hollow of her neck
where the scent of the powder lingered, and when her eyes
strayed from the book she held, she looked down the V
between her breasts and watched her own breathing. The
weight of the book pressed heavily upon her lap. One of
the edges was sharp against the yielding flesh of her thigh;
the binding smelled of masculine leather.

She found on page 119 in the third volume of *Los Toros*
a formal tauromachian biography of BELLO GARCIA (LUIS).
Studying the photographs and the portrait drawing by
Cabral that accompanied the dry text, before she began
to read the facts of the matador's life, she decided Luis
Bello was a very attractive man.

Cabral's drawing showed cruelty in Luis Bello's mouth,
yet she did not find it echoed in his eyes. A man with a face
like that must think barbarous things nevertheless, she
thought. He probably did them too. A torero must have an
enormous life. Her gaze left the book and wandered down
the V as she thought of Luis Bello's mouth, remembering
the white teeth. He was undoubtedly barbarous!

BELLO GARCIA (LUIS), born in humble circumstances at Hacienda Aguabendita, State of Guerreras, Mexico, October 29, 1916. First of a large family born from the union of Francisco Bello, soldier of the ranks in the Revolution, and Natalia Garcia, daughter of a day laborer. Before and after the Revolution, the father was employed as a vaquero on the Aguabendita; he died of pulmonary tuberculosis in 1928, leaving the widow in poverty with seven children and an unborn son. From tenderest years Luis Bello, the future diestro, worked as a hacienda herdsman for a few centavos a day. In 1929 the family moved to the City of Guerreras and came to live with a brother of the widow, a Pedro Garcia residing in the barrio of Los Posos of that city. Garcia was one of the grooms of the famous Spanish horses of Don Angel Pedrazo, haciendado of Guerreras State. The boy Luis Bello worked as a helper to his uncle tending horses.

Jaime was a horseman too, thought Linda, but he never tended any.

The situation of his family precluded continuance of his studies beyond the elementary grade.

He's never been to school.

While delivering horses to the renowned Las Astas establishment of Don Tiburcio Balbuena in Zacalisco, young Bello saw brave bulls in their pastures for the first time, and was present at the operations of a tienta. What he saw fired his imagination. He first dressed in the suit of lights in the diminutive plaza at Pilares de Santa Ana, July 26, 1933, during a country fiesta, and was awarded the ear of the first bull he ever killed, for

his valor with the sword. At a novillada in the plaza
of his home city Guerreras, September 24, 1933, he
was severely gored in the right thigh. The wound kept
him from further appearances until June 10, 1934,
when . . .

So many names and dates, Luis Bello! She began to
skip some of the closely packed text.

. . . seasons of bitter struggle and repeated gorings.
He received his Doctorate of Bulls on November 21,
1937, at the *Plaza de Toros San Marcos* in the City
of Aguascalientes. . . . In December he went to Peru
. . . at the plaza *El Toreo* in the City of Mexico confirmed his alternativa on March 6, 1938. His first bull,
Bandolero of Torrecilla, was extremely brave. . . .
Bello buried the sword to the hilt and was awarded
ears and tail and a thunderous ovation . . . making
a *quite* with the fifth bull, he was most gravely gored
in the left armpit. The horn wound carried him to the
door of Death.

She wondered what horn scars were like, and if they
showed.

. . . of 1942 the eminent *Tio Curro* wrote in *Taurino:*
"The season has made Luis Bello an ace of first cate-
gory. He is that rare thing, the completely emotionated
killer of bulls. . . . he is all a senor and master of
his muleta . . ."

Rare, indeed, she was sure!

. . . in Madrid *Al Sesgo* wrote: "No more interesting gift to the Brave Festival has come from the recent exchange of toreros between our country and

Mexico than the phenomenal swordsman Luis Bello. His style with the cape is sound, he places banderillas with the ease of his compatriots, but the real value of his work is his devotion to the Hour of Truth. He brings honor and meaning again to the third period of the lidia in these days of the ballet masters of the red cloth.

So technical, and nothing about women.

. . . he emerged from his labors in full apotheosis after the award of four ears, two tails and a foot, and being carried to his hotel on shoulders.

What a life, Luis Bello. All done in satin trousers!

He called her on the telephone at twenty minutes after five, when she had returned from the hairdresser's. She used her low voice with a kind of anticipation in it, so that he could hear the rich intake of her breath when she laughed and answered what he said.

She would love to have dinner with him. At ten would be fine. Wherever he liked. He didn't? Well, Ciro's was clearly very public. La, Luis Bello! No. She liked Club 123. Very much indeed. She would be ready.

She was also spectacular, in a gray gown and white furs, when she came into her drawing room a little after ten, smiling at Luis. The handkerchief showing from his breast pocket was very carefully folded, and he was smoking a cigarette.

Outside by the driveway gate he helped her in the front seat of his car, and walked around to get in at the wheel. He hadn't dreamed it up. Here it was. And that damned Tacho insisting on driving for him tonight! The hell with that nursemaid Tacho. What if there were bulls on Sunday? This was only Friday and look at it now!

Sitting there beside him in the convertible, the flower and cream was not so formidable. It was nice. Luis felt nice himself; his self-consciousness withered away before he had driven out of the Lomas.

"Raul Fuentes says you will be very busy now," Linda said in her low mellow voice, "for three months, every Sunday in the plazas, and then maybe you will go to Spain again in May."

"I hope so, God granting."

"I haven't seen you in the ring, you know," Linda said.

"You haven't? Maybe that's better."

"Why do you say such a thing?"

"You like the brave festival?"

"To be truthful I have not seen much of it, Luis Bello. We lived so long in the Argentine and Paris and Cuba. Raul Fuentes says you are the best."

"Raul is an agent. Did you know Raul a long time?"

"Our families were friends."

"Big Lawyer Fuentes. Raul fixes everything. Eight years my manager. He knows the atmosphere of the bulls and a lot more. Most managers have once been toreros, but not Raul. He's distinct."

"He's charming. His love of the atmosphere of the plazas comes from his father, I think."

"Old Don Faustino Fuentes owned a bull ranch and a bullring too. He made Raul a lawyer and the bulls made Raul a rascal. Not really. What I have I owe to Raul."

"He is very fond of you."

"Well, he presented me to Senora Linda Castillo de Calderon. I am enchanted. You like being in Mexico again?"

"It's very interesting to be back."

"I would like to call you Linda because the name fits."

"La. I suppose I should be calling you Don Luis — Luis!" Her eyes laughed at him in the moving lights as they turned into a side street from the Paseo.

"I think it's good enough, just Luis."

On Calle Liverpool he parked the car a few spaces away from 123, and they walked into the lights under the striped awning. The doorman looked surprised, grinning at Luis Bello; he opened the door with a flourish. "Ole!" he allowed himself to say.

"It will be all over town tomorrow," whispered Linda as they stood waiting for the maitre to seat them.

"The same, if we were having barbecue together in Tlalpan," laughed the matador. "Jabber, jabber."

Their table was in a pleasant unnoticeable corner; they sat beside each other on the upholstered seat built along the mirrored wall. They ordered coq au vin while a pianist played sentimental gringo ballads from an alcove beyond the chef's salad table. The dim light added art to Linda's gray gown and pearls, to her dark golden hair; she seemed flawless, smiling at Luis.

In some way she communicated this flawlessness to him, so that Luis felt he said the right thing, did the right thing, smoothly, there in the dim light with the music, sitting with her, eating with her, talking with her. It exhilarated them both, as if they each were demonstrating triumphs to each other. It was better than the wine they drank.

"How did this happen?" asked Luis, when the waiter had taken their plates and brought them brandy.

"Isn't it nice?" she answered.

They lighted cigarettes.

"I don't believe it," said Luis.

But he did. The dirt floor, the bulls, were far away. Linda turned to look him full in the face.

"Why don't you believe it?"

"It doesn't happen to me."

"In all the places you go? With all the fame? Luis Bello!"

"Nothing like this. Nothing."

"Now I'm the one who doesn't believe."

"You should."

Quite suddenly the intoxication, the feeling of intimacy, changed pace.

"You've been in love, Luis? Been married?"

"Both."

"Your wife?"

"That was the first year I was matador de toros. While I was in Lima she died. Typhoid."

"I'm sorry, Luis. I shouldn't have asked."

"Why not?"

"You loved her? Tell me her name."

"Barbara. I was a kid."

"I loved Jaime. When I was a kid, as you say."

"Lucky man."

"Not so lucky I guess."

"Raul told me about him. Killed playing polo. But Christ in Heaven we all get killed! Or else die. Just die."

"Oh Luis, do we live any, before that?"

He believed she meant it. He took a swallow of brandy; the bulls, everything, always came back.

"You do, Linda. Carai!"

"Jaime didn't love me."

"Tell me," said Luis, looking at her after a pause, "what are you doing like this, Linda? I'm torero. It is something that you are with Luis Bello tonight. It gets more every minute. But — I don't know your type because you are better than that. You got a family. You're — "

"Their disgrace if you want to know, Luis Bello. I have only aunts and uncles and they are stupid. Stupid! Jaime's family is a barbarity. In Buenos Aires. I am finished with them all, completely. Luis, I have nothing I can do well, and nothing to do now but — "

"Don't tell me," he broke in, holding up his hand. They both laughed. "Let's have a brandy."

"And *your* family?" She could be cruel, too.

He answered her slowly. "People like Bellos don't exist," he said, "except in a family. To keep living we got to help each other from the time we're born."

She decided not to be cruel.

"Raul told me about your little brother, following your steps."

"He's some kid."

"Tell me, Luis, how does one learn to be a torero?"

"Well, I guess you watch the bulls, and the bullfighters, and then you try it yourself," said Luis. "The main thing is to stand still while you're trying." He was smiling.

"Don't you take any lessons, read any books, practice a lot, to learn?"

"You learn all the good stuff from the bulls and yourself while you're standing there."

She leaned on the table with her chin on her hands, looking away, thinking about how to learn to fight bulls. "It's rare," she said. "How does it happen?"

"It's hard to say. You really want to know, Linda? I'll tell you. To fight bulls a little worm has got to bite you. He gives the fever. The little worm bites a lot of people but it takes a real man to get the real fever. Bullfighting starts from here." He indicated his middle, somewhere below the table. "Then, it goes up here." He pointed to his head. "And it comes out here." He worked his wrists. "That's all."

"Starting with that little worm," she said, laughing with him. "I see!"

"The little worm. He starts some other things I think. He brings fevers. Ai, Linda, a burning — "

"Luis!"

The girl with the camera came up to their table, offering to take their photograph as a souvenir.

"Absolutely not," Luis said quickly.

"That's all we need!" Linda said when the girl had gone pouting.

The singing band of mariachis that took the pianist's place changed the tempo of Club 123. The tenor smiled at Luis as they started "Guerreras, The Place Where I Was Born."

"A scandal is arming itself," said Luis. "Let's get out of here. Shall we go someplace where it's darker, and dance?"

"You ought to take me home, Luis. Don't you have to fight bulls Sunday?"

"They'll wait."

"You really had better take me home," she said when they were in the car. "Luis, I want to see you in the plaza Sunday."

"It's not a very good cartel," he said. "But you come. Maybe I can show you something."

"I know you will."

"I'll ask Raul to take you. He can explain it as it happens."

"That would be wonderful."

"I'll know where you're sitting. I'll try to put a bull in my pocket for you."

"I'll probably be nervous."

The trees of Chapultepec whished by fast as they passed under the wide branches; the stars were bright between the dark clustered leaves.

"Am I really taking you home this early?" he asked, as the car climbed the Lomas hills.

Oh, it was there. It was there for sure and he was just taking her home.

"Here is the turn, to your left, Luis. You are really taking me home."

She had a key that unlocked the gate in front of the dark house and another that unlocked the door and she was trembling. Even her lips were trembling.

"O Luis, no, O God," she whispered, "O — "

"Here," said Luis Bello, "and here and here. And here," with the wave mounting in the yielding trembling softness under the furs, in the dark.

"And here," he said when they got to the canopied bed on the satin with the lips and the wet and the hot. "Here."

The morning star was up when he headed the car for San Angel. He stopped on the way and had a bowl of warm broth at the street stand by the carbarns of Indianilla.

SIX

ELADIO GOMEZ CONSULTED the gold watch in his vest pocket again. The train should have arrived in Cienleguas five hours ago; Gomez was upset. He should have known better than to travel on Friday. The toothpick he had whittled from a match was chewed to shreds and he spit it out.

For the hundredth time he took the folded telegram from his breast pocket and read it to look for something he might possibly have missed. He knew it by heart.

COME TO LAS ASTAS AS MY GUEST TO SELECT REQUIRED BULLS DISCUSS TERMS HERE CORDIALLY

T. BALBUENA

He was too far in the trap to get out now.

Yet he had to admit to himself a certain pride. He had never been asked to Las Astas but he was going now. To the greatest bull ranch in Mexico, on business. He fingered the yellow paper of the telegram, the final bait to the trap.

The wheels on the rails said only click click clack in a tentative way. Five hours late. Powdery dust churned into the chair car. It lined the nostrils, stung the eyes in the hazy light from the lamps over the long dusty aisle. It reduced the passengers to a torpid state of resignation. Most of them had closed their eyes, trying to doze on the gritty plush, while Gomez sat staring into the darkness outside. A baby cried somewhere ahead. The train jerked, and the cuspidor sloshed by the empty beer bottles at Eladio Gomez's feet.

He remembered Cienleguas, passing through it on the trains, on other trips, and it worried him, Cienleguas after midnight. It was one of those stations with a cattle pen and a pump house and a few adobe houses sprawled along a ragged line of tamarisk trees. What if nobody met him? What if they never got his telegram saying he was coming tonight? Las Astas was a long way from the station, he knew. Way out in the country. It was twenty minutes past twelve.

He folded the telegram again and put it in his pocket, next to his billfold. When he heard the door open at the back end of the car he felt the cold and smelled the billow of new dust that rolled in with the louder clicking of the wheels on the rails. He turned in his seat to look back.

It was the brakeman holding a lighted lantern. He pointed his finger at Gomez.

"Cienleguas" he barked.

"By God," mumbled Eladio Gomez, jamming the brown hat down on his head, reaching for the overcoat and the pasteboard suitcase on the rack over his head, in a great hurry. He set his suitcase down on the thick dust in the vestibule and put on his overcoat, while the train slowed to a stop in the darkness.

"Cienleguas!" said the brakeman again, hopping off with his lantern.

Gomez went down the steps with his suitcase and stepped off in the dark. Far up the track he saw the one dim light of the station house, up by the engine. Nothing else. He started walking.

The brakeman waved his lantern and the train jerked. Before Gomez had gotten halfway to the station house, the last car clicked by him, shrinking down the right of way, the lights dimming to pin points and then going out, leaving him walking alone.

Somewhere off in the dark a dog barked the long bark of a country dog, challenging Gomez to Cienleguas.

"Dirt in the milk," he answered.

A cold wind blew the dust by the side of the track. It

whipped around his ankles, penetrated his thin rayon socks, worked up his pants legs and under his overcoat. His teeth chattered a little when he scuffed up to the lighted door of the station house. It was locked.

"Jesus Christ in all His truth!" said Eladio Gomez, pounding on the door.

A man carrying a mail sack came around the dim corner of the station. Gomez could see the patent leather shining on the bill of his stationmaster's cap. The man's shoulders were hunched up with the cold. He was very surprised.

"Senor?"

"I came in on the train," said Gomez. "I was expecting to be met here. Is anybody waiting to meet me?"

"No," said the man. "Nobody."

"Nobody from Las Astas? I am the guest of Senor Balbuena."

"Las Astas," said the man. "That's where most of them go. Mail, telegrams, the same."

"Well, how do I get there?"

"It's far. They go in automobiles."

"Listen, are you sure nobody came to meet me?"

"No, senor. Who knows?"

"Well, for God, can you get me out of the cold?"

The man set down his sack, found his keys in his pocket, and unlocked the door. They walked into the waiting room.

"Is there a telephone?" asked Gomez, looking at the cold concrete benches and the unswept floor.

"At the store. It will open tomorrow."

"Is there anybody else around here?"

"No senor. Just those sleeping in their beds. It's late."

"Oh is it?" He clenched his teeth.

"It is possible an automobile will come tomorrow," said the man, obliging.

"It is possible Jesus Christ will too." Gomez was bitter.

"Eh? Senor, with your permission, I will tend the mail." He picked up his limp sack and went out, closing the door behind him.

"Mother of dirt. O mother of whores!" said Eladio Gomez to himself. He looked at his watch. "Four hours until the sun. Four frilling filthy hours."

He was about to throw the butt of his third cigarette, sitting there in the silence with his eyes stinging, when he heard it. First it was a dog, far away, as if it were barking from the other side of the Sierra. And then another dog, closer, and then two others, closer yet, and then a regular nigger-supper of barking dogs out there in the dark brought him to the dirty window at the end of the room. Headlights. He could see them. Then he heard the rumble with the dogs barking, and the rattle and the sound of the motor as the headlights came toward the station. Picking up his suitcase he went out the door.

It was a five-ton truck when it rolled up and stopped. Loaded on the flat bed behind the cab Eladio Gomez could dimly see shapes that made him happy. The truck was from Las Astas all right. The shapes were boxes for shipping brave bulls.

"Senor? For Las Astas?" the driver said, getting out of the cab.

"Yes."

"Ah, senor," he said, taking off his vaquero's hat

"Policarpo Cana at your orders." He bowed his head with old back-country courtesy, and reached for the suit-case.

"Eladio Gomez. Much pleasure."

"The hour is late," said Policarpo when he had gotten the gears shifted and the dogs were barking again. "I feel deeply. I saw the train from the hill. I hurried." He cut in sharply at one of the dogs but missed.

Eladio Gomez was very tired and somewhat confused. The empty bull boxes rumbled and rattled behind them on the rough road that led out of Cienleguas.

"The automobile coach broke itself tonight," said Poli-carpo. "I had to bring a truck. I feel deeply."

"The train was more than five hours late. I feel deeply myself. There isn't much at Cienleguas; I'm glad you came."

"I am glad in all manners," said Policarpo.

He accepted a cigarette Gomez offered him and they lighted up. The cab was warmer and Eladio felt a little better.

"How far is it to the hacienda?" he asked.

"Twenty-two kilometers, more or less," Policarpo said. "A short way, by machine."

He pulled his sombrero down tighter and pushed the accelerator. The truck lurched forward in the darkness, eating the uneven ribbon of the road that turned and twisted ahead white in the headlights, bumping by the thickets of nopal, the dark mesquite in the draws where the dust whirled out under the wheels, and the long rat-tling flying stretches through the grass over the hills. The chalky pale road plunging toward him had an effect on

Eladio Gomez's eyes. He closed them, and nearly fell asleep bouncing on the seat with the cigarette burning in his hand.

At the top of a rise Policarpo got out and opened a gate, drove the truck through, and closed the gate again. Down a long slope they came at last into the headquarters of Las Astas. They drove in past the dark adobe huts and stone walls, through a narrow lane, and ground to a stop in front of the big house lurking in the darkness behind a court-yard wall.

"This way," said Policarpo, carrying the suitcase. A dog growled at their heels. "Shhuh!" he said. A roosting chicken squawked from a vine by the wall. The sour fer-mented smell of silage tainted the air. From the darkness out beyond the walls they heard a bull grumbling, deep down in his throat, to himself.

The ancient arched doorway to the big house was wide open; Eladio Gomez followed his guide into the patio beyond. A single bare light bulb cut a pale hole in the gloom of the battered columns that flanked them as their footsteps sounded on the flagstones around the patio.

"The toilet," whispered Policarpo, pointing to a dark door. "And here is your room."

The door squeaked. Inside, Policarpo groped around above his head, and found the light bulb, and turned it on. The room was pink. It had a venerable beamed ceiling twenty feet above Eladio Gomez's head, and it was im-mense. Over in a corner by a small rug was a brass bed with a purple spread, a bureau, a wardrobe that leaned at an angle, and a straight chair. The rest of the vast room was bare. Tacked on the wall over the bedstead was a

colored calendar lithograph of Manuel Rodriguez, Manolete, the matador of Cordoba.

"*Manolete*," whispered Policarpo, pointing. "He slept
there, in that bed, when he came to the tientas. May God
care for him now in Glory! Good night, senor."

Eladio Gomez stood alone in the middle of the pink
room, before he went to the toilet.

Las Astas. Where they raised the greatest bulls in the
Americas. Where a bull cost six thousand pesos.

SEVEN

HE FELT DRY and brittle when he awoke in the dim pink room and the cold. He dressed quickly, shivering, and took a nip of tequila from the bottle in his suitcase before he stepped out into the patio, into a day at Las Astas.

Ruddy light from the early sun warmed the weathered arches and carved stone tops of the columns on the opposite portico, but the rest of the patio was still in chilly blue shadow when he stepped down on the flagstones and looked up between the columns at the pale spotless sky. He took a deep breath then, smelling the air tinged with silage and wood smoke, and looked around.

Under the portico on the other side of the patio he paused to examine the stuffed head of a black bull looking down on him there. It had a Roman nose, and lacked ears. From somewhere in the unknown around him he heard faintly the jangling of spurs as someone walked across a stone floor. Then there was silence again. He scuffed his feet, self-consciously, to make a little noise, and he gave an artificial cough, continuing his circuit slowly, peering at closed doors.

At the far corner he was rewarded. A door opened and a tall old woman with a brown Indian face and gray hair looked out at him. Her two hands were on her stomach, under her black apron. He had found the kitchen of Las Astas, at least.

"Yes senor?" the woman inquired.

"I arrived in the night. A guest of the dueno," said Eladio Gomez. "Do you know if he is up and if I could see him?"

"Well. He's up with the first light, and gone out," said the woman. She made a sign outward with her hand and followed it with her eye as if her patron had gone to the end of the earth.

"Well," said Gomez. "Well. Could I ask you for a cup of coffee to start the day?"

"How not?"

She came out and opened the door next to the one she had stood in.

"Enter, senor. Be seated."

He stepped into the dim dining room and sat down at the long empty table covered with checkered cloth.

The coffee was black and thick when the woman poured it in the bottom of the big cup and then added the steaming milk to the brim. When he had drunk it, smoking a cigarette, gazing at the ornate crockery on the plate rails, he felt fortified. With his hands in his pockets he sauntered out into the morning where the sun was warming the walls.

Peons stood around outside, waiting for their foreman. They lounged by the tall open door of the saddle house, by the truck with the bull boxes, by the sunlit walls, warming themselves in the light from the sky, the "stove of the poor" that climbed bright and promising over the hills in the east. They stood in the sunlight gathering unhurriedly the direction and the desire for the work of the day, while the dew dried, and the horses were saddled. In the west the Sierra rose up pale blue and beautiful, like a promise, above them.

"Good morning," said Eladio Gomez, walking out the courtyard gate. Something in his city dwelling heart expanded there in the open sunlight. His senses reached out beyond the clay they lived in and found the tidings good.

He looked out across the markings in the sunny dust, the tracks of hoofs and paws, the tangled prints of cart wheels and truck tires, of boots and sandals and naked feet, and out beyond the open space he saw the stone pile

of the bull corrals with their heavy gates, and walked out
to examine them.

As he came around a corner, three horsemen appeared
in the lane under the pepper trees. He recognized the rider
on the big sorrel. Drawing closer, the horse pitched forward suddenly, answering the spur. Ten paces from where
Gomez stood, it reared high, spinning on its hind legs, coming down facing Gomez smartly as the rider grunted "Ho!"
and dismounted, throwing down the reins.

"Senor Gomez!"

Don Tiburcio Balbuena came forward, extending his
hand. He was tall, spare, with white mustaches, and he
was dressed in tight leather charro clothes, well worn,
under a magnificent sombrero with a hat string biting into
his monumental chin.

"You arrived, Senor Gomez. Now you know where your
house is." His voice was deep and strong as a bull's.

"Eladio Gomez at your orders, Don Tiburcio."

"At yours, Senor Gomez. I feel deeply I did not meet
you last night. . . . The lateness of the hour — "

He walked over and caught up his reins.

"This morning we have been cutting out horses for the
charro Iturbide here, to take to Michoacan." He turned to
the two riders who had come up.

"Iturbide! My friend Gomez, impresario of the plaza
at Cuenca. Senor Gomez, I might mention that Iturbide is
the proud and happy father of twenty-six children, at last
tally."

"Only twenty-five," said the charro smiling, shaking
hands.

"This is my foreman," said Balbuena, pointing to the

other horseman in the crimped straw sombrero and the old rawhide leggings with the iron buckles. "If he will permit me, I will mention that my foreman is a boar hog in the swill when he's drunk, Senor Gomez! The Whore of Babylon on Saturday nights. But he knows the bulls, Gomez, he knows them. He has faculties. Tuerto, shake hands with the dueno of the plaza at Cuenca."

The foreman took off his hat, grinning at Gomez with his mouth like a bear trap, and his one eye.

"Doroteo Paz," he said. "Your orders."

"You had some breakfasts?" boomed Balbuena, looking at Gomez.

"Not yet."

"Neither have we," said the old man. "Tuerto, take these horses. We are going to eat. And saddle one more while we're gone. Senor Gomez wants to see brave animals."

My God, thought Gomez.

"We'll get Serafina, that old cow, to put something on the table," said Balbuena. His spurs were like bells, on the flagstones. "Serafina!"

They had a tumbler of claret first. Then canned asparagus laid out on a platter, soaked in vinegar, to whet their tongues; then Spanish sardines and claret and fried beef and frijoles with plenty of chili and more claret.

"You need a foundation to look at bulls in their pastures," said Balbuena, picking his teeth. "More claret, senores?"

At the courtyard gate Gomez eyed the bay horse the one-eyed foreman had saddled for him. "I didn't bring any boots," he said.

"Don't think of it," said Balbuena. "El Tuerto has mounted you on velvet, on baby hair. Here."

El Tuerto had also sent the peons to work. "You want me with you?" he asked his patron.

"Come along," said Balbuena. "We might need you."

They mounted and rode down the lane.

"Too bad you weren't here yesterday, Senor Gomez," said Balbuena. "Tonio Algara was here. He drove out from Mexico to look at some bulls for his El Toreo. But you'll see the ones he picked. We'll load them for shipping tomorrow."

The sun climbed high and strong in the sky. The horsemen jogged across the grassy hills.

"The charro here, he probably doesn't know our Brave Bulls, our Toros de Lidia, are greater of family and purer of blood than thoroughbred horses. Do you think he knows that, Gomez?"

Gomez and the charro smiled.

"Of course I knew that," said Iturbide.

"We like the stuff with the horns, don't we?" said the dueno of Las Astas.

"Well armed with points," added El Tuerto, half to himself.

"Which points are you talking about?" asked his patron. "Anyway we like them. Let's go in this pasture and see the cows."

Tuerto took down the cedar poles across the narrow opening in the mortarless rock walling that divided the pastures of Las Astas, and the horsemen rode through.

They found a herd on the slope beyond the spring in the thicket of cottonwoods. Gaunt and baleful-eyed, the black cows lifted their sharp-horned slender heads and snorted at the riders. Their calves jumped from their nursing or from their rest in the shade, nimble as goats, and stood braced on their wiry legs, snuffing.

"The old cow at the right, the one with the twisty horns," said Don Tiburcio, trying to whisper, "she's the only one left that was dropped in Spain."

At the sound of the voice the cows and calves started away on their spring-steel legs, more like deer than cattle.

"You see the heifer turning to watch us? Can you see her shoulders? Twenty-seven times she took the iron at the tientas three weeks ago! Twenty-seven times before she had enough iron in her shoulders. Oh, she will make formidable sons! Tuerto, the shoulders are healing nicely."

"Don Tiburcio," Eladio Gomez said, "it would be a privilege to hear from your own lips how you do things here at Las Astas."

"Thank you, Senor Gomez. Of course you know everything here is purebred fighting stock which I originally, myself, brought from Spain — the casta of Saltillo, later refreshed with Murube and Pablo Romero.

"All the breeding is based on selection for bravery alone. Nothing else. As a real fighting bull can issue only from a brave sire and dam, it follows that everything depends on creating a breed herd distinguished by fighting spirit. To build it, each animal must be tested before it can be placed in such a herd.

"That is the function of the tienta, the test for fighting spirit.

"It is performed by allowing each individual heifer and young bull, at about the age of two years, to charge a mounted picador armed with a lance bearing a steel point that is sharp but which cannot penetrate to any damaging extent. The animal is then classified according to the fierceness with which it charges the horseman and receives the pain of the lance point in its shoulders.

"Bull calves are never allowed to charge more than three times, and they are never worked with the cape. This is to keep them unspoiled and innocent when they enter a bullring two years later.

"The heifers, on the other hand, are allowed to charge as much as they will; and they are worked hard with the cape to further test their desire to fight.

"I find, for my purposes, about one heifer in five brave enough to join my breed herd, where she will pass her exceptional bravery on to her sons.

"Even so, of those sons I find only about one bull in three meeting my standards at the tienta and worthy to go to a plaza wearing my ribbons.

"Certain rare, completely exceptional bulls I choose to retain at Las Astas as herd sires, to mount my cows. These seed bulls must be of the best blood lines and display the most extraordinary bravery at their tientas. After choosing them, I retest them, to make sure.

"The culls? I sell them to butchers. Or to less particular men who breed them, or sell them to plazas, calling them 'brave'!"

The remark made Eladio Gomez slightly uncomfortable. "How do you put the seed bulls to the cows?" he asked.

"I allow them to mount from June to January only, so the calves will come when the grass is good. There is a bull with the cows in this pasture now. Old Cantarillo.

"A vaquero is assigned to watch each bull, to note down upon paper the branded number of each cow his bull mounts, together with the date. Nine months later when the calf is born, I have not trusted to fences and guesswork. I have an accurate record for the registry."

"How far does the Las Astas book go back?" asked Iturbide.

"Fourteen generations now. Of course we lack data for the time of the Revolution. In our book we record not only the heredity but the history of each animal, in this order: branded number, name, description, sire, dam, date of birth, tienta date and rating, and if the animal has gone to the ring we note behavior in plaza. With this informa-tion we can breed selectively."

Around the slope they sighted Cantarillo, in the shade of a tall nopal. His man Teclo sat on a horse, keeping his distance. Cantarillo pawed the dust. He tossed it high over his shoulders, grumbling, as the horsemen went through a gate.

"Here the sucking calves stay with their mothers while their brands and earcrops heal, getting strong and learning to eat grass before they are weaned," said the dueno of Las Astas.

"The branding of brave calves is a work of talent. Tuerto here, he's a genius, wrestling the fighting devils to the mat. You ought to see it. We throw them on a pad, you know, handling them like angels. Their horn buds must not be injured, nor dirt get in their eyes, to cause defects later.

"Now we go into the big bull pasture."

He swept his arm out in a great curve.

"See it? Grass, water, and shade. See the bluffs and the breaks down that draw? Protection. See those hills? Strength of leg. See those stony ridges? Hardness of hoof. You see what gives Las Astas bulls their form?"

The sun was past the zenith, hot and bright. Eladio Gomez could feel it burning the back of his neck. His pants legs had worked up so the wrinkles chafed his legs against the stirrup leathers. He could feel the saddle soreness coming in his groins and backside. He had not been so happy in a long time.

"Here my bulls live from the time of their tientas," said Balbuena as the horses paced through the high grass, "until I put them in feed lots to fatten for the ring. Two years they live their lives here, untouched. Born of a fierce breed, living the most of their days like ranging wild animals, their power and savagery develops. They learn to use their horns among themselves.

"The festival has symbolisms that sometimes strike me, gentlemen. I love the brave bulls. For them there is no coming of old age and weakness and dying fire. No servitude, no toil. Yet we deny them the benignity of reproducing their kind. Certain of their male relations will stay home to take care of the cows and carry on the breed with those formidable sacs that swing between their legs. But not our fighters to the death. They are virgins. It is a curious thing, our festival.

"Ah," he said, trying to whisper again. "Look at them! We will not talk. Ride slowly, with care."

In the tawny grass beyond a huisache thicket a score of black bulls had tossed their heads up, gazing at the intruders squarely with their horns held high, their legs ready. The horsemen reined, stopping. From the distance of forty yards they heard the snorts, the breath plunged from the massive lungs. One bull lowered the horns, backing two steps, head down, and pawed, throwing dust. The horsemen stood rooted, facing the bulls. A breeze rippled the grass and carried the dust away in silence. Then a bull blew, whistling the air through his black nostrils, and turned slowly away, stepping with majesty through the grass. The others turned, following.

"Precioso!" whispered Eladio Gomez when they were gone.

"Some of the three-year-olds," boomed Don Tiburcio again. "They will be going next year. There should be two oxen with that bunch, Tuerto."

"The oxen are somewhere close," said the foreman. "I saw their tracks."

The horsemen rode on.

"It is strange," said Eladio Gomez, "how the herd instinct makes it possible to husband such beasts. The herd makes the tranquillity, the feeling of well-being. Take a bull suddenly from that divided responsibility of herd thinking, make him an individual, and he tries to kill you."

"Exactly!" said Balbuena. The old man winked. "The symbolism there may be why I prefer the country life!"

"The most symbolical part," said Gomez, "is the ox. Our castrated friend. Our servant with the empty sac, who is traitor to his kind. We use him to trap the savage bull from freedom, to manipulate him by deceit to where he would not go."

"Clearly symbolical!" said Balbuena.

Eladio Gomez was surprised with himself, talking like

that. Symbolically. Riding a pacing bay horse in a bull pasture.

The sun was down so that their hat brims no longer shaded their faces when they stopped at the old well La Noria under the trees, and drank the cold water, and rode on toward the walled lane that led to the bull corral.

"Along this lane," said the dueno pointing to the gates along the side, "are the feed lots for the bulls being readied for the plazas, the four-year-olds. I give them several weeks of heavy feed to build their weight and strength before they leave."

"You have any trouble getting them to take grain, after bringing them in from grass?" asked the horse buyer, Iturbide.

"Sometimes. They have to be taught. This is done right after their tientas when they are not so hard to handle. They are penned in a lot where there is nothing to eat but cracked corn in individual stone troughs. Most of the young bulls take to it and learn right away. A few refuse. They learn to eat corn from a trough, or they starve. When they are four and come in to the feed lots, they remember.

"There is a little bull in a pen back of the house where I have him now, taking his lesson. He has refused to eat for nineteen days. He is a black bag of bones. If he does not eat his cracked corn he will die, and I will let him. Starving or not, at this moment he is as full of fight as any animal at Las Astas. In a brave bull, spirit withers last of all."

"When do you bring the four-year-olds in from the grass?"

"I try to time it so they will be finish-fed, rounded out

but not too fat, at my delivery dates during the bullfight season which in Mexico, of course, is from November into March. Late in September I divide the four-year-olds into encierros, groups of six which will go to the same ring together for the same corrida. Each encierro goes to a separate feed lot, along with a couple of extras, so I'll have six for sure at shipping time. Bulls kill and injure each other, and they can get sick.

"Let me tell you the kind of heavy feed they get in the lots. Two feedings a day, one in the early morning, another soon now. The total daily ration for each bull is forty-odd pounds. About thirteen of corn, twenty-two of silage, and five or six of boiled frijoles! All this in addition to what a bull will munch of dry corn stover between feeds. Daily each bull gets a little more than an ounce of saltpeter mixed with his corn, to quiet the natural urges of bullhood. Bulls will masturbate, you know.

"Here come the feeders, the only men at Las Astas that work afoot among the bulls. They are rarely attacked, for the beasts identify them agreeably with the bringing of aliments."

A vaquero on a tired old nag preceded the squeaking, tall, two-wheeled cart that came up the lane, drawn by a team of shaggy burros. A driver sat on the cart beside the sacks of cracked corn and the frijole cans, with the sour-smelling silage stalks piled up high at his back. Another peon walked alongside. They stopped by the gate at the side of the lane where the four horsemen had dismounted.

When the feed was down from the cart, the gate was opened quietly and the vaquero on the old horse rode in. Behind him silently walked the peons carrying feed. They made four slow trips with their burdens, while the mounted man stood motionless between the feeders and the bulls that watched from among the thorn trees fifty yards away. Silently the peons portioned the feed into the troughs, then filed back to the gate, the horseman following them out as the shielding rear guard. The eight bulls came up to their troughs like milk cows and began eating.

A flock of blackbirds from the sunlit tops of the thorn trees flew in by the bulls and hopped around for crumbs.

"Pretty?" asked Balbuena in his rumbling whisper, after the long silence. The bulls looked up toward the gate, their ears cocked forward. "You want to go inside where you can see better? They are gentle while eating."

"This is fine," said the charro, Iturbide. "From here."

Eladio Gomez stood with his eyes fastened to the bulls, saying nothing. Oh, they were beautiful! A peon closed the gate, and the cart creaked down the lane.

The sun stood on the edge of the Sierra and the shadows were long and violet when the horsemen rode up to the courtyard.

"I'm dry, dry in the throat," said Balbuena. "Serafina! Serafina, brandy and some glasses — in my room."

At a rickety card table in his bedroom, the dueno of Las Astas tallied his account book for the day. He wore little steel-rimmed spectacles, penciling in the figures slowly from a paper his foreman had brought him. El Tuerto stood by, with his hat in his hand. Then they discussed tomorrow's work, while the dueno had a brandy and ate tortillas from a saucer on the spotted table.

Gomez and Iturbide sat happy and relaxed in straight chairs tilted against the wall, with brandy glasses in their hands. Gomez gazed at the framed enlargement of a bull photograph over Balbuena's iron bed. He had read the lines of white lettering at the bottom, "The Noble Bull FINITO of Las Astas. Died by the Sword of Lorenzo Garza at the Plaza El Toreo on Christmas Day of 1935."

There were tumblers of claret for dinner, and marinated fish in fiery sauce. There was a hard mountain ham from Spain, and fried beef again and more frijoles and stacks of hot tortillas. When Serafina brought in the coffee and Fundador, there were dried sweet pastries in a round tin box from Madrid.

"Of course I have been gored," Don Tiburcio was saying, "but never gravely." He knocked on wood. "I carry only a scar here on my leg and these three stiff fingers. I have had horses ripped to shreds while I lay on the ground beside them, but nothing serious. El Tuerto lost his eye here at Las Astas, falling with his face in a cactus when a bull knocked over his horse. Most of us carry the marks of the bulls. But they are usually too eager with their horns; their first thrusts are not often accurate. They butt and bump and seldom cut meat. In forty years we have had but two fatalities from bulls at Las Astas. Victims are saved by diverting actions, most often by the horses. If a man is mounted and careful, as he should be, accidents are foolish.

"Some wonderfully foolish things happen," the old man laughed, "when a bull gets hot and goes on the prod. About a month ago two agrarians from San Ysidro came over here riding one burro about the size of a dog. A handsome trio, 'on a visit to relatives.' I was standing in front of the house when they came ambling across the road.

I heard Policarpo yell from down the lane, and he yelled loud, 'Here comes a hot bull!'

"It had climbed a wall of the feed lot, I found out later. It was really hot, coming around the corner of the corral. When something like that happens, all my people take cover. Fast. They know what it means.

"I yelled to the idiots on the burro, 'Get off! Run for the wall!'

"The fool in front didn't even turn around. I heard him say, 'He will do nothing. His anger is not for us.'

"But the man by the tail took a look. He flailed the burro in the flanks and yelled, 'Oh yes his anger is —'

"I crossed myself, seeing the vision of a lawsuit before my very eyes. The donkey and the two passengers all sailed into the air. As the bull ripped the burro's belly, the front man lying down very flat said to the rear man praying flat on his back, 'Juan, this bull has anger for us.' That's what he said!"

"Yai!" said Iturbide, slapping his breeches. "What happened?"

"Nothing. They had to walk home to San Ysidro. Tuerto made a fine quite, taking the bull away with his horse. Policarpo had oxen with the bull in no time. They led him back to the feed lot.

"But handling bulls is no dull way to earn bread, gentlemen. Have more brandy. We eat early and go to bed with the chickens at Las Astas. Tomorrow we ship Tonio Algara's encierro to Mexico."

"Tomorrow I go with the horses to Michoacan," said Iturbide.

"Tomorrow I take the train," said Gomez.

"Tomorrow we find you some bulls for Cuenca," said his host.

"Don Tiburcio," said Gomez with the supper and the brandy warm and fine in him, "permit me to say I feel the privilege tonight of being the guest of a happy man."

"Gomez, you are kind." Tiburcio Balbuena fingered his brandy glass. His voice was not so loud. "I am getting old. In a long life I have lost much. I lost my wife, my two boys. I have lost a great part of my patrimony. Revolutions, agrarians, misfortunes, they have taken five sixths of the Balbuena property and I have wasted and rioted much else besides. But I have had luck, Gomez. In all of it I have found more than I could lose. I was born, as the Marques de Bradomin said of himself, 'ugly, Catholic and sentimental.' I was also born ready. I'm still ready." The old man grinned. "My family furnished the formalities. The common sense is my own."

"And the bulls of Las Astas," said Gomez.

"The festival is brave, friend Gomez, and the bulls are the finest part. Listen. I will tell you and the charro the story of a spectacle I saw with my own eyes in Sevilla when I was young.

"The old Conde de la Plata had a daughter. She rode hot-blooded horses and she loved the bulls. One of De la Plata's herd cows died and left a bull calf starving and the daughter of De la Plata saw the calf and said, 'I will tend it.' By the bottle she fed that calf for five months. The animal grew big and strong with her care, and was weaned and turned out to grass.

"At the tientas everyone wanted to see how this pet calf that showed affection for a girl would charge and bear

against the iron. The little bull was very brave; De la
Plata classed him superior and pastured him with his
best. The bull was savage to all but the girl; to her he
came when she called the name she had given him — Caribello. And he ate from her hand.

"When the bull had four years the girl pleaded with her
father to spare Caribello. But the father refused and this
bull went in his box to Sevilla.

"And, womanlike, the daughter went to save her bull.
In Sevilla she told friends of her family why she had come.
The aficion and the bull critics heard of it. The papers
printed it. On Sunday the ring was jammed.

"I was there. Caribello was the fifth bull. He killed four
horses and was very brave. When the time came for the
faena, and the matador Antonio Montes brought out his
sword and muleta, Caribello was still strong, ready. People began to understand they were seeing something. Not
the pet of a daughter of a Count, but a noble bull. He
gave pass and pass again to Montes: it was enormous.
Montes and Caribello. Dancing the strange dance
with the scarlet cloth, with Death looking down upon
them.

"The time for the sword arrived. Caribello stood fixed,
tired at last.

"The rare thing began. Someone shouted for the indulto,
the indulgence, the pardon of this bull's life. Then the sand
of the ring shook, with a shout from twelve thousand
throats, for the indulto.

"Montes walked to the center of the ring, head up, and
looked to the box of the Authority. He received the sign.
With the crowd roaring, slowly he put down upon the

sand first the muleta, then the sword, and last of all his hat upon them. Thus was granted, according to the old and yet very rare custom, the indulto.

"But that was not the spectacle.

"When the oxen came out to lead the bull away, the daughter of the Conde de la Plata walked down into the ring and held up her hand for silence. A breathless quiet came over the plaza. 'Caribello,' the girl called. He raised his head. Slowly she walked up to that hot and bloody bull, and then stroked him between the eyes. The oxen were not necessary. With her hand upon one of his horns she walked Caribello from the ring."

He poured their glasses full and they drank.

"The strange thing about breeding bulls is that you never know how successful you have been until a few minutes before your bull dies. The man who has bred a brave bull has bred a quality without measure, a spirit, that may be tested only in the destruction of it.

"To get a fighting bull you study blood lines and you balance your breed herd and hire cowboys to see that the right bull mounts the right cow. You watch the little bull nurse his mammy, and you brand him with your mark, and you study him closely when he takes the iron at his tienta. Carefully you tend him, building his size commensurate with the spirit you hope he has. You speak very confidently to impresarios like Senor Gomez here, and you sell your bull and you ship him. And it is very possible that after four years of your work and hope and expense, people in the plaza will whistle and throw bottles at your bull that is not brave.

"The bulls are a gamble. You hope they will be fine

some Sunday afternoon when they are four, but you never know until that Sunday comes.

"Meanwhile, you are grateful. You know the light of morning on the grass where your cattle are feeding. You know the smell of horse sweat and cow pens at noon, and the dry squeak of your stirrup leathers coming down the lane from the feed lots, and the dust, and the taste of brandy clearing your gullet after a ride.

"You know the long slanting afternoon light that makes the thicket of nopal seem so high above the old spring where the calves are bawling, and the water ripples going down to the corn patch. You know the smell of wood smoke at dusk when your cowboys sing going home to supper, and always you are hearing the talking of your bulls.

"You know the fun at the tientas; and the strong feeling that comes up in you, there with the crowd, when your bull comes out of the toril and charges the men resplendent with crimson and gold in the sunlight. You belong to an ancient art. It is an art that speaks to the hearts of men who understand violence. It is," said Don Tiburcio Balbuena, "a thing for glory, and to stir the multitude."

That night, asleep on the bed where Manolete once slept, Eladio Gomez in his dreams saw the most majestic bull in the history of the world. It was huge and black. He saw the immense muscles sliding under the fine-haired glossy hide. The short head was narrow at the nose and wide at the forehead where sharp and smoothly tapered horns sprang outward, then forward with upward tilting curves. The weaponed head was drawn up proudly on a massive neck where a crest of muscle, swollen into a hump, joined with a curve of brutish power into the deep shoulders. The line

of the back was concave in connecting those shoulders with
the high rounded rump, and the flanks were slick. The
hindquarters were all rippling muscle; the lower legs were
light-boned right down to the small sharp hoofs. There
were glossy curls between the angry eyes and the silky tassel of the tail touched the ground. Upon the left hip was
burned the brand of Las Astas, the mark of Tiburcio Balbuena:

EIGHT

THE DRIVER GOT IN, started the engine, and moved the truck forward slowly, inch by inch.

"Hold it!" yelled Policarpo from on top of the bull box at the end of the truck. "Back a little!" The truck backed, barely moving.

"Stop!" Policarpo signaled the driver to cut the engine.

"One more now," said Balbuena, standing by Eladio Gomez.

The truck had moved into position so that the last box stood squarely at the mouth of the loading chute. Policarpo reached down and pulled up the sliding gate on the near end of the box. When it was raised, squeaking up its grooves, the inside of the box formed a fitted terminal to the chute.

Policarpo kept his station behind the raised end gate, ready to lower it at the proper time. The box he stood on was exactly like the other three on the truck. Built of almost a thousand pounds of wooden planking reinforced with iron straps and lined at the forward end with iron plates to keep bulls from shattering the planking with their horns, each box was a standard eight feet long, six feet high, and thirty-two inches wide. Trap doors were cut in the end gates for handling feed and water, and there were ventilation slots along the sides near the top. The three loaded boxes on the truck were queerly alive. They shook, creaked, and thumped with the blows delivered against them invisibly from the inside where in each one a bull pounded with raging hoofs and horns.

"Ready!" Balbuena shouted. He and Gomez took up their stations on the masonry ledge built along the outside of the chute where they could duck down out of sight, or raise their heads to see over the wall.

The gate to the trap at the far end of the chute opened silently, manipulated with ropes handled by two peons lying flat on their bellies atop the wall at each side of the gate, and three belled oxen trotted into the trap leading and flanking a black bull. When they had led the bull in far enough, the oxen circled away and headed back out of the half-closed gate where the foreman El Tuerto, mounted on horseback, whistled softly to the oxen, cleverly speeding them out, leaving the bull alone, shut in the trap, in the silence, facing the chute with the box at the end.

The bull's great neck muscle swelled and he bellowed, pawing the dust and scouring, furious with the sudden solitude and stillness. Shut within the high stone walls the bull searched for some hint of movement, some target for his horns.

The target appeared suddenly. Up the chute near the box Tiburcio Balbuena lifted his head above the wall and swung his arm over the top, shaking his hat at the bull. "Huh! Toro!"

The bull charged through the chute after the lure, snorting and hooking at the hateful movement of the hat — and ropes pulled a gate shut at his tail, trapping him further, his head almost inside the dark box.

Without allowing the bull a pause, Tiburcio Balbuena reached over the top of the chute with an electric prod pole in his hand. He jammed it under the bull's tail, pressed the button, and with the shock the bull gave a wild snort and lunged involuntarily forward into the box.

"Now!" thundered Balbuena, and Policarpo slammed the end gate down its grooves, scraping the top of the bull's tail, hitting the hocks as they plunged while the gate came down all the way and latched into place.

"Ho!" said the dueno of Las Astas. He was smiling. "Another encierro. All safe. We had good luck this morning." He turned towards the corrals where heads had appeared from behind most of the walls. "Well done!" he boomed out. "A good faena!"

Policarpo climbed down. The bulls were jarring the boxes. plunging and bawling; he walked around peering up at the ropes and wire that fastened the load on the truck bed.

"When are you leaving?" Balbuena asked, coming down from the side of the loading chute.

"As soon as we eat," Policarpo answered.

"I will mention your responsibility again," Balbuena said. "As mayoral you have complete charge. Keep the trucks in sight of each other all the time. You ride in the lead; go slow, and take no chances. You know how many pesos are in those boxes. Take care of them. You ought to be in Mexico before sundown tomorrow. When you get to El Toreo you tell Morenito to unload you immediately. Send the trucks back Tuesday morning; you stay, and see that the bulls are cared for exactly the way we would do it here. Be there when the vets make their examinations and watch the scales when the bulls are weighed. Remember you are responsible for the animals until they come out of the toril Sunday. Don't get drunk in Mexico. You'll hear from me later in the week."

"Yes, patron." Policarpo got in the cab.

Balbuena and Gomez waved as the truck lumbered down the road. One of the bulls was bellowing.

Balbuena sat down on the ledge by the chute in the bright sun and wiped the sweat from his face. Gomez lit a black tobacco cigarette. They were alone. Gomez knew what was coming next, and tried to plan what he would say.

"Now tell me what you have in mind for your corrida, friend Gomez."

"Well," said Eladio, drawing a breath. "Don Tiburcio, as you know, my plaza is modest. The corridas there are the best I can afford, but the box office is limited. I am forced to practice economy to keep my enterprise sound. I seldom pay the high fees currently received by ranking toreros, nor can I afford the kind of bulls great plazas buy."

"I understand clearly."

"The season at Cuenca usually opens on the Fourth of December, as the main feature of the festival of our town's patron, Santa Barbara. This year I thought I might make that first corrida something special, if I could manage. I am about to sign Luis Bello as First Sword."

"Luis Bello," Don Tiburcio said. "A real torero, and my good friend. He's in the Plaza Mexico this afternoon; we'll listen to the corrida on the radio. Luis says his career was born at Las Astas: he came here as a boy herding horses. The bay you rode yesterday, Gomez, is out of a Pedrazo mare Luis Bello drove to Las Astas. To be honest, I don't remember him then. There were so many kids wanting to wave their shirts at the bulls. But I do remember the Bello uncle, an old man with spurs on his sandals. He delivered the horses. Luis is in the grand tradition all right: his people were hungry enough! He has fought many bulls from these pastures — "

"He wants Las Astas bulls at Cuenca, Don Tiburcio. I want them too — " Gomez added. "That's why I came — "

"You ought to have them. Who's alternating with Luis?"

"He wants his kid brother Pepe on the card."

"The kid, eh? Who else?"

"Nobody yet. And if I get Las Astas bulls, I can't afford six of them, nor three toreros. I can't."

"Raise the price of seats for a gala festival on the Saint's Day."

"I'm afraid of that, Don Tiburcio. Circumstances — the people of Cuenca, they — "

"Then what you are thinking is this: a mano a mano, a hand to hand, between the two brothers. And only four bulls."

"What do you think of it?"

"Well — why not? A short one. But quality not quantity. Something special. The Great Swordsman of Guerreras with bulls of the first class from Las Astas. What's wrong with that?"

"The only thing is the kid. Pepe. That part don't seem so strong. It's no mano a mano because it's no heated competition."

"Luis insists on the kid of course?"

"That's it."

"Go on, Gomez. You know Luis will put on a show. You know that. And the kid will be trying. Trying hard. Suppose he did take his alternativa a little early, that the public remains, shall we say, somewhat cynical regarding Pepe Bello. He will be trying, with good bulls. And the two brothers together in the ring will give a color, a certain interest."

"The Cuenca public is hard, Don Tiburcio."

"The public anywhere is hard, my friend. It's a gamble. From my standpoint, from yours, from the toreros', from the public's, it's a gamble. Everybody risks something. Whether it's the price of a back row seat on the sunny side, or death on the horns, everybody has to risk something."

"It's the only thing to do, I guess," said Eladio Gomez.

"I'm going to take you out now and show you some bulls for the Bello boys at Cuenca," said Balbuena. "I have something in mind."

Out at the feed lot they leaned with their chins on their hands, looking over the high wall. The peon that went with them threw rocks at the bulls in the enclosure, so that they stood up, alert, in the shade of the huisache.

"I will take the two reserves from this encierro, Gomez, and two from another. You understand that these are absolutely Number Ones. I will show you the book when we go to the house. Write down those numbers, 74 and 107, and we will check their ratings in the registry."

"They are wonderful bulls, Don Tiburcio. But I can't pay the price you get for them at the big plazas. Have you got — "

"I have something in mind," said the dueno. "Now let's look at the other pair I want to show you in the lot down the lane."

The peon got the other encierro up, throwing more rocks. "Ho! Toros! Ho!"

One of the bulls in the enclosure stood out from all the rest. His horns were good, turning slightly toward each other, like parentheses. His barrel and legs were well shaped and powerful, matched in size and line with the other bulls. But he was ugly. He had a marked Roman nose. Coarse hair grew under his jaws like a beard, along the brisket, under the belly to the pizzle. And the tassel of his tail was missing. He was a whiskered, bobtailed bull.

"What's that one doing in there?" asked Gomez. He sensed the impending offer. He understood now what Balbuena might have in mind.

"Listen," said Balbuena. "That nose and that hair are just one of those rare matters that crop up in breeding. There is nothing wrong with that bull, Gomez. Unfortunately a coyote nipped the end of his tail off when he was a calf, and left him rabon. But I gave him four stars at his tienta. I'll show you in the book. Number 23. Write that down. You can see he's the amo, the master of that encierro, now. I've had my eye on him since he lost his tail. He deserves a torero. I say he is a Senor Toro!"

"People expect something different from that, wearing the green and gold ribbons. No, Senor Balbuena! That buffalo would make people laugh and then get mad and throw things!"

"Senor Gomez. That bull is out of the best cow at Las Astas. He will give a torero worth the name a real time. The horns are nice to work. Look at them. Turned in just right."

"With the whiskers and that rabon? No, senor! Begging your pardon, it is a cartoon of a bull. Like the funny papers."

"All right, Gomez. Look. Granted I can't sell Rabon to the big boys. They say he's ugly. All right. I say I like the bull. I say he will wear my ribbons very well. You are looking for four Number One Las Astas and — if we must be brutal a moment — you cannot pay what I ask for them. I can only make you this offer. You take the bobtailed bull along with three other Number Ones, and we will do business. I'll give you that Number 37, the pretty one by the wall, to go with Rabon."

"How much?" Gomez asked. He was sweating.

"What do you offer? You know the worth of the bulls."

"Well — "

"For four selected Number Ones I can get above twenty thousand pesos in the Capital this season. What can you afford?"

"Nothing like that, Don Tiburcio."

"All right. You take the bobtail. What can you afford?"

"Fifteen thousand?" Gomez asked.

Tiburcio Balbuena broke into a laugh. "Gomez, the devil sits on the shoulders of hagglers. Take the bulls for sixteen thousand."

"I'll take them."

Gomez had to laugh then himself. "That bug without a tail!"

"That's a bull. You wait and see. Of course the Bellos will be mad. But they won't stay mad. They'll see. The crowd won't laugh long. They'll forget the whiskers."

"You've settled it, Don Tiburcio."

"Good. Now. I want to find Tuerto and have him put your four together so they'll get used to each other and not cause injuries in the pens at Cuenca."

Sitting alone on a bench in the courtyard sunlight, waiting for his host to return, Gomez probed at the work and the worry he saw ahead, promoting the half-born corrida. It was hard to wait until he could notify Raul Fuentes, to get that signature on the dotted line. He wished it were train time. If the Bellos refused a mano a mano with the four bulls . . . well . . . that would be the fat pearl in the crown! That would chill him. He was glad when Don Tiburcio walked into the courtyard.

Gomez had not seen the parlor in the big house. He was surprised it was there, when his host opened a door from the patio and asked him in.

"The radio's here; I can't move it because of the antenna attachment into this window," said the dueno. "It's about time for the corrida. Serafina is going to bring refreshments. Except for the broadcasts, I seldom use this room." He extended his arm as if in explanation, indicating the oil portrait over the mantel and the two large elaborately framed tinted photographs on either side. Gomez understood by the gesture these were portraits of the wife and the sons Balbuena had lost. He nodded, and said nothing.

The rest of the room was a dusty museum of tauromachia. Gomez noticed first the dim crimson and silver wallpaper with its design of garlanded plazas de toros and its beribboned bright instruments of the lidia. Up toward the ceiling, extending around all four walls, was a papered frieze of matched hand-colored lithographs by Daniel Perea, a hundred scenes of all the pageantry of a nineteenth-century corrida de toros. Hanging on the walls were stuffed heads of bulls with engraved plaques under them. The bulls' necks were encircled by braided silken cords of green and gold. There were elaborate banderillas with sharp barbs and dusty satin flowers held by ribbons to the wall. Two picador's lances and a picador's wide beaver hat were fastened above a torero's rose silk cape draped on the wall by the scarlet wool of a muleta formally folded over the blade of a matador's red-handled sword. In the corner by the door was a great silk rosette lettered LAS ASTAS in gold, with wide satin streamers of green and gold hanging from it almost to the floor. A long double line of photographs stretched along one wall, action scenes in bullrings, pictures of bulls, autographed portraits of toreros. The radio sat on a scratched old library table by tall stacks of bullfight magazines, and chairs upholstered in worn, torn leather, and a tall brass spittoon.

"Enormously interesting," said Gomez.

"No," said Balbuena. "It's a warehouse. There's no one to tend it. Before the Revolution this room was different. The draperies were all embroidered toreros' capes held in place by the polished horn tips of Las Astas bulls. There were Moorish rugs and the furniture was carved with bulls and gilded in Sevilla. On a night in 1915 bandits threw everything into the patio. They had a bonfire. No, Gomez. You see only remains. Some souvenirs accumulated since those days. But all the great figures have been in this room — Bombita to Manolete — all of them."

Serafina brought in the manzanilla rack, loaded with food on the compartmented wooden plate that formed the base around the tall bottles in the center and the circle of thin cylindrical wineglasses.

"Help yourself, Gomez," said the host, pouring two glasses of manzanilla and starting to eat. "It's good."

With the cool wine they ate creamed goat cheese and tortillas, spiced mountain ham, cold fried anchovies and little green olives soaked in lime juice, and they poured more wine.

"You know how I saved the casta of my brave bulls when the revolucionarios took this place, Gomez? Have you heard the story? I loaded my great seed bull, Flamenco, and eight of my best cows in boxes. I armed my people and we hauled those boxes on wagons, fighting, in the night, all the way to my father's old house in the city of Zacalisco. We tended those animals in four bedrooms of that house in town with mattresses hung in the windows to keep out bullets, for fifteen weeks, and by God we kept the casta! Your bulls, Senor Gomez, come from animals we fed in my family's bedrooms long ago."

Gomez had another glass of manzanilla.

"Ai! What time is it?" Balbuena asked. "We're forgetting the corrida!" He turned on the radio. "What station do you get it best in Cuenca?"

"XEW," said Gomez.

"The same out here," said Balbuena, twisting the dial so that the red needle pointed straight up on the kilocycle band. "Don Verdades is not a bad narrator."

When the tubes warmed, a blare of sound blasted out at them.

"Ho!" Don Tiburcio shouted, as if the radio were a horse. He turned the volume down, tuning.

" — and, there go the third pair! Served by Monkey Garcia fast and badly placed," the radio said, intelligibly.

"That's it!" Balbuena said. "We're late. They're nailing banderillas."

The two listeners lit cigarettes and settled back in the leather chairs.

"Luis Bello has the sword and the rag in his hand now, he's coming out. He walks over and looks up to the Judge, and salutes the Authority. He will now make the dedication of his bull, the third bull of the afternoon here at Plaza Mexico."

"We are really late, Don Tiburcio," said Gomez.

" — the dedication is to an individual. Ah! It is to Bello's manager and friend, Senor Raul Fuentes, sitting in the first row. I beg your pardon, ladies and gentlemen, it is not to Senor Fuentes. The dedication is to a beautiful young lady sitting next to Fuentes. A very beautiful girl. She is smiling. She catches the matador's hat when he tosses it up to her. Bello is now walking around the barrera to face the bull, which has taken up a position near the toril.

"Bello is citing the bull with muleta in right hand. There! No, no. The bull did not follow! Bello chopped with the rag from horn to horn. He is having difficulty adjusting. Now he tries again, approaching, for a two-handed pass with the cloth held high. There! But a very mediocre high pass. The bull does not turn for a repeat. Luis Bello is trotting after the bull. There is some whistling from the crowd.

"This is very dull, friends of the radio audience. Bello is angry. The Swordsman of Guerreras has not shown us anything yet this afternoon. He has not shown his usual feeling of domination.

"He is chopping at the horns again, without undue risk. There is more whistling. Loud remarks from the sunny side — "

"Bad!" Eladio Gomez said.

"The bull won't charge past him," Balbuena said. "He's sweating a bull made of lead."

"Friendly listeners," said the voice on the radio, "Luis Bello has just made two inconclusive passes with the right hand, and has continued chopping at the horns. Bello is

being intelligent and discreet with a difficult bull, but his
work is without spirit. The crowd demands more. Bello
has given up the idea of developing a faena. He is trying
to square the bull for a sword thrust. There is whistling
and booing.

"The sword hit bone! It's still in Bello's hand! He's
squaring again, mounting the sword. Oh! Bello is having a
bad time! He hit solid bone again and the sword bent and
whistled into the air. He's disarmed, the muleta is hanging
on the horns. Somebody has just thrown a cushion. More
cushions! Bello is at the barrera taking another sword and
rag. He's sweating ink."

"Fiasco," Gomez said.

"There!" said the radio voice. "Bello has delivered half
the blade. It is on the bias. It is not sufficient to bring the
bull down! There is a strong demonstration arming against
Bello from the sunny side. There is a scandal of cushions
and whistling. Bello is attempting to sever the spinal cord
at the base of the skull with a descabello. One jab. No
good. Another. O ladies and gentlemen! The Plaza Mexico
is the scene of a near riot!"

The roar blurred the broadcaster's voice.

"At last." Balbuena and Gomez heard it with difficulty.
"The ninth intent to descabellar is successful. The ninth!
The bull is dead, the mules are coming out. The demonstration continues. Bello is walking very slowly now, across
the ring. His head is down. I see tears on the face of Luis
Bello, ladies and gentlemen. Police are making arrests of
demonstrators in the stands. The monos are clearing the
cushions from the ring."

"Holy Mother," Balbuena said. He filled his glass. "But

they all have afternoons like that. They all have them. It starts with something very small, and once it's started, the devil builds a monument. Imagine that funnel of fifty thousand screamers pouring their venom down on you, flooding your brain."

A gloom descended upon the impresario of the plaza of Cuenca. Luis Bello would be a savage this week. He would be a son of filth to deal with, signing a contract with a fiasco still in his teeth. He might not come to Cuenca at all. He might go into a slump and be terrible even if he came to Cuenca. Gomez looked up at the bull heads, the bull pictures, the bull business, that surrounded him, and he thought of sixteen thousand pesos, and he hated the bulls. He wished he owned a grocery store.

"This is Don Verdades bringing to you a regular Sunday afternoon chronicle of bulls from the Capital of the Republic, sent to you for your listening pleasure over radio station XEW."

It happened suddenly during the fourth bull. Skinny Salazar had been the soul of caution, the competent old craftsman on tired legs, working his last animal of the afternoon, for money. The glory for Juan Salazar was past and no longer necessary to him; Don Verdades droned the period of the cavalry, the period of the sticks, and now, the period of the blade. Salazar was making a pass with the sword and muleta in his right hand, a pass he had made ten thousand times, when the bull got him.

The tone of Don Verdades's voice jerked Gomez and Balbuena up in their chairs.

"Sacred Name, the bull has Salazar! Ahh! *Ai ai ai!* Oh, friends! *Ai!*" The voice was silent. The static popped and crackled. Balbuena jumped up and turned the volume knob, waiting, with a wrinkle like a gash between his brows, with the static crashing.

"Ladies and gentlemen," the voice resumed, trying to control itself. "Friends. This is Don Verdades at the Plaza Mexico. I will try to recount the tragedy just witnessed by the plaza. Juan Salazar has been gored, horribly gored, by the fourth bull of the afternoon. They are carrying Juan to the infirmary. His blood stains the sand, stains his clothes. He appears unconscious.

"Ladies and gentlemen. Salazar was intending a low pass with the right. It is impossible for me to say at this moment the reason for what occurred: the bull cut in from his charge and the right horn caught Salazar in the right thigh, tossing him. Before intervention was possible, the horn found Salazar again on the ground, and again. At least ten capes were at the rescue. It was very confused. I believe Salazar's swordhandler pulled him from under the bull while a cape was over the beast's face. Someone had the bull by the tail, twisting. It is impossible to give details at this time, ladies and gentlemen. Salazar is now in the infirmary. This announcer will give you full word from the operating room at the earliest possible moment. Stay tuned to Don Verdades, XEW."

Balbuena and Gomez were standing, looking at each other.

"Luis Bello," continued the radio, "whose cape was prominent in the rescue, Luis Bello has muleta and sword, is walking out to kill the Salazar bull. The bull has a wet horn, ladies and gentlemen. The horn is red. Bello is squaring, mounting the blade. There it is! *Now* we have the great

Swordsman of Guerreras! A tremendous lunge in over the horns, ladies and gentlemen. An enormous volapie by Luis Bello! A revenge by Luis Bello. The bull is dead! A terrible drama. Bello stands over the beast. Bello has thrown the muleta on the ground; he is walking to the barrera, wiping the blood of the bull from his sword hand."

The voice of Don Verdades was hoarse and tired as it came with the static to the two waiting listeners at Las Astas. It recounted without excitement the regular progress of the fifth bull toward death at the hand of Luis Bello before an unresponsive, almost silent plaza.

"The crowd is not seeing the ring. The crowd is imagining a white room under the plaza. It is waiting for word from under the bright lights in the white room," said Don Verdades.

Young Chato Palacios was placing a pair of banderillas on the last bull of the afternoon, his bull, when the word came.

"Attention! Attention, all Mexico. Juan Salazar, beloved veteran matador of Teotihuacan, is dead. He died in the infirmary of the Plaza Mexico in the Capital of the Republic approximately three minutes ago, as a result of wounds suffered at the horns of a bull in this afternoon's corrida, reported to you by Don Verdades, radio station XEW. The name of another glorious martyr is now inscribed on the golden catafalque of the brave festival! Juan Salazar is dead. The nation's heart mourns. Rest in Peace, Juan Salazar, torero."

The loud-speakers at the Plaza Mexico boomed and rattled above the voice of Don Verdades on the radio.

The crowd was not interested in watching Chato Palacios

finally kill his last bull on the day of his doctorate, in the center of the world.

"I've got to get the train tonight," Eladio Gomez said to his host. "The train to Mexico, not Cuenca!"

"We'll get you to Cienleguas in time. I think I'll go with you, Gomez. To pay my respects to the remains. Salazar sat in this room many times. I didn't think the bulls would ever get him. He wasn't the type. The public will make him a hero now for a couple of days while they bury him, after making him a cynic while he lived, past his day. Dying on the way down."

"I'm wondering about Luis Bello," Gomez said. "My corrida."

NINE

IN THE PASSAGEWAY and patio under the towering plaza the crowd was jammed too tight to move. A squad of soldiers guarded the infirmary door, blocking and shoving with their rifle butts, trying to hold back the flood. Police blew their whistles around the edges of the packed mass of the crowd, ordering, pleading, threatening without any effect on the morbid mob. It was too big to put under arrest; the police were angry.

At the dense rim of the crowd by the cuadrilla gate that led from the ring, Luis Bello and Chato Palacios with all their toreros pushed and swore at the packed backs that blocked their way to the infirmary door. By tradition, and by their own deep desires, the toreros owed an appearance in the infirmary, now that the corrida was over, now that the bulls were all dead. Juan Salazar was dead too, and they could not get to him. The police were helpless, trying to clear them a path to where Juan Salazar lay.

A wailing chorus of sirens moaned down the ramp from the outside of the plaza. Motorcycles roared with the sirens, and the sound ripped into the enclosed passageway blasting at the walls and racking at the mob. Ringed around a black hearse in the dim light the motorcycle police plowed into the side of the crowd. It fell back upon itself stumbling, shouting, melting in front of the wheels that would not stop but slowly rolled with the sirens screaming like doom's approach, to the infirmary door.

"They're getting him out, they're taking him away!"

The crowd swirled like a wave lifting itself and lapped around the white-sheeted stretcher swallowed by the black hearse doors.

"No use now! No use!" Palacios shouted in Bello's ear.

The sirens screamed, the motorcycles popped, the exhaust smoke fogged the dim passageway as the hearse plowed through the other side of the crowd, carrying Juan Salazar away from a bullring for the last time.

"Now break it up, you bastards!" roared the police,

charging. "There's nothing more! Get the hell out of here," they howled, and the rim of the crowd broke in pieces. The sirens were screaming yet. Caught in the drift of the backing mob, the toreros were pinned and surrounded in the passageway, and the crowd turned its curiosity and its remarks upon the trapped cuadrillas, sweaty and mussed in their soiled satins and bloody glitter. Luis Bello heard the phrase in the crowd and heard them laugh, "The Axman of Guerreras!"

"I'm tired of this," Luis Bello said between clenched teeth. "But not too tired to show you, you herd of filth. Gimme one of those swords, Tacho! Open that case and gimme one of those estoques. Open it, goddammit! I'm going to kill me a few dirty filthy lousy bastards that like blood! I'll give you some blood, I give you some blood out of your own dirty whoremother hearts that like to see blood," rasped Luis Bello, grabbing at the sword cases under Tacho's arm. Goyo Salinas held the matador. Bello was crying.

Raul Fuentes broke through, with the police. He was bareheaded and white-faced.

"Let's go, Luis. Let's go home," Raul said, putting his hand on Bello's shoulder. "Let's go."

A cordon of police escorted the bedraggled procession to the outside gate. Swordhandlers' assistants lugging loaded cape baskets and empty water jugs brought up the drooping rear. No one said a word. The Bello cuadrilla climbed in Luis's car.

"Thank you, Chief," Raul said to the captain of police, handing him something when he shook hands. "That mob of — "

"Infamy, canaille!" said the policeman. "Thank you, Senor Lawyer Fuentes."

"You go with them," Tacho said to Raul. "I'll drive Goyo's car and bring the stuff." He gave Raul the key to the Buick, and Raul got in at the wheel.

The sun was down behind the mountains when the crowded car got on the boulevard and turned toward San Angel. Nobody said a word. There were heavy clouds behind the dark peak of Ajusco. A wind swayed the tops of the trees along the parkway in the fading light.

When the Bello cuadrilla fought in Mexico they dressed for the ring at Luis's house; afterwards they always returned together to San Angel where they could bathe and change to their street clothes again. On evenings after triumphs, friends and fans swarmed to the house where Luis held open court with his cuadrilla, accepting congratulations while his callers rehearsed his exploits to each other and prolonged his triumph. It was different after an afternoon without luck. The fans went to pay court to a more fortunate matador then; or if they were confirmed Bellistas, they went home glum, to wait for another day. Only a faithful few would come to offer their comforts after a gray afternoon in the plaza.

But this evening as Raul drove up the narrow lane there were cars and a crowd by the gate to the matador's house. Tonight Luis Bello was no hero; he was contact man with a tragedy, to be touched if possible, morbidly, and to mourn with.

When Luis and his men got out of the car in the garden they were surrounded. Stiff and sore, with the sweat drying cold on their silks, they wished for no company, neither mourners nor enthusiasts, but they had them. Luis allowed a few of the faithful and the influential to embrace him, but he answered none of their words. He felt numb and gutless now that he had quit trembling with his rage. His jaw muscles worked as he walked into his house.

Tacho came driving Goyo's car into the garden; the watchman lifted out the cape baskets and the swords. He had a score of anxious volunteers to help him take them to the house. Raul Fuentes skillfully assumed the public relations of his shaken matador.

Upstairs, with no less skill, Tacho drew a hot bath and got Luis Bello's hair unfastened from the black velvet button of the pigtail pinned on the back of his head; got him out of the scuffed slippers, the bloody gold-crusted jacket with the black band on the left sleeve, the spangled vest and the sash and the wrinkled satin tie, the skin-tight glittering taleguilla, the stained embroidered shirt, the dirty pink stockings, the gritty white sox, the long sweaty underwear, the shining silver medals of La Virgen de Guadalupe and Santa Barbara from around his neck.

Luis Bello got into the bath where his flesh seemed to melt outward away from him in the hot water, pulling the tense knots out of his flat empty belly, away from his arms and his legs floating in the heat, dissolving the knots out of his shoulders, and finally from the inside of his tired skull. He felt better when Raul came upstairs.

"Raul, I never even noticed. What in hell did you do with the girl? I forgot."

"Some people took her home. The Galvez Ramiros were sitting next to us. They took her; I went to find you. Listen, you ought to get out of this house now. We'll go to my place. The cuadrilla can meet us there after they've eaten. Then we'll go out to Salazar's, all of us. You better stay with me at the hotel where I can block the fans and the phone calls until after the funeral. It's no good being around here. Everybody can get at you and make you nervous. There are two reporters downstairs now, more coming, and everybody seems to think the idea is to cry. Tacho, you can handle them here; I'll handle them at the hotel. We won't tell anybody where Luis is."

It was raining when they drove into town. The windshield wipers clacked and the water whished, thrown by the wheels on the black shining streets, in the silence. There was no talk. Raul hunched over the wheel, intent on driving. Luis sat with his hands in his trench coat pockets. He had an unlighted cigar in his teeth.

The newsboys were screaming the name of Juan Salazar in the rain, along with the lottery tickets, by the hotel door. At the lobby desk in the Ritz, Raul left strict instructions. He was not in. Luis Bello was not with him.

They ordered dinner in the room. On the day of a corrida a torero never eats a meal until his work is done; Luis Bello was usually ravenous after an afternoon in the plaza. Tonight, as he sat at the table the waiter brought to Raul's rooms, the food stuck in Luis Bello's throat.

"Can you give me a brandy, Raul? I'm not hungry."

The cuadrilla knocked on the door about ten. They were feeling better with food under their belts. They were beginning to look back on the afternoon more professionally, with less emotion. The Jackdaw was limping.

"That goat of a second bull," the Jackdaw said. "He jumped like a goat."

"He knocked you off like a goat, too," said the Little White. "Why didn't you start with enough stick?"

They discussed the corrida lightly around the edges and had a drink. Nobody mentioned the third bull, nor the fourth.

Damp and crowded together, they drove out the wet streets that led into the Colonia Roma. The mass of the city seemed drawn into itself, huddled in the dark with the rain beating down. The modest parlor of Juan Salazar's rented house was dimly lighted and jammed with people when Luis Bello and his men came in out of the rain. The guests in the dead man's house smelled of damp wool and alcohol as they crowded together talking low.

An uncle of Juan Salazar led Luis alone into another room where the women of the house sat weeping with black veils over their faces.

"O how did it happen?" Juan's mother asked herself aloud. She did not expect an answer. It was simply a refrain for her grief. "He never regained his senses. His tongue could not shape a last word for those who loved him."

"I did not feel it when Juan went away," said his wife. "He was in the suit of canary and silver. I didn't know."

Juan Salazar's three small children were in the room with the women. The little boy said to Luis, "A bull killed Papa."

Luis groped through his mind hunting for some words. He did not find them. There was a kind of embarrassment joined to this suffering; there were real tears in his eyes and he wished there were none.

"Juan was, Juan was my friend," he said to the women.

"I came to tell you. If you need anything. If I can help. Ask me, senoras. If you need anything."

The undertakers brought the body a little after midnight. Juan Salazar's swordhandler came with them. He had just dressed his matador for the last time. In a blue serge suit. Tonight was the end of his matador, tonight was the end of his own career. Nineteen years in the plazas and the bulls finally got Juan. The swordhandler's eyelids were puffy and red.

They wheeled the coffin in on a metal stand, lifting it over the doorsill, then placing the stand with its burden in the center of the room. An undertaker brought in four tall candlesticks and arranged them on the bare floor at the four corners of the coffin. He fitted them with high white candles, and when he lit them the flames cast a new light on the crowded faces all turned and fastened on the long black box.

There were many kinds of faces. Most of them had looked out upon a thousand sunny afternoons when the bands played and the applause was loud, but now the candlelight leached that from them, took it all away, left only the ends of those afternoons when the darkness came.

Garza and Silverio were there; Fermin Espinosa with his brown bony face, by his brother Juan, and fat Don Felipe Mota. The Briones stood together; Gregorio, Chucho, the old Tiger of Guanajuato with his forelock in his eyes. Valles looked down over the shoulders of Ochoa and Vasquez Alas with Luis Procuna at his side. The Balderas were there, remembering a coffin like that; the Algaras and the Madrazos flanked Chimo, who remembered Linares and a grave in Cordoba. Rivera, Manolo, Castro. Carlos

Rojo looking bitter. The kid Chato Palacios and Luis Bello
with Raul Fuentes and the cuadrilla and a waiter from the
Tupinamba. Whatever they all felt for and against each
other, whatever feuds or friendships burned for them in
the sunlit plazas, the candlelight now did not reveal. The
hungry faces of bad luck, the tired faces of mediocrity,
the well-known and the obscure faces of adversity, bru-
tality, loyalty, and everything else written from the human
heart and the horns of the bulls, were crowded to the
corners in Juan Salazar's parlor.

A priest made the sign of the cross and said a Latin
prayer by the coffin; the undertakers opened the lid to
show Juan Salazar's face, under glass; the women of the
family cried aloud coming up to the bier to see their man
who was home again.

The face was not a true likeness of Juan Salazar. It was
thinner than ever. It was too pale and too quiet. Juan
Salazar did not look as if he slept, either well or poorly.
Juan Salazar looked dead and it did not matter how he
slept. Juan Salazar had gone, leaving some clay.

Valles placed a great bouquet of red carnations at the
feet of the clay.

It was raining harder than ever when Luis and Raul
drove back to the Ritz.

"I had to get out," Luis said. "Father Jesus of the Great
Power! I had to leave."

"Sure, Luis. You had plenty today. Plenty."

"It's true what they're all saying, Raul. If the bulls
can get Skinny, then nobody's safe. Nobody. He knew the
answers, so many years. It shows you. It don't seem right,
the bulls getting Salazar."

"How did it happen, Luis? His back was turned to where I was sitting. What really happened?"

"The wind. A little puff of wind. It blew the muleta back, and the bull did the rest. It caught him unlucky. It just happened. It happens a thousand times out there on the sand, and luck takes care of you. Then it happens one more time."

The headlines were black with the name of Juan Salazar on all the newspapers at the desk in the Ritz.

"Remember I'm not in," Raul told the clerk. "Send up all the papers when I call in the morning."

"I don't give a damn what the papers say," Luis told Raul when they were in Raul's rooms. "I did what I could."

"Everybody knows that. If anybody thinks different the hell with them and their mothers."

They undressed by the twin beds.

"I want to know, Raul, what did Linda say? I knew I shouldn't have toasted that frilling glue-footed ox to her. I knew it when I did it. I knew it was no good. But I hoped. What'd she say, Raul?"

"Don't worry about it. She felt terrible, on your account. She knew you were trying, don't worry."

"I thought I could make a faena anyway. I couldn't. I toasted her a fiasco."

"Quit worrying, Luis. There's plenty more Sundays when things will be different."

"It won't take many more Sundays like this one, senor mine."

"Quit worrying. Go to sleep." He turned off the light.

"Salazar died broke. His family hasn't got nothing."

"Juan was never the torero you are."

"He was pretty damn good. Raul, I want to be smarter with the money. Will you help me be smarter? A real program. I'll listen."

"You'll do all right, twin. Sure I'll help. If you're serious."

"I'm serious, Raul. This don't last forever. It don't feel like it used to."

"Knock off that. Go to sleep."

"The horn was wet right up to the hair. It was red and sticky."

"For Christ's sake, Luis!"

"Meat for the bulls. They say it about me. They always have."

"What the hell do they know about it?"

"Who knows?"

"You know, goddammit. Get to sleep!"

"I don't know," Luis Bello said.

In the morning the rain rolled down the windowpanes and it was very gray.

"We won't do a thing today," Raul said. "We'll hole up. Thank God the funeral isn't until tomorrow. Look at the rain."

"They'd have to bury old Skinny like a sailor," Luis said. "In the ocean. Let's order up some breakfast. I'm hungry."

"I'm glad you are," Raul said.

Eating their breakfast in the sitting room, they looked at the newspapers. When they had finished, there was a great litter on the floor. The press bulged with the tragedy

of Juan Salazar. The sob sisters even brought the weather
into it. They said the heavens joined Mexico's mourning
and wept for a brave torero.

Luis looked mostly at the pictures. *Esto* carried seven
full pages of corrida photographs, including two blurred
views of Juan Salazar dead in the infirmary. Luis did not
read much of the text detailing the afternoon. Big words
gave him difficulty; his reading was painfully slow. He
left that to Raul.

They lit cigars and the smoke hung in lazy layers in the
closed room.

"The critics were fairly decent, Luis. They should be.
They gave no prominence to the third bull. Everything is
a flood of tears for Salazar. After the way the poor devil
has gone begging for corridas in wooden plazas lately!"

"They like a torero better when he's dead. Oh, how they
love to mourn, feeling no pain," Luis Bello said.

"The rest of the corrida yesterday is more or less for-
gotten. You don't lose any cartel, or very little, over that
third bull. They forgive you with that sword thrust you
made on the fourth."

"The coyotes make me sick," said Luis. "There's some
lousy pictures of me here offering the apple to that
third ox."

"But the stuff about Salazar," Raul said. "They dig
their tripes out, hanging the crepe. They shovel it. Listen
to this: 'Rather than eulogies, than poems, than ballads on
the streets, may this torero who has gone from us receive
in simple farewell that sweetest of prayers for the eternal
rest of his soul: Our Father Who art in Heaven —' Here's
another one: 'No torero of the highest summits, no favorite

child of the Goddess Fortune, Juan Salazar yet bathed himself in the sweat of afternoons of triumph. He was a brave one amongst the bravest in a festival that calls itself brave, but has no surplus of valor. He fell a victim of his valor; he fell a victim of his honor, lest he leave a plaza cheating the fans, many or few, who paid for a ticket to see him. Yesterday afternoon he gave a pass with his muleta to immortality!' "

"He fell because there was a little wind and it caught him unlucky," Luis said. "He gave a pass with his muleta to the infirmary! Where we all go, with Doctors Ibarra and Rojo de la Vega looking down at us. Raul, it may be this festival business has no surplus of valor like it says there, but it's got enough bullshit. Plenty of that. Poor old Skinny! We got to order a wreath for him. The biggest damn funeral wreath ever made."

"You're going to save your money, Luis. You're serious."

"I'm serious all right. But I'm not starting on it until after this wreath I'm talking about. I want them to put with white carnations ADIOS JUAN. Something like that. FROM YOUR FRIEND LUIS. All written with flowers."

He picked up the phone and called the house in San Angel to tell Tacho to order the wreath, right away.

"The best," he said.

Tacho asked if he had received the long distance from Sain Alto, Zacatecas; he had referred the operator to the Ritz.

"No, I haven't got it," said Luis. "That must be Pepe. Look Tacho, if you want me for anything, make the operator ring this room."

Luis clicked the receiver to get the hotel switchboard.

"Did long distance call me from Zacatecas? Well, if they do, I want the call."

He hung up and turned to Raul.

"Pepe, I guess. He probably listened to the corrida."

"He's probably anxious about his bookings, too," Raul said. "We ought to be hearing from Cuenca. Eladio Gomez."

"Still hooking at the wind?"

"Probably, but it's worth a whack."

Luis sat down and relit his cigar. He did not feel as well as when he first awoke, and he settled back in the overstuffed chair, staring at the blue smoke from his cigar. The rain outside made a discouraging sound on the windows. His eye caught idly at words on the newspaper near his feet. The words formed slowly in his eyes; their meaning and import slowly came into his mind. The words were under a cut of Juan Salazar at the moment of his goring. They said something about "the destiny of toreros who go on fighting 'one more time.'" It sounded like a hell of a thing to print about Juan Salazar. About anybody. Luis Bello knocked on wood.

"It's dead around here, Raul. Makes me nervous. Let's do something. Is your radio working? Let's go somewhere."

The phone rang.

"For you, Luis."

Pepe Bello was calling from El Sauz; Luis said yes, he would accept the call collect. The connection was poor and the brothers had difficulty hearing each other.

"Sorry about the corrida yesterday, Luis. That's bad about old Skinny."

"Very bad," said Luis. "What you doing? You coming down here?"

"You got any bookings for me?"

"Not yet."

"Then I'm going back to Guerreras."

"Why?"

"A cow stepped on Loco. Broke his collarbone here at the tientas. I'm going to take him back home in his car."

"Can't you kids stay out from under cows? What you trying to do? Milk them?"

"No, fight them. Loco lost. We nearly died laughing."

"Fighting cows is a losing game, kid. Specially from underneath. Ole! When you coming to Mexico?"

"Jank and I and Abundio will be there the end of the week. Tell Raul for God's sake I want a corrida. I'm going broke."

"Come on down here. I'm going to Guadalajara Saturday."

"I'll see you when you get back from there."

"Stay out of trouble."

"You too. Luck, Luis, for next Sunday. I want a booking, tell Raul."

"He knows it. See you, boy. Keep off the horns."

Luis put the phone on the hook.

"I owe you for that call. Damn kids! They have the fun. A cow stepped on one of Pepe's pals and broke something. Pepe's taking him back to Guerreras. Raul, let's get out of here. Let's go downstairs and sit in the bar and see people. I got to do something. Today makes me nervous like being in jail."

They sat at one of the low tables around the corner of

the bar, where Chucho the waiter brought them beer and roasted pumpkin seeds. In twenty minutes there were twenty men around the table, and the crowd grew. Chucho went to the phone: reporters and bull critics came galloping from the battered tables of the Cafe Tupinamba a few blocks away, to sit in the red leather seats of the Ritz Bar and get a story. Most of them had been to Salazar's house earlier in the morning.

Old Skinny would not have believed it, they said. Crowds were pouring into the short street in Colonia Roma thicker than the rain, invading the house of the dead matador, to view the remains. They were about to wreck the place. There were fifty policemen out there. It was a scandal.

Now the press was anxious to know everything Luis Bello thought and felt about yesterday's tragedy. Everything. How about a firsthand account of his part in rescuing Salazar from the horns? Could he explain the goring? Could he please take off the sunglasses for the photographers?

"I had the bull by the tail, twisting," said Luis Bello. The flash bulbs popped. "We did everything we could."

"How about the public yesterday? Your reaction, Luis?"

"The public is one of those things," Luis Bello stated. "Very variable. The public is like one of those toy houses with a little old woman that comes out and points to 'Fair' while it's raining oceans. You can't tell about the public. One day it whistles and hoots, the next day it wants to kiss you and carry you around with flowers. The opposite is just as true. Three left-hand passes with one de pecho can put the public in your pocket. The same passes — when you don't make them — can put you in jail. In the

case of Juan Salazar he makes one pass which puts him in
Heaven. The public likes it fine. The public makes Juan a
hero. The bull makes Juan dead — "

"Say," Raul Fuentes broke in, "don't write it like that.
You know what Luis means."

"Sure they know. The public's as hard as a mountain
ham. It takes a hell of a lot of knife to slice it."

"Luis means the aficion is hard to please. It makes great
demands, which a torero's honor supplies. Put it like that."

"Yeah," said Luis Bello. "Print it like that. We all eat
off the ham."

A half hour later the crowd around the table was thicker
than ever, and Luis was finding less and less to say. The
talk in the bar had the flavor of the pieces in the newspapers.
The crowd handled the big words and the big thoughts the
way they handled the beer and pumpkin seeds. Sitting in
the middle of it, Luis felt farther and farther away. It was
just as bad as being alone. Maybe worse. It was worse.

"We ought to be going, Raul," Luis Bello said. "We got
a lot of things to do."

"Well," his manager said when they were alone in the
car on the rainy street, "I told you it would get you. What
do we do now?"

"We might as well have been in the screeching Tupinamba. The bull crowd that warms the seats and stands
behind the barrera gives me the pain. The great pain. They
talk bigger and braver than any bull or any bullfighter
that ever lived and a two-year calf would scare the Jesus
out of any one of them. Maybe they think they buy the
balls they lack by buying tickets to a plaza. Maybe it's
what a bullfighter gets paid for: to sell a brave feeling to

a man who lacks it and has to buy it so he can talk about
it like it belonged to him. I never thought much about it
before. I been thinking a lot since that damn trip to Guerreras. The old uncle got me. Now Salazar. I been thinking
too much. Let's go out to the house and have Pomposa
make some chili. The fire like I ate when I herded horses
and didn't think. Hot enough to dry this rain. Hot enough
to burn rust from this ass!"

The cook made enchiladas for him at the house in San
Angel and they were hot enough. The friends who came
to call joined the matador and Raul Fuentes at table; together they wore most of the afternoon away playing
conquian with the taurine cards marked in suits of swords
and cups, tambourines and banderillas. The twelve of
swords was a painting of Luis Bello. It brought him no luck,
but a bottle of tequila capped and carried along the heat
from the enchiladas, and the parlor was a cosy fortress
against the fading gray light at the windows. The radio
played music.

Raul came back from a trip to the telephone in the hall
and touched Luis on the shoulder. Raul was smiling.

"Luis, that was Gomez. He's got your bulls!"

"What bulls? No! You don't mean the Cuenca Gomez!"

"He's got 'em. He wants us to sign."

"Must be something queer, Raul. It's the end of the
world!"

"Number Ones, from Las Astas!"

"How do you know?"

"He's telling the truth all right. He's been to the ranch.
Don Tiburcio came to Mexico with him for the funeral.
He said we could ask Don Tiburcio what's going in the

boxes to Cuenca. Gomez says he's bought four. For a mano a mano between the Bello boys! No third alternate. And now, a booking for Pepe Bello, matador de toros!"

"Wait a minute! I'm not going to any Cuencas until I find out more about this business."

"You will. I told Gomez to come on out here now. We'll see old Balbuena tomorrow. You're signed!"

The radio was playing a new ballad, the announcer said, "The Tragedy of Juan Salazar."

> Juan died at dusk
> In the gloaming.
> When the day was dead
> So was Juan.
>
> They took him from the plaza.
> It was empty. The wind blew
> An Ole of gray ashes and then the rain
> Washed everything away.

"Turn that goddamned thing off!" Luis Bello said.

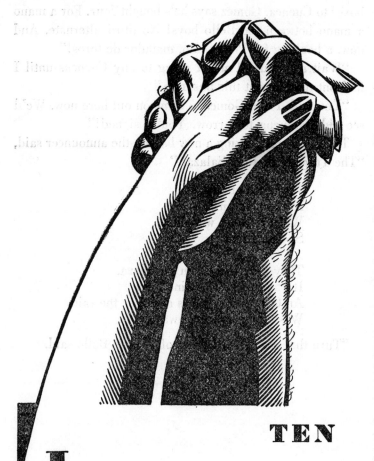

TEN

IT WAS LIKE an island in a black ocean made of
air. Just the dark air all around and in the middle the
island where it was completely warm and easy not to move
or see or try but only feel how soft and smooth and still it
was being alive and tired, so tired, and easy now upon the
island without eyes.

And then the black ocean shaped away from nothingness. Waves and tides and currents grew within it, moving across the deep to find the hidden place, to wash at its blindness, to melt its mindless shore, to cast it finally adrift, no steadfast island after all, upon the voyaging sea.

"Are you asleep?"

"Not asleep."

"Content?"

"Ai Linda! Linda in the dark without seeing you, Linda."

"I'm glad."

He lifted his head and rested his chin on the heel of his hand, looking down, trying to see her in the darkness. Then he turned, sliding his arm under her neck so that her head rested on his shoulder. Lying on their backs they both looked up into the black ocean.

"Just so you don't think I'm as bad as I was Sunday."

"Luis. Why do you keep talking about Sunday? I don't want to remember that man and the bull."

"I meant about me Sunday. Dedicating the bull. I was ashamed. I still am. I was afraid to call you after that. Then the funeral and a lot of things. I had to be there. I had to help carry the coffin. And the mob. It was terrible, the whole business. The part you saw probably finished you with the bulls. I thought it finished you with me too. It was all bad."

"Why are we talking about it? But why do you do it, Luis? How can you go on doing that? The scars — I'm glad I can't see! Why do you do it?"

"It's what I do. You know that. Luis Bello without bulls? Nothing going back to nothing. Linda. You saw only the bad. There is something to it, something great sometimes about it. I wish you could see it then. I would like to show you when it's good. I mean sincerely in my heart some afternoons there is something. I haven't felt it for a long time; I don't know why. I try, and I wish I could. But I didn't show you — "

"Luisito. You show me — "

"Hola! I'm the one that gets shown."

There was a flexible line of warm softness along all his side, all of it, from his shoulder to the very end of his toe.

"Is your arm getting pins and needles?"

"My arm is happy. Linda. Will you go to a plaza again, so I can show you? . . . In the plaza! Devil!"

"It's important, isn't it, Luis?"

"It's what I do."

"I'll go."

"Look, my next one here is three weeks from Sunday, on the eighteenth. We'll have a real one, God granting. One for Linda. And look, we'll celebrate, if it's good. Christmas week. What do you say? Maybe go somewhere."

"We'll see. Tell me what you do till then. Torero."

"Day after tomorrow to Guadalajara."

"How do you go, Luis? The train?"

"Often in my car, but this time the train. Raul wants a car this week end and I told him to take mine. He's going on some kind of party. Big lawyer business."

"Will the corrida in Guadalajara be prominent?"

"It's a kind of a competition, with a fellow named Carlos Rojo. I don't like him and he don't like me. The public makes us rivals. We fight on the same cartel a lot because we contrast. I don't work the way he does, jumping around swishing a cloth and grinning. It's a competition. It will be fairly prominent."

"And then?"

"And then not so prominent. On December Fourth a queer one. One I don't want except for my kid brother Pepe. We go to the great metropolis of Cuenca. Just Pepe and me on a four-bull card. Raul signed for it day before yesterday. It was funny. You know how small bullrings are. I said I wouldn't show in Cuenca unless Pepe fought with me and unless we had real bulls to fight. I didn't think it would happen. But I thought if it did happen I would make Pepe a chance to advance his campaign as matador by fighting serious bulls."

"God! Aren't they all serious?"

"The brave bulls with the breed in them are serious. Without them, the whole thing's a pity. You got to have them or there's no chance for the thing I was telling you about, what I want to show you.

"Well, like I said, I got surprised about Cuenca. I didn't expect the man to get the bulls, but he fooled me. So Pepe and I are going. It's something for the kid."

He moved in the darkness so a whole new set of fine places twined and found the lovely long line of smooth warm closeness.

"Tell me more. About bulls, Senor Bello!"

"Talk, talk, talk."

"More yet."

"So then — oh, well. About Cuenca? All right. What a subject! Yesterday a friend of mine from Spain showed up at the house in San Angel. A torero without contracts.

Shall we say it, maybe not very good in the plazas, but a good boy. From Seville. I got well from a goring — this one, right here — at his mother's house in the barrio of San Bernardo. She took me like my own mother when I got out of hospital. She made paella I still remember like a dream; you should taste it, the way she made it! The boy's name is Paco. Paco Saya. I'm taking him to Cuenca with the Bello cuadrillas. He's going as the sobresaliente, the substitute like they always have when there are only two matadors on the card. I can't get him anything else now, but he's a good boy and at least he can swing his cape on a few quites with us and get his name on a Mexican cartel. So the queer corrida has got a Spaniard for a substitute matador because of some paella in Seville. Is that enough about Cuenca? Is that enough talk, talk, talk, Linda Castillo de Calderon?"

It was.

"Luis. Darling. I wish it would stay like this."

"It's staying."

"If everything would stay away like this! All gone away. Keep everything away, Luis."

"Linda, don't cry!"

"I'm not. Nothing really stays away, does it, Luis? It comes back. You turn on the lights and there everything is. All over again."

"There are some good parts."

He kissed her and brushed her cheek with his hand, feeling her tears. "What's the matter, kid? There are some good parts."

They lit cigarettes. In the flare of the match she smiled at him. Propped on the pillows with an ash tray between them, they each held little round points of fire that glowed orange in the dark.

"Nobody knows how it comes out, kid. Nobody can tell till they get there. But Linda. You'll be all right. Believe me. You're someone. I know that."

He could see her dimly in the glow when she drew on the cigarette.

"Linda, you think the bulls are bad but I thank them very much. Without the bulls it never—you know I was kind of scared of you at first, kid."

"I'm still scared of you."

"Ha! The faithful ox named Bello?"

"Luis! But tell me. How long do you go on with those bulls? That business Sunday. Really! Don't you plan to retire? Why don't you?"

"Not yet Linda. Raul and I have been talking it over. We're making a program. We figure two more seasons. That ought to fix it. I want a ranch. All toreros want a ranch sometime and I guess I'm no different. They say the money you make belongs to the bulls. It's the bulls' money. They give it to you and they can take it away, anytime. It don't actually belong to you until you retire. That's why I spent so much, before the bulls could take it back. I know that. It's not yours until you can walk away telling the bulls good-by forever. Then if you got anything, it's yours. Manolete had forty million pesetas of the bulls' money and they took it back before he could walk away. But you know — there is something about the bulls. And the crowd. And feeling what you can do, and the big afternoon. Most bullfighters don't know nothing else. Remember the little worm? I told you about him."

"I remember him. He's terrible. I don't see how you can do it."

"I don't either. I'm going to quit someday, Linda. Still — "

"Still you are proud, Luis Bello. They say pride is a sin and I suppose that it is. But oh, Luis, I wish I could be proud like you! I'm not proud of anything for so long, long. I was taught to be proud of myself. I remember my grandfather's house where I lived in Toluca."

"It wasn't anything like my uncle's in Guerreras."

"Don't be like that, Luis. It makes you very proud. And foolish. Not all the difficulties in the world are yours!"

"Thanks to God. I got enough. We all have. But no difficulties with Linda. None. I'm sorry. Let me put the ash tray on the table. There. Now isn't it better?"

"I'd do so many things differently if I could go back, Luis."

"You can't, and besides, you don't have to. You'll find out because you're wonderful. Tell me about when you were a little girl, in Toluca."

"The most fun was the family picnics in the summertime up to the lake of the Nevada de Toluca. We'd stay overnight. The servants would pitch tents and make barbecues, and the musicians would play at night around big fires. We'd have games, all the cousins. Once we had fireworks. We could look down, down into the whole valley in the morning and point out Cruces, my grandfather's hacienda in the tiny trees and the whole city of Toluca not big enough to be a toy. I had a chestnut mare and we cousins would ride along the slopes in the flowers. At night we could reach up and touch all the stars from the beautiful high

Nevada. The musicians would still be playing when we children were put to bed in the tents, and we could hear the grown men singing by the fires, and laughing. My grandfather had a wonderful laugh, Luis. He laughed most on the picnics with all the family around. You know what he used to do when he was very old? He sat under the gallery in front of his house in town on Sunday mornings, in a chair, holding his walking stick, and he would give the boys who came by a silver toston and a whack with his stick and say to us in the family, 'They may be mine! How do I know?' "

"I wish I had seen you when you were a little girl — ah Linda! The other day, the day it rained so hard, I had me some hot chili because I was thinking about things. About being a kid. About the Aguabendita where I was born, about climbing in the bell tower and getting the squabs and the pigeon eggs and stealing the bell ropes from the priest. In Guerreras my uncle took care of horses for the Pedrazos and I was a helper. The thing I liked was in the early morning when the sun was just coming up and we rode the race horses to the edge of town. There was a five hundred vara track out there. I got to exercise the horses on the track with the soft dirt and I remember how it used to be, flat against the bareback, holding to the mane, running so the wind made my eyes water, going fast, fast, whistling, leaving dust in the shadows. That's the fastest I ever went in my life. Coming back through town, the sun would be on the streets warm and you could smell the cook smoke from the houses. The kids would look up at me on a horse blanket and run along beside the horses and I felt big enough to run my hand along the roofs."

"Can you remember anything in the Revolution, Luis?"

"Sure I can remember. When they burned the big house at the Aguabendita. I can remember when my father came back. He was a soldier with Villa."

"They killed my father. I never saw him. He never saw me. My mother used to tell about the Revolution. She carried me on a refugee train. I'm glad I can't remember anything about it."

"I think we remember plenty, Lindita. Lindissima. Remember the good things. I can remember everything, exactly, about you."

"Luis! *Ai Luis* — Bello!"

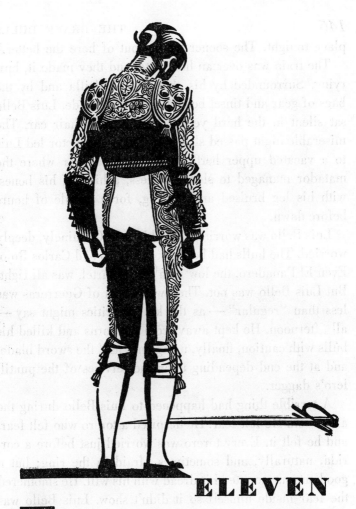

ELEVEN

THE BELLO CUADRILLA was not a team, when it drove back to the hotel from the bullring in Guadalajara. It had fallen apart into single morbid pieces.

"Tacho," Luis Bello said, "find out if the train is late enough so we can catch the damn thing to leave this frilling place tonight. The sooner we get out of here the better."

The train was over an hour late, and they made it, hurrying. Surrounded by his cheerless cuadrilla and by the bags of gear and tinsel belonging to their trade, Luis Bello sat silent in the hard yellow light of the chair car. The miserable night passed slowly until the conductor led Luis to a vacated upper berth in the Pullman car where the matador managed to sleep, restless, aching in his bones, with his leg bruised and hurting, for a couple of hours before dawn.

Luis Bello was worried about himself. Genuinely, deeply worried. The bulls had been good, and so had Carlos Rojo. Even El Panadero, the low man on the cartel, was all right. But Luis Bello was not. The Swordsman of Guerreras was less than "regular" — as the kinder critics might say — all afternoon. He kept away from the horns and killed his bulls with caution, finally, using only half the sword blade, and at the end depending upon the services of the puntillero's dagger.

A terrible thing had happened to Luis Bello during the afternoon. He felt fear. He despised a torero who felt fear, and he felt it. Every torero was worried just before a corrida, naturally, and sometimes afraid in the ring; but a good one surmounted his dread with his will. He smothered the fear inside himself so it didn't show. Luis Bello was afraid he had shown his fear, and he despised himself, helpless and angry. He had never been afraid like that, feeling the fear eat at him like a tumor, squeezing his heart pale. But now he had.

Two ears for Carlos Rojo, a circuit of the ring with applause for El Panadero. Nothing for Luis Bello. Except the discovery that he was afraid. Afraid of the horns. Afraid of what horns do.

He cursed the moment of silence at the beginning of it, with the big silly sign UN MOMENTO DE SILENCIO and everybody standing voiceless and still in the Guadalajara ring, with their hats off. The moment of silence to the memory of Juan Salazar, like they had for every dead one, at every ring in the Republic, the first corrida after a fatal goring. It upset the tempo and the pace of a corrida from the very start. The moment of silence in memory of Luis Bello. Sainted Christ of the Health!

When the train finally came into the station at the Capital, Luis Bello was so worried with himself, so genuinely worried and irritated and lacking sleep, that he thought nothing strange at seeing Pepe and Jank Delgado standing waiting for him. He gave his brother the abrazo and shook hands with Delgado, not accounting for Pepe's white lips or the Jank's constraint. In his preoccupation with himself he interpreted their manners as solemn sympathy for the failure that had grown inside himself on the way home from Guadalajara. Pepe hurried him through the station, motioning to Tacho, while Delgado helped quickly with the bags.

"Let's get to San Angel," Pepe said. "Come on, Tacho! Goyo, you boys take another cab to your houses. We'll see you later." With his face turned away from Luis, Pepe made a furtive grimace to the cuadrilla. There was anguish in it, and they saw it. The Bellos, with Tacho and the Jank, got in a cab.

The ride to San Angel seemed endless to Pepe Bello. Luis was so deep in his moodiness he was only gradually aware of his brother's unnaturalness, of Delgado's silence, of Tacho's puzzled, silent concentration on the younger Bello's obvious strain.

"What's the matter with you?" Tacho finally asked aloud.

"Nothing," Pepe said, shooting a look at the sword-handler.

Luis caught it.

"What's eating you, Pepe?"

"N-nothing."

"Christ's sake!" the older Bello said, scowling. "Like somebody rammed a sausage down your throat. The corrida wasn't that bad yesterday! But I got enough worries, Jesus and Mary. And Joseph!"

They got the bags out and were paying the fare when the watchman opened the gate, looking hard at Luis and then at Pepe. Saying nothing, he carried the pigskin traveling case initialed LB, and the swords. The cook Pomposa was red-eyed at the door of the house.

"A hell of a home-coming after a fine corrida. Beautiful all over! What in the Name of God, Pepe?"

"I wanted to get you home, Luis! I just wanted to get you home!" He motioned everyone else out of the room.

"Huh?"

"Luis." The tears Pepe Bello had been holding back, holding back tight, finally glassed his eyes and rolled out, two big round drops, down his brown cheeks. "I got to tell you something. It's Raul. Raul got killed."

Luis Bello stood perfectly still. He did not move, with his hands down at his sides. He stood still as a stone.

"Raul?"

"He got killed. In the car. Coming down from Cuerna-vaca. On the mountain. Last night."

"Raul?" Luis did not move. "Dead? Pepe! Listen, Pepe! How do you know that?" His fists clenched, still at his sides.

"Everything. The police chief on the phone. Then every-body. It's in the paper this morning, and I was afraid, afraid you'd see it! Before I could tell you, before I could get you home!"

Luis Bello sat down in a chair. He sat very straight.

"Raul. My right arm." He felt his right arm. "My right arm gone." It maimed his mind and his mind backed away from it, numb. It would have to come back. But not now, not now!

"Huh." He looked at Pepe. "In the car? Wrecked my car?"

"It's junk. Nothing. Forty meters off the road."

"Huh." The clock on the mantel ticked in the silence. "Raul and the car." The clock ticked on. "Anybody else in the car?"

"Yes."

"Dead?"

"Yes."

"How many?"

"Just one, one besides Raul."

"Who? What was his name?"

"It was a girl. O Jesus Christ, Luis my brother — and I got to tell you! The girl was Linda de Calderon."

Luis stood up.

"With Raul? Killed with Raul?"

Pepe put his hand on his brother's shoulder. Slowly Luis pushed him aside, with his eyes coming wide open;

Luis looking up seeing himself standing there clear and plain in the parlor mirror. His hand found the back of the straight chair. He took hold of the smooth round wood slowly, firmly. Then sent it hurtling. It smashed the mirror, shattering pieces into the air. The crash brought Tacho and Jank Delgado running through the door. Luis stopped them, wordless, motionless, looking at them as if he held a sword in his hand. He looked past them then, trembling; he spoke very calmly, in a low voice, almost whispering.

"Now. Get out, please. Go away. Get out. GET OUT! And close the doors."

He stood at the window alone, with the clock ticking.

His mind approached it, then backed away. The sweat came cold on his forehead. Slowly, slowly then, Luis Bello walked up to the horns, unarmed. He walked up to them numb, and let them come, let them touch and slide sick into him, and twist him, and when they got there inside of him, he cried.

One of the horns was Raul dead and one of the horns was Linda dead and there was still another horn and that was Raul and Linda together alive. That was a horn too many for anything real, O God. It was a horn he had never seen and how it cut and tore!

One horn at a time, O Father Jesus, one horn is all I can bear. Old Raul my right arm. Raul that took care of everything. Raul that put me up there and taught me and kept it all going in the green times and the ripe ones. Old Raul, my sword arm, and I lost him.

And Linda. The flower and cream not like it sounds but truly, and it's gone. Gone. Linda that had troubles, I never

knew what. I'll never know now at all. Nor help. Linda
that was beautiful, by God, with the real casta in her who
pardoned a torero.

Linda and Raul. Did you really do it? To me? I won't
ever know. Maybe you didn't. I hope I never find out.
But I'll think, O God, I'll think. Raul doing it to me.
Maybe he didn't, going in the car. Taking my blue car
and making everything a pile of junk.

I was always going to be the one, the pile of junk they
worried about. I was going to be the one that got it all
the time, the dead one, and here I am.

The clock ticked, measuring off the silence with the
horns in him. He heard the phone ringing in the hall, and
the footsteps going and the voices around him in his house,
the strands and colors he had woven in wrappings around
the central strange shape the days beat out upon their
anvil forming him, the wrappings that padded Luis Bello
and hid him from himself. Now these integuments of vanity and ornament, of necessity, of service, of faith and
affection, were torn away suddenly: he had smashed the
mirror that showed him the shape of himself without them.

Nothing is yours until you walk away telling the horns
good-by forever, Luis Bello. But you got nothing worth
carrying away then, have you? Are you afraid?

What is it you fear, Luis? Is it the horn that rips so fast,
and turns you twisting dizzy in the air, and comes out red
and sticky? Is that it? Is it the smell of ether when things
go gray in the infirmary? Or is it the bed with the pus,
the thirst, the fever at night? What is it now, looking at
yourself, Luis? What else did you see in the mirror?

There's something that hasn't happened yet, Luis Bello,

and horns or no horns it finds you. It found the old uncle
the week before last, and last week it found Juan Salazar.
This week it came to Raul and Linda. Now it's headed for
you. You'll get it.

And this week you'll have to go again to the hushed
place and look down into the box. Not one box but two,
O God. With the smell of the wax and the sickly flowers
in the candlelight you'll hear it again, the Mass with the
voices on the rim, the terrible high mysterious rim that
crumbles away forever from the sun and the color and
the crowd and falls away, into dust, into —

Luis Bello could name it. He knew what it was, and he
looked at it there in himself, all alone. When he had seen
it and named it there was something finished about it,
and because he was alive, he turned away from it.

He turned away from it the only way he knew how.
Standing by the broken mirror he blew his nose and put
on his sunglasses, and he walked out.

"I'm going," he said to Pepe. The whole cuadrilla was
standing there.

"Where?" said Pepe. "How?"

"I'm leaving for a while. I'm making a circuit."

"I'll go with you," his brother said.

"Nobody's going with me. Understand? You understand
that? You leave me alone."

"Luis, for God, take it easy!"

He walked out the front door bareheaded, across the
garden, unlatched the gate and went through, pulling it
closed after him. Pepe and all the cuadrillas watched
him go.

"O Christ of the Pains!" said Tacho. "The first night

Luis went for that honey-headed whore I tried, I tried to get him not to go. I saw it arming. Oh, I saw the great foul frilling father and senor of all filth arriving. Look at it! I'm going after Luis!"

"Wait a minute!" Pepe said. "You want to get him real crazy? Raul used to handle him, but we got to do it now. And do it right. We got to let him go wherever he thinks he's going. But maybe we can tail him till he cools off. And bring him back."

"I know him. He ain't going to cool," Tacho moaned.

"I seen the bull's ear twitch, and John of the Palms, boy, the horns are here. They're on top of us now!" Goyo Salinas said. He spit.

"Goyo, you and the boys handle things at the house," Pepe said. He started down the lane with Tacho, and the Jank.

Luis saw them when he turned around to look. A hundred yards behind him, helpless, silly, devoted. It made him angry. He stopped and made the sign he made in the plazas, motioning his peons to get away, get behind the barrera. Then he walked on, faster.

They saw him step into a taxi by the convent square, and they were too far away, too far.

"Why the hell didn't we get in Goyo's car? Why didn't we?"

"He'll be all right," said Jank Delgado. "He'll take care of himself."

They watched the taxi drive away, down the slope from San Angel.

"Get off the boulevard," Luis ordered the driver. "This is worth your while."

The cabman hoped it was; he knew who sat behind the sunglasses on the back seat of his cab, all right. Toreros were characters. This one didn't want any talk today. The cabman drove.

Leave it, thought Luis Bello. Get out of this week. This whole week. I got to. I don't want to see it. I can't look at it. I can't see them, and smell the flowers and hear the Mass and go to the graves. Leave it. Leave it.

Leave everything. Leave the bulls, everything about the bulls, the people, the places that know bulls. Know Raul, know me — know Linda. Leave it.

The cabman drove a long time. Luis sat alone with himself. Leaving, leaving all of it. Then he wished he had a cigar to leave with. He didn't have one. Not even a match. He didn't have a drink either. And he didn't have a place to go, leaving everything.

They even wrecked my car. I can't go no place. I got no place, except with the bulls. Because I never made another kind of a place and I never thought about it before. The damned bulls and I'm through with them. I'm through with anybody that knows anything about the bulls. And where's that? Where's that around here, where they won't find me? Never find me. Where I can get a cigar and have a drink away from the bulls.

"Driver. You know the Tenocotle? That little three-sided dump of a plaza, Tenocotle? You know it? Well, take me there."

He paid, and let the taxi go away, around the corner out of sight, before he moved from the curb. Then he crossed the street and hurried a block and knocked at a door painted green.

He stood there waiting a long time for an answer. When it came, the door opened only an inch or two. He had to lift his sunglasses and show his face before they let him in and he was angry, with his red eyes.

"Senor Bello! Truly it *is!* Don Luis of the bulls! And so long since we've seen you, since we had the honor. O mother mine! And at such an hour? Monday morning? Ai, the girls — "

"Get this, Mamacita. This is important," Luis Bello said. His voice grated. "No Senor Don Luis of anything. Understand? None of your damned dash and scratch. Understand? I came here. That's all. It's a place."

He pulled his wallet from his hip pocket and handed it to the old lady.

"Here — you keep this for me. Take what you need to pay for what I want. I'll tell you what that is, when I want it, and to hell with your beauties! Understand? I want to sit under the grape arbor in the back. See? I want to sit at a table with some cigars and a drink. I want you to keep bringing me cigars and tequila until I quit asking for them, or until I ask for something else. I want to sit. See? Quiet. Frilling goddamned quiet, you old hag. Get it?"

I'm proud, eh, Linda?

TWELVE

Callers came to the house in San Angel, and the telephone rang. There were questions Luis could answer, situations Luis could resolve, and Luis was gone. Tacho had no luck all day, trying to trace the taxi Luis had taken.

Pepe went searching in Goyo's car. He went to the morgue, to the undertakers', asking if Luis had been there. He called at Raul's mother's. After inquiry, with embarrassment and hesitation, he even took flowers and presented himself to Linda's relatives, looking hopefully for Luis and not finding him.

Back to San Angel, frustrated, Pepe answered the telephone while Jank Delgado handled the callers. Impresarios, managers, agents, bull breeders, parasites, worried about agreements and contracts with Raul Fuentes, called anxiously to express sympathy — and to inquire about the new Bello management. There was no new Bello management. There was no Luis Bello.

His men did not want to say Luis Bello had walked out. It sounded queer; they had a story they told instead. Luis was emotional over the tragedy. He was caved in, he was secluded, he was not seeing anyone. Not even dear friends. Repeated over and over, the story was a strain. And the reporters did not believe it.

When evening came the cuadrilla became a search party making the rounds of the cafes and bars where the bull crowd collected. They asked for Luis at the desk in the Ritz, the Reforma, the Regis, and went down the line, while those in the house at San Angel waited and wrangled.

"What would you do," asked the Jank, "if the Bomba Atomica went off in your face? What would I do? Get drunk. Pig-dirty pulque drunk. If we could find the right saloon we could find Luis — "

"Fix yourself!" Pepe was angry. "You ain't Luis. Luis is responsible. He complies. Like he complies in the ring till the mules take the last bull out."

"Yeee, he complied all right. With himself. He blew a big fuse."

"Oh, he blew one!" Tacho said. "And I hate the policia but we got to call the cops to find him."

"The only thing the cops will do is give it to the newspapers," said the Jank. "Luis'll be back. He'll come back when he's ready."

"And when's that?" Pepe asked bitterly. "Raul's funeral tomorrow afternoon. The corrida at Cuenca Sunday — Jesus Christ!"

At a quarter to ten that night Don Felix Aldemas Leon, his round face very sober, walked into Luis Bello's parlor.

"Pepe. Where's Luis?" There was authority in his voice and in his question. It was too heavy for Pepe.

"Don Felix, we don't know."

"I thought it was queer. Nobody seeing him all day. Where did he go?"

"We don't know. He just walked out of the house after I told him this morning. After he got home from Guadalajara."

"He hasn't been to the Fuentes'. Has he been to the woman's? Do you know?"

"No, I went there myself."

"You've looked everywhere for him all the places he goes?"

"The cuadrilla's out yet. We been looking and worrying all day."

"Then he's out on the town. Drunk. I know these bullfighters. Have you asked the police to help?"

"No sir."

"That must be done, done properly. Where's the phone?"

Pepe, Tacho, and the Jank stood looking at each other like children.

At the telephone in the hall, Don Felix called the Chief of Police. "Scour the dives, Jefe," they heard him say. "You know these artists."

"Now," said Don Felix, returning from the hall. "They ought to have him by morning. His face is as well known as the Bronze Horse on the Reforma.

"Pepe, I came out here to San Angel after dinner because I felt some worry. Luis is an artist — one of the great artists of our country — and artists have temperaments. They also have curious attitudes about the money they make and throw away.

"I came out here to speak to Luis. Until I can speak to him I will mention a few words to you. I was a friend of Raul Fuentes, and a friend of Raul's father. God have them both now in His glory. As lawyer for Raul's family it is my duty to attend Raul's tangled affairs after the tragedy of last night. His financial affairs are greatly involved with your brother Luis.

"As you know, I have been a friend and admirer of Luis Bello for years. I feel deeply the aficion for the bulls. I intend to see your brother's affairs properly straightened out, along with Raul's, though God alone knows the difficulties of justice.

"I wish to say this. And impress it upon Luis, and upon you too, at the beginning of your career. It is criminal to throw away the money you make in the plazas at the risk of your lives. Unless Luis changes, he will end with nothing. Like Salazar, like a hundred more anyone can name. It is time Luis changed. And this sad day is a good day to determine that change. I have only affection for the memory of Raul Fuentes, and understanding for irresponsibilities and ill judgments of young men with hot blood. But I do not wish to see your brother make any more mistakes.

"I offer Luis my services now in handling the increment of the remainder of his career, and guarding it for his benefit, for his family, for his old age — if God grants him old age. He must do it. And you must do it too, young man.

"In my position at this sad time, and in future if you so desire, I can manage the Bello money affairs. I cannot of course manage the Bello affairs in the plazas and box offices and journals, up to carrying a sword case — as Raul did. That is for some manager within the professional atmosphere of the bulls. But! I see my duty. I intend to speak to Luis Bello clearly.

"Now. I will see him when they find him. I hope he is in shape to pay his respects to the remains of his friend Fuentes tomorrow. You tell Luis I am acting on the presumption that he will fulfill all contracts and agreements just as his now deceased manager arranged them. And that I will help him in any way."

Don Felix put on his gray fedora hat and his topcoat. "I hope Luis is all right, Pepe. It has been a blow. A hard blow. With the woman and all that, too. Good night."

"Yai!" said the Jank when Don Felix had gone. "He wears the whiskers. That's what this encierro of artists needs around here. A man wearing the whiskers!"

"He wears them," Tacho said. "He calls the cops."

Goyo Salinas phoned after midnight.

"We been everywhere. Nobody's seen him — "

"Get some rest, Goyo. Tell all the boys to get some rest. We done what we could. We even called the cops."

"The cops? You hit bone there, kid. That's bad."

"Come on out in the morning, Goyo."

Pepe and Tacho were up with the first light, drinking coffee in the kitchen.

"He must have left town," Tacho said. "I thought about it all night. You know, he blew once before. In Lima, when he got word his wife was dead. Just blew. Missed a corrida when he needed corridas. Showed up looking like a picador's nag with the saddle gone. Ten years ago. It's where he got the medal of Santa Barbara, now I remember. Mother mine! No torero ever wore Santa Barbara in the ring, that I ever heard. She's for storms and earthquakes.

"His wife was named Barbara. That's why he got it. That's why he wears it."

"I know that. But she is the saint of storms. Not so bad for a torero. Eh? Storms and earthquakes. Christ, but Luis has been bad since you saw him in Guerreras! I never seen him afraid before. I never seen him so bad. Now this thing. Washing him up!" Tacho knocked on wood, shaking his head.

"Listen, Tacho. He'll be all right. He's got to be all right. Next Sunday. It's my chance. Las Astas bulls at Cuenca. Luis has got to be all right. So we can go."

"He ain't getting in any ring to kill himself if I can help it. Not in his shape!"

"He'll be all right by Sunday."

"We don't even know where in the name of the dirty milk he is! No telling what's happened to him — " There were tears in Tacho's eyes.

"Fix yourself, swordhandler." Pepe walked out of the kitchen angry.

A police inspector arrived to ask questions. He stayed almost an hour. The cuadrillas came, dressed in their dark suits, for a funeral. Paco Saya, the torero from Seville, showed up in a beret, and a scarf knotted around his neck. The crowd grew. Two more policemen came. The phone rang.

The crowd was glum, sitting around smoking Luis Bello's cigars. They talked about him. About Raul, about the blonde. Carai! Too many funerals lately. The blonde was really Luis's babe, all right. Eehoh, and Raul Fuentes with her! What a pity. No wonder Luis jumped the barrera!

"Tacho," said Jank Delgado, when he got the swordhandler alone in the hall, "you and I ought to think about money. The bull is loose in the plaza now, and we got to think of it. I'm not putting a long nose on my face; I just want to help if I can. What about money? For instance, Pomposa ought to feed this mob before we go to the funeral, or afterwards, and there ought to be drinks."

"She will. There will be."

"You handle the funds for the house? Have you got some?"

"None of your frilling business, Delgado. I'm a swordhandler. I pay the cuadrillas. I handle the money on trips, I make reservations, I send telegrams, I work like a dirty dog. I pay the expenses here at the house from money Luis gives me. But I don't keep no account book if that's what you're swinging a rag at. I'm honest, see?"

"Don't get so tender. I don't mean anything about what

you do with the peluco. That's your business. I mean do you have enough now? Until Luis shows up?"

"I got some. I also got the check from the Empresa de Toros in Guadalajara, for that corrida. Right here." He patted his pocket. "Luis trusts me, if nobody else don't! I deal with real stuff. Not garbage."

"For Christ's sake. Ram it. I was just going to tell you I had a little in my pocket if we got stuck — "

The Jank had fully two pesos in that pocket.

"You're not a bad kid," Tacho said. "Some of these bull followers — "

"Bulls ain't the only thing I've followed, twin. Ram it."

The phone rang again and Pepe came into the hall where they stood. He picked up the receiver.

"Who speaks?" asked a female voice on the wire.

"Pepe Bello speaking."

"Is this Luis Bello's house?"

"Yes. Who is this?"

"You Luis Bello's brother?"

"What do you want? I'm his brother."

"Listen, Bello boy. Come and get him!"

"Huh? What's that?"

"Your brother. Just about wrecked my place, sonny boy."

"Where?" Pepe Bello yelled into the phone. "Where is he?"

"You come and get him."

"Where, goddammit?"

"Tenocotle. Tenocotle 6 and be quiet about it. No policia! You hear that?"

"You just hold him. Hold him. I'm coming from San Angel!"

He slammed down the phone and turned to Tacho and the Jank.

"Get Goyo and let's go!"

Goyo's car worked hard, going fast, going toward town. The four of them sat in it, trying to help it go faster, sitting on the edge of the seats, not going fast enough.

"Tenocotle, Tenocotle, where's that? I never heard of it," Pepe said.

"I know where it is all right," Goyo said. "I wasn't born in this town for nothing. No wonder we couldn't find him. Tenocotle."

"I was right all the time," the Jank reminded them. "He just went off for vacations. Remember what he said, 'I'm making a circuit'? Remember?"

"He's making a circuit, que tio! A fluffing house at a time like now! I thought of saloons," Goyo said, "but I never thought of the feathers! No wonder we didn't find him. Que tio padrote! That Luis! Last night fluffing the feathers. Ole!"

"The mama says he was wrecking the place," Pepe grinned.

"Oh, he's a peril when he's drunk," Tacho said. "I know him."

"We know him," said Goyo. "Que tio!"

The green door opened immediately. All four of them went in.

"Well!" Pepe recognized the voice on the phone. It came from between all the lipstick, on the old lady. Three of her girls in very short dresses were standing in the patio with her. "You get your torero out of here! What's the matter with him, anyway? He used to be a nice man."

"Where is he?"

"He's in a room."

The girls rolled their eyes at the gentleman callers. The old lady unlocked a door and they all walked into a dim place lighted only by the light from the opened door. Luis had been sick. He was lying across a broken bed with his head down. His shirt was torn. They could see the immense scar in his left armpit. There was a long red scratch across his cheek and his knuckles were bloody.

A leg of the bed was broken and so were a chair and a crockery washbowl and a pitcher smashed on the bare floor in a corner. The room was a dirty wreck and so was Luis Bello.

They knelt down and felt him and listened to him breathe. Pepe wiped his brother's mouth and chin with a handkerchief.

Luis Bello groaned.

"O Sacred Name," Tacho said. He looked up from where he knelt by his matador. "What happened?"

"What happened? O what happened!" the old lady said. "Thank God there wasn't a sword in the house last night. He thought we were bulls."

"How long was he here? Did he drink much?"

"Did he drink much! Pig! He came about noon yesterday. There was something wrong." She pointed to her right temple and rolled her watery eyes. "Crazy. He just sat. And drank. Too quiet. Until last night. Ai! He made me lock the door to the street! We had to turn a quantity of respectables away unhappy from our door. This torero here said the plaza was closed, the encierro was his. Then he said he wanted a band of music and all services of plaza, complete. He tied ribbons on the girls for divisas and he used my good shawl for a cape. O the scandal! Everybody's got a cold this morning. Listen, boys, get that goddamned bullfighter out of my house! He got rough when he began calling for a horse and a pic! Never again! Crazy, that's what he is. I had to hit him over the head."

They found the knot on his skull. Goyo could hardly lift for laughing. "O Luis! Que tio! Que tio mio!" They pulled on his pants and coat.

"Did he pay?" Pepe asked. They carried him across the patio.

"He paid all right," said the mama. "I'll say he paid." She pulled the wallet from her bosom and handed it to Pepe. "Here. I kept the money. The damages are terrible. I run a nice place here, boys. Come back sometime. But by the sacred name of the little virgin of dew, you better not come like bullfighters!"

The green door went shut and they loaded Luis into the back seat of the car. He was violently sick on the Insurgentes. They got him out of the car on the parkway grass, hoping no one would recognize them.

When they put him back on the seat, Luis opened his eyes.

"Huhh," he said. "I'm sick. O I'm sick."

"Fine, Luis, fine," Tacho said, holding him up. "We're going home." His matador did not respond.

"Eleven-thirty," Tacho said, seeing the clock on a barbecue drive-in. "We'll get him a bath and soak him good while Pomposa is making him menudo. A bath and some good strong tripe gruel, that's what he needs."

"We'll get the barber to the house too," Pepe said,

"right away. Luis needs him, and he needs the back of his neck rubbed with that hot stuff, like a barber can do it. That will fix him."

"My friends," said the Jank, "what Luis needs is the doctor with the penicillin. The wonders of the modern science. He needs some very modern science."

"O the bulls he worked last night!" Goyo said. "They got the splintered horns! What you call that stuff, Jank, pencillin?"

The crowd at the house in San Angel all watched Luis being carried upstairs. Everybody followed, jamming into his room.

"Plastered," Goyo said, explaining. "Just plastered."

"Poor Luis," they said. "All emotionated."

"He'll be all right," Tacho said, "if you will get the hell out of here and let us fix him up. How about the menudo, the barber — and that doctor, Jank? I'll draw the bath.

"How you feel, Luis, big goat with the whiskers, how you feel?"

Two hours later he could hardly feel at all, except feel sick and feel shame. In a silk dressing robe he sat up in a chair, trying to eat menudo, after the bath. The doctor had been there; the barber was waiting. Luis Bello was weak and silent.

Long distance from Guerreras was calling Luis Bello.

"I'll take it," Pepe said. He went downstairs to the phone in the hall.

It was Carmela Bello asking for Luis.

"You can't speak to him," Pepe said. "Haven't you heard? We got tragedy."

"Tragedy? Help us God, what is it?"

"Raul Fuentes has been killed."

"Oh. But you and Luis?"

"Luis is emotionated. I'm fair, but very busy."

"Thanks to God you are safe. I called because we have trouble in Guerreras."

"What now?"

"Alfredo's in jail. We can't make his bail."

"Good," Pepe said.

"You sound like Luis! Don't you make me mad! The disgrace — "

"What's he in for?"

"Bad checks. In Monterrey."

"We got enough worries, Carmela. Leave him in."

"Pepe! I want to speak to Luis! This instant!"

"You ain't speaking to any Luis."

"Oh Pepe!" He could hear her crying.

"Pepe. Aguilar has cut off our credit at the store. You remember the bill? The forty-seven hundred pesos Luis got so mad about? It hasn't been paid. Aguilar won't charge any more. What will we do?"

"Name of God, we got enough to worry about without a grocery bill! Why don't you get somebody in that house to go to work and *earn* some groceries? Huh?"

"Beast! I'm telling you, little man! I've had enough! I'm going into a convent! There!" She slammed the receiver in Pepe's ear.

"The happy day! The good life!" Pepe said, going upstairs. He spit on the floor. "I'd like to get plastered too."

Luis was drooping in his chair, holding his head. "What was it?" he asked.

"Carmela. The usual. The difficulties in Guerreras. Alfredo's in jail. The grocery bill not paid. Carmela taking the veil — so she says."

Luis Bello did not answer.

"Luis," Pepe said, after a long silence. "In about an hour there's the funeral. Will you go with us? You know — "

"The hell with it."

"I know how you feel but — "

"Which one, Pepe?"

It took him a moment to understand. "Oh! Raul's — it's Raul's."

"The other?"

"That was this morning. It's over. Yesterday I took flowers and went there. For you. Would you go with me now, Mano? The public expects — "

"The hell with it. I can't."

The Jank came into the room.

"The frilling phone again downstairs. It's long distance from Cuenca now. Wants to speak to Luis Bello."

"I'll take it," said Pepe, fast.

"And listen, Jose Antonio Bello, you go tell Cuenca to take those bulls and ram them," Luis said. "I'm through. The hell with the bulls."

Going out the door, with his face turned from Luis, Pepe winked solemnly at the Jank.

Eladio Gomez was on the wire.

"Bueno? Luis?"

"No, Senor Gomez, this is Pepe. Pepe Bello. Luis can't come to the phone today. He sent me."

"Pepe. I feel deeply the tragedy of Fuentes. Accept my

sympathies. I called about the corrida Sunday. I want to make sure of my contract — " The worry was in Gomez's voice.

"Naturally, Senor Gomez. Naturally," Pepe delayed. "I will tell you. We are upset. Very bad. Luis, he — he's sick. But I will tell you. I think he will be all right. I think he will be there — "

"I want to know. From Luis himself. The cartels, the bulls. The corrida in five days only! Jesus Christ, man! I got to know!"

"Naturally. Naturally Senor Gomez, Don Eladio. I will tell you. I will let you know if he can't. Otherwise, go ahead. I think he will. I am pretty sure."

"Listen. You're saying he might not come! Breach of contract! You are responsible, you are liable. Are you *both* coming?"

"You go ahead please, Senor Gomez. I will be there and Luis, Luis is coming too — "

"That's your word! Five days only. I'm counting on it. I want a telegram from Luis saying it. You hear? In writing!"

Pepe was sweating all over when he came back upstairs to Luis.

"Did you tell Gomez?" Luis asked, scowling.

"I told him."

Pepe sat down. The barber was rubbing Luis's neck.

"Luis," Pepe said.

He had to ask him again about things. He had to. One thing at a time.

"Luis, you going to the funeral with us?"

When the barber quit rubbing, Luis looked up. The

color was gone from his face and his eyes were sunk in their sockets. They looked too dark and unnaturally wet. The long red scratch marked the pallor of his cheek.

"I feel terrible. I'm sick. But old Raul. Jesus and Mary, I guess I ought to. I ought to go."

THIRTEEN

THURSDAY MORNING Eladio Gomez was dulled with gloom when he walked into his bullring. Looking up at the forlorn empty seats of his lifeless plaza in the harsh morning light, he perfunctorily told Sanchez to hurry and get done with the red paint on the barrera. Then he went through the toril on his way to the shack by the corrals to find Chon Munoz.

Chon was as familiar at the bullring of Cuenca as the sign over the main gate. He was an old banderillero. In his prime he had spent two seasons in the cuadrilla of young Gaona; those were the days of his glory and he liked to talk of them, and of his friendship with Ojitos. Living now in poverty with his big family in the shack by the plaza corrals, he still devoted himself to the golden illusion of his life, to the bulls. He took care of the bull corrals, and the bulls before they died, and the toril door during the corridas. He handled the livestock for his employer, Eladio Gomez.

"You got to clean up those chiqueros soon, Chon," Gomez told him, talking about the small, dark, manure-caked pens he had passed by, under the plaza, where each bull spent his last hours in solitude before his exit to glory through the toril door. "The Las Astas are coming today. Are the corrals and the feed ready? What about that leaking water trough in the big corral? And Chon, what about horses? What about those two nags Landeros wants to sell? How cheap will he go? Will you see about that?"

"I think we need them," Chon said. "Number One bulls will be a pity to our Rosinantes here. Look at the four bone-bags we got in the patio for Sunday! They need help."

"Not if it's expensive," Gomez said. "You see about it."

Vicente Domingo, the pockmarked caretaker of the Cuenca plaza, met his boss at the door of the workshop under the stands on the sunny side.

"I have the sign artist today," Vicente said. "And Jacinto is finishing the banderillas."

"Why can't you learn to paint lettering yourself?" Gomez asked.

He stepped in the shop. It smelled of fish glue and black tobacco. Strung on wires above his head, scores of paper-frilled and flowered banderillas colored the gloom. The hunchback Jacinto grinned when Gomez came up to his side by the table littered with bright tissue, scissors, wire, knives, and glue pots.

"These are the ones for the brega, the combat, here, Don Eladio," Jacinto said, pointing. "I got the barbs from the blacksmith yesterday and ground them myself."

"Be sure there are two dozen matched pairs to show to the Asesor," Gomez told the little hunchback. He hefted one of the colored sticks.

"And here are the pretty ribbons, the divisas of green and gold," the hunchback said.

The sign man was in the corner by the window, lettering the time, the place, and LAS ASTAS, on lithographed one-sheet posters of Luis Bello haughtily dressed in a shining traje.

"These are the ones for downtown?" Gomez asked.

"Nine," Vicente said.

"Get them placed today." Gomez stood watching the sign man's hand, with the letters coming so easy out of the end of the brush.

Walking alone across town to his office on Hidalgo Street, Gomez was in a bitter mood. He was like the sign artist, he thought, without any paint on the brush. He was writing dry, in the empty air, lacking the paint. Luis Bello was the paint. And Luis Bello, that son of a whore of a bullfighter, had not yet said he would be in Cuenca.

Today, if no word came, Gomez would have to act. He would have to scramble for a substitute for Luis Bello. And lose money. Because he mentioned the wrong name at the Plaza Club one morning. He remembered with disgust how it all happened. He cursed the worries it had brought him. Along the street, window cards peered at him like reproaches, with that name in red at the top, Luis Bello.

The office of the Empresa de Toros of Cuenca was cold on winter mornings. The yellowish light over the box office window where old Lara sat, and the light over Eladio Gomez's desk behind the railing, spread no cheer in the dim place where the impresario of Cuenca promoted his sunlit spectacles. Before he sat down at his desk, he ripped the November sheet off the calendar on the wall and December looked at him. Then he noticed the unopened telegram Lara had put on his desk.

Gomez saw it with foreboding. It was bad. He could feel its badness staring up at him from the desk. Bello won't come. He picked it up and tore it open and read it.

LUIS AND PEPE BELLO WITH CUADRILLAS AND SOBRE-
SALIENTE SAYA ARRIVE CUENCA BY TRAIN SATURDAY
FOR CORRIDA AS CONTRACTED.

FELIX ALDEMAS L.

"Huhh," Gomez breathed, letting the air come out slowly. "It's about time! Huh." The heaviness began to slide from his shoulders; he felt light all of a sudden, and fine.

"Take a look, Lara!" he said. "Who is this Aldemas? You know any manager named Aldemas?"

"Nobody. It is an unfamiliar name in the atmosphere."

"I wonder who is this Aldemas; I hope this telegram is all right. I think I'll go over to the Plaza Club. If Santana comes in, tell him now I will buy a little of that radio time."

The window cards he saw in the shops along Hidalgo Street were different now, with that red name at the top. Eladio Gomez had paint on his brush.

Only a few early birds were at the Plaza Club bar when he walked in and ordered lime and salt with his regular tequila. It tasted fine as he stood there gazing pleasantly at the cartel on top of the stack of handbills asking for takers by his elbow on the bar. "Grand Corrida de Toros," he read, "Festival of the Day of Santa Barbara, Sensational Presentation, LUIS BELLO — "

He could taste the cartel along with the tequila.

Nobody at the Plaza knew any manager named Aldemas. Never heard of him. Too bad about Raul Fuentes, wasn't it? When were the bulls coming? Were they really Number Ones?

Salvador Cofino hurried in, and ordered a beer. He greeted Gomez in deep-voiced Castilian; he was on his way to the ranch now, to look at some sheep for his father. But he would be back! Back in time for the corrida, of course. Luis Bello hadn't looked so well in the plaza lately, had he? In a slump, probably. He hoped that Sunday —

"Salvador," said Gomez, "you knew Fuentes. Bello too. I got a telegram from a new manager of the Bellos I never heard of. Aldemas. You know him?"

"Aldemas? No torero manager I know, named Aldemas."

"Felix Aldemas L."

"One moment!" Cofino said. "That's Aldemas Leon! Naturally I know him. A friend of my father, a great friend of the Fuentes. One of the big lawyers of the Capital. Everybody knows fat Don Felix. Don't tell me he is managing bullfighters!"

"He signed a telegram from the Bellos this morning."

"Oh! Then he must be helping. In the business Raul left. He must be helping Luis, until things get straight. That must be it."

"He's responsible?" Gomez asked, to make sure.

"Responsible? My God, Gomez, Don Felix?"

"Good!" Gomez said. "Have another beer."

Cofino laughed. "I start for the ranch, thanks. I will be in the first row Sunday!"

Eladio Gomez felt expansive with the tequila and the telegram when he got back from the Plaza Club.

"Santana in yet?"

"Not yet," Lara said.

Gomez put a yellow sheet of paper in his typewriter. "I think I will write a little propaganda myself."

For Radio Diffusion on XECU

TEXT: T O R O S ! ! !

Here is a marvelous, a stupendous, a truly formidable announcement to provoke tumult and rejoicing in the ranks of the passionate partisans of Our Brave Festival!!!

LUIS BELLO, The Enormous Swordsman of Guerreras, the grand master of the steel and the cloth, the emotional dominator of bulls, the virile and valorous idol of the plazas of the New World and the Old,

YES, LUIS BELLO! will be in the plaza of Cuenca Sun-

day demonstrating his art with magnificent bulls of
Las Astas,
YES, LAS ASTAS bulls, bravest in the Republic!!!
And with Luis will be Pepe, YES, PEPE BELLO, alter-
nating with his brother, unfolding his magic cape to
feast the eyes of the fortunate with his gallantry and
alegria!!!
TWO SUPERB TOREROS! FOUR BULLS OF LAS ASTAS!
DON'T FORGET! SUNDAY! PLAZA DE TOROS, CUENCA!
FOUR O'CLOCK SHARP!!!

"Enthusiasm," said Gomez, pulling his work from the
typewriter with appreciation. "That's what that coyote
Santana needs. Enthusiasm."

Gomez's mind settled to details with relish, now that
he might make some money, now that Luis Bello was
coming. The paint flowed from the end of his brush, add-
ing busy little dots of color to the stage he dressed for the
bulls.

He wrote memos to himself about a discount on ice for
the beer vendors' buckets; about the hundred newly covered cushions for renting at the ring; about a bass drum-
mer that would stay sober enough, at least, to hit the drum
when the band played "La Macarena"; about a new head
usher — since the trouble with the colonel last time who
took eight seats without tickets and threw the head usher
in jail for protesting, Gomez had to be careful about ushers.
The colonel was still mad; it was bad to have a mad colonel
around. A new head usher.

"Lara," he called, "will you get word to Prado and
Olanda that I want to see them today? We got to keep the
union business straight." Jose Prado and Gonzalo Olanda
were on the cartel for Sunday, fillers for the cuadrillas.

They were local members of the Union Mexicana de Picadores y Banderilleros, and they had to be hired to meet
union regulations. "It's a crime," Gomez said to Lara
again, "when even bull stickers and rag wavers organize."

Still feeling expansive, Gomez decided to go ahead and
get the pretty blue neon light repaired over the altar of
his bullring chapel, and to speak to Vicente about some
fresh flowers there. The paper ones were getting kind of
faded. He even decided to buy the two nags from Landeros,
now that Luis Bello was coming.

The afternoon was wearing away, carrying with it some
of Eladio Gomez's enthusiasm, as he plotted propaganda
with Santana by his desk. He was talking about a little
free time on XECU, a radio interview with Luis Bello upon
his arrival in Cuenca, to stir up the fans, when one of
Chon Munoz's kids came breathing hard in the office, with
word from the bullring. The boy was excited.

"Don Eladio!" he said. "The bulls! They're here. The
truck from Las Astas!"

"Ha!" said Gomez. "You hear that, Santana? Good,
heh? I'm going to the ring, Lara. Take care of the office.
If anyone wants to see us disembox, tell them to hurry!"

Approaching the ring with Santana, Gomez recognized,
by the horse patio gate, the familiar dusty truck with the
brand of Tiburcio Balbuena painted on the door of the
cab. He saw the four big bull boxes lashed to the truck
bed; he saw Policarpo Cana squatting in the shade by the
gate talking to old Chon. Policarpo had brought the pastures of Las Astas to town with him. He brought them with
the cut of his striped charro pants, with his short jacket
wrinkled with sweat and pale with dust, with his big crimped

straw sombrero and red chin string — and most of all with his leathery face, and his eyes squinted from looking all his life into the sun. Policarpo was part of something good — something far from business — Gomez remembered that morning in the sunlight in front of the big house at Las Astas.

"Policarpo!"

"Senor Gomez, at your orders!" They shook hands smiling.

"You got them here."

"Yes, senor! All in shape, well arranged." He reached into his jacket and unbuttoned a shirt pocket. "The papers. From Don Tiburcio, who sends salutes and respects."

"How is the dueno? And all Las Astas?"

"Well. Thanks to God, very well."

"How was the encierro I saw loaded for El Toreo?"

"Credit to the ribbons. Three lost ears before they left the arrastre. Procuna and Canitas cut them."

"Are these going to lose some ears Sunday, eh?" He pointed to the truck.

"How not?" Policarpo laughed. "Senor Gomez, one lacks a tail already! Ho!"

Gomez frowned. He was sensitive about that one. "A brute. Truly a brute," he said, opening the papers Policarpo had given him. The sheet on top gave the names and numbers of the bulls.

A crowd had collected around the truck.

Gomez read aloud: "*Tramillero* 74, *Bandolero* 107, *Regalon* 37, and — for God, Balbuena named him wizard! *Brujo* 23! Well, we'll see."

Vicente the caretaker, the hunchback Jacinto, the poster

artist, and Sanchez the painter with all his helpers, came out to join the crowd by the truck.

"Here's the names and numbers — for the toril door," said Gomez, looking at Vicente and then the poster man. "Take care of that."

Don Alberto Iriarte, the Engineer Vilar, and a whole Packard sedan full of aficionados from the Plaza Club drew up by the patio gate smiling, and got out to watch the faena of the disemboxing.

When greetings and handshakings and cigar lightings were over, Gomez looked up at the Las Astas truck, and then at Chon Munoz.

"Corrals ready?" Gomez asked. "Shall we?"

"All ready."

"Then, Policarpo, if you will drive the truck around to the chute — "

The disemboxing was dramatic and fascinating for everyone who loved the bulls. It was better than setting off dangerous fireworks, standing close, lighting them with a short fuse. The crowd took up silent stations on the platform built atop one of the high walls on the far side of the plaza corrals. The truck drove to the mouth of the unloading chute so that the head gate of the first bull box fitted against it squarely. Chon Munoz and his helper Miguel, who wanted to be a torero, entered the corrals; Gomez climbed with Policarpo to stand atop the bull boxes.

The very wood of those boxes seemed alive, squeaking and shaking queerly with the power confined within them. Gomez could feel the impressiveness of that dark invisible power so close under him. The least movement and shifting of his weight brought violence. Horns struck the planking so hard they stung his feet through the soles of his shoes.

Chon Munoz, standing at the end of the runway directly facing the mouth of the chute, signaled he was ready.

"Let the amo, the master, out first!" he shouted.

Policarpo reached down and pulled up the head gate. They heard the bull grunt. They waited in silence. Then the great beast, with a snort that whistled, plunged out of the box, pounded with its cramped uncertain legs as it charged snuffing down the runway, ravening to get Chon Munoz on its horns. The old banderillero calmly lured the bull past the gate into the corral, then dodged behind a burladero in the corner.

It was the bobtailed bull with the whiskers; it lunged against the burladero after Chon, its black-tipped horns thudding into the wood, tearing again and again, throwing chunks and splinters of the planking into the air.

Gomez felt a moment of panic: the horns might be broken and ruined for the corrida.

"Miguel!" Gomez bawled, with the fear clutching at him. "Fool! Get him away! Ai! Start him!"

Miguel ran out where the bull could see him. He ran waving his arms, shouting, "Huh huh huh! Toro! Huh!" and the bull spun around and charged him, across the corral. Miguel disappeared through a narrow slot in the adobe wall. The bull skidded to a stop at the opening, hooking at it, then turned fast and stood still, surveying the empty, silent corral. Hot and furious, with its neck muscle swollen high, head up, alert for killing, the bull challenged the emptiness, the silence, ready. The challenge went unanswered in the quietness.

The truck made a noise adjusting the next box to the

mouth of the chute and the head gate screeched as Policarpo pulled it up the grooves. Chon Munoz stayed hidden
behind the burladero. The second bull advanced down the
runway uncertainly on its numb legs, head down, snorting,
breathing the smell of the strange new hateful place. Trotting, it passed beyond the gate. Then cautiously it entered
the big corral, lured by the sight and smell of its encierro
mate. The two bulls squared off for a moment in the silence
as if they must fight, then lost interest in each other and
looked around, their ears cocked, hearing the sound of the
truck from over the walls as it started to move again along
the mouth of the chute. The third bull came fast, grunting, into the big corral. The fourth was slow leaving the
box; Chon showed himself as a lure again, and the bull
bellowed as it went through the gate. Chon came around
and swung it shut, grinning as he dropped the bolt into
place.

Gomez drove with Policarpo around the outside of the
corrals and they parked the truck behind the walls of the
horse patio. The dueno of the plaza was very anxious to
join the aficionados on the platform who stood peering
down at his bulls.

"Well! What do you think?" he asked, sweating, coming up the steps.

"Excellent," said the Engineer Vilar, puffing his cigar.

"Really Number Ones," said Zeferino Ramos.

"Too bad about that 23," said fat Rufino Vega. "A
damned buffalo."

"Ugly, it is true. Not aesthetic," judged Don Alberto
Iriarte. "But you don't know anything, Rufino. Didn't
you watch the way that bull came? The way he went after

Miguel? The way he held the head, the way he turned —
and no lingering? Ho! He has got something behind those
whiskers!"

"Casta, that's what he's got!" Eladio Gomez said,
proudly. "From the best cow at Las Astas."

"He's got no tail," Rufino Vega said.

"Name of Jesus. You think a bull fights with the tail?"
asked the Engineer Vilar.

They all stayed an hour, until the bulls had cooled, until
the bulls were chewing quietly, in the blue shadows under
the high curved wall. They liked to stand and just look at
the bulls.

Eladio Gomez walked alone to his office at dusk. It
was in his mind to ask his Physicians of Plaza, please, to
check again the condition, the equipment, of the infirmary.
He could still feel those horns through the planking. Oh,
there was something about the horns! There was something about the dark bulls in the shadows at night. There
was something about the bulls in the sunlight with the gold
and the music.

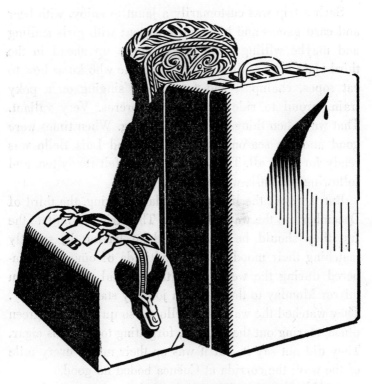

FOURTEEN

THE TWO BELLO cuadrillas traveled in style to Cuenca; the swordhandlers were proud of the accommodations they had arranged to make the trip easy, after the emotions and uncertainties of the week. Luis and Pepe, with the sobresaliente Saya, occupied the drawing-room compartment on the Pullman, and each torero had his green-curtained berth to rest in during the night on the way.

Such a trip was customarily a jaunt to enjoy, with beer and card games and high conversation; with girls smiling and maybe willing; with guitar music up ahead in the third class to pass the time, with people who knew how to eat sopes, chalupas, and fat gordas, singing on a poky train, proud to ride with valiant toreros. Very valiant. That was when things were going along. When times were good and the season held triumphs and Luis Bello was ready for them all. Then the cuadrillas felt ready too, and following the bulls was the life!

But it wasn't the life on Saturday morning, the third of December, on the way to Cuenca. They tried to imitate the fun they should be having, without having it, secretly matching their moods with a multitude of omens remembered during the week, from the scandal of the broken mirror Monday to the risk of a journey started on Friday. They watched the way Luis Bello sat so quiet on the green plush, staring out the window, forgetting to light his cigar. They did not say it, but it was on their minds every mile of the way: the corrida at Cuenca boded no good.

Outside the morning sun beat down upon the brown earth and thorny brush that slid by along the right of way. It glared upon the dry glitter of the plain, it paled the blue sierra high beyond the speckled hills. A wind blew hard through the faraway sky, through the leafless trees by the wells and walls of lonesome ranchos, across winter fields and wide waste places, raising thin sad streamers of tan dust like mournful divisas.

Luis Bello felt hollow inside. Don Felix Aldemas, the son of a whore Leon, had done it. He talked too well. He made going to Cuenca sound easy. He made Luis Bello ashamed, sitting in his parlor at San Angel, refusing to fight bulls. Luis Bello was torero, he said.

He put my tail to the squeeze. He put me on this frilling train. That fat Aldemas — and Pepe that goat of a brother — they got together for the devil's work. They got me to say I would. And here I am.

A shadow reached out for him when he thought about it. Sometimes it made his heart beat fast, and a big lump come high in his throat.

Yesterday he unfolded a cape again in his garden, just to see. His people ran the horns for him all morning. He sampled his timing as the cloth whirled, feeling how his legs held and handled under him, testing his wrists and the sinews moving, swinging the rag again, worried.

And not a drink, not a drop of anything stronger than tea since Tuesday, since the funeral he went to. Ai, Luis Bello! It was serious.

Only tomorrow. All wrapped up in a package with the name, with the name framed in black. He had tried his escape from it; he felt silly remembering. The package was coming on the horns tomorrow, and Luis Bello would reach out his hand then, and take it. He could take it. You damn right Luis Bello could take it, he hoped.

The blue sierra was coming close; Cuenca was not far. He would take it. He turned away from the empty land outside the window, and lighted his cigar.

"Paco," he said when the cigar was drawing well, "what you think of Mexico?" He pointed out the window.

"Dry and lonesome. Very frilling dry and lonesome."

"I drove horses through here when I was a kid. It's drier and lonesomer than that."

"For the very soul of dryness and lonesomeness," said Paco Saya, "you should sit on that hill out there and eat a salted fish for the complete sensation."

"What you need with the fish?" the Jackdaw asked.

"Jesus's Apostles!" Goyo Salinas said. "Remember the time we ran into the Spanish fish wagon, Luis? That time in the car on the way from Santander? God of mine, we smelled of fish for five corridas. I even caught 'em in my sox. The Aztec fishmongers, killing bulls at the fiestas of San Lucar! Remember how the fans held their noses when we opened the capes at the tablas and how this damned Monkey Garcia would stand by the barrera making a face like a fish blowing bubbles?" He slapped Garcia on the back of the neck.

"We had some times in Spain," Luis said. "You got a pretty good place for rascals, Paco. You got the atmosphere over there. It's different here, for toreros. The only important atmosphere of the bulls in Mexico is in the Capital. Nobody pays any attention to corridas out in the States, except the local fans. In Spain you got to be good in every wooden plaza to have real cartel; in Mexico it don't matter — except when you are on the make, when you are pointing. The only place where you are expected to really rip your drawers is in the Capital. The critics and the press rate you from there."

"A pity," Paco said, "and I will tell you why. If the bulls are good, the plazas of the provinces are the places to get the real flavor of the dish. The great plazas make a grand spectacle, but the little ones without boxes, they are the ones for the true festival. Close up, intimate. That's where you get the valor, the alegria right in your throat, in the little ones."

"Well, there's some real bulls in the pens at Cuenca this morning, waiting for us. And the plaza there lacks boxes and Governors' daughters with flowers in their hair. It's little enough. We'll see about the valor. The alegria." Luis felt the eyes of the cuadrilla when he said it. He felt their uneasiness.

"We will," Pepe Bello said. "We'll arm the big father and senor of alegria."

"We'll give them a package," said the Jank. "Listen, Saya, when you going to start talking Spanish so people of decency understand what you say?"

"Father God. I speak it. You speak something else, I don't know what, some barbarity of farmers."

"So that is Spanish," said the Jank. "And I'm a farmer. Imagine!"

"And the bull speaks also," said Paco. "You know what he says? He says, '*Mooo!*' "

"I understand every word the bull says."

"You got the knowledges, Delgado. You know what the cows say?"

"I know what they answer when I say '*Mooo!*' "

"When you sit on the horn, Delgado, see what it says when you say '*Yai!*' "

"So soft, so smooth."

"God of my life," said Luis Bello, "do we have to listen to the wind blowing the pigtails?"

"We are coming to Cuenca," Pepe Bello said. "I can

see the brewery. Four hours late on this slow freight."

"We got a Cuenca in Spain," said Paco Saya. "Not one of the large pearls of the true virgin."

"You might find a pearl or a virgin in this Cuenca, maybe. But I doubt it, Paco," Luis said. "Did you ever look for anything like that in Cuenca, Pepe? This Cuenca?"

"No senor. I was just looking for the barrera, the time I was in this Cuenca. Loco Ruiz and I got sand in our shoes and holes in our pants. There was some little black pearls down behind the slaughterhouse, but no virgins, they told us."

"They can stay behind that slaughterhouse," said Pancho Perez, "but they probably won't. There's fiesta in Cuenca, for the Saint."

"A feria?" asked Paco. "Like in Spain?"

"Something like that. A carnival with popcorn and dancing. Not so fancy like Spain."

"Just as drunk," smiled Monkey Garcia. "Maybe drunker."

"Impossible."

Luis Bello spoke up, looking around at the brown faces crowded in the compartment. "Listen. No drunks in these cuadrillas at Cuenca! I'm serious. You hear that? We got work. We face bulls, and that's tomorrow."

There were never any drunks in the cuadrillas on the night before a corrida. They decided Luis was talking to himself, aloud. It made an impression; it brought a silence.

"We'll just look around at these Cuenca fiestas."

"You'll see some big black things moving fast, tomorrow afternoon, without half looking," Luis said. He spit on the carpet and rubbed it with his foot.

Tacho knocked on wood, then saw it was metal. There wasn't any real wood around.

The train slowed coming into the switchyards, and the porter carried their bags to the vestibule, while they ran pocket combs through their hair, carefully, and adjusted their ties.

"Cuenca," said the conductor, stepping into the compartment to shake the Bellos' hands. "Luck tomorrow," he said. "I wish I could be here to see it."

Eladio Gomez, with a spontaneous committee of welcome from the Plaza Club — and bars of less cartel — met them as they came down the steps. When the handshaking and the abrazos were done, the picadors picked up the long ash-wood shafts of their lances and held them like tall badges of their trade, in the middle of the crowd, while Tacho and the Little O hurried around the sword cases and cape baskets, hiring porters and haggling.

"Our rooms are at the Europa," Tacho said, speaking for the Bellos. "The cuadrillas are staying at the San Andres."

Salvador Cofino came pushing through the crowd, arriving late and out of breath.

"Hola, Luis!" He gave the matador an abrazo. "Let me take you in my car."

"Good. This is my brother Pepe — and Paco Saya, here, from Seville."

The cuadrillas, with the Little O in charge of their gear, got a ride with Rufino Vega, who drove them to the San Andres, the hotel on the side street not far from the station. Rufino was disappointed to carry only cuadrillas; he had hoped for a matador.

Breaking away from the crowd, the Bellos and Paco Saya climbed into Cofino's car with Eladio Gomez and Tacho, who stowed the baggage, and they drove away. The gray stone façade of the Europa stood on the main plaza of Cuenca, looking out over the square, and across it, to the high tile-domed church of Santa Barbara. Cofino had difficulty getting his car to the hotel entrance. Holiday crowds at the market booths and carnival concessions jammed the sunny square and overflowed into the streets.

They got out of the car to the sound of wheezy music from a carrousel and the jangling of church bells marking high noon above the murmur of the crowd. Idlers on the street spied the sword cases when Tacho lifted them from the car; a crowd gathered around to gawk at the toreros and grin, while hotel porters took the baggage and led the guests inside. Cofino and Gomez went with them.

Two big ramshackle connecting rooms on the second floor front were reserved for the matadors. Shuttered French doors opened out upon rusted ironwork balconies from both rooms, overlooking the color and movement and noise filling the square.

"Day of fiesta," Cofino said as they watched it. "The people come in from the whole district for today and to-morrow."

"Racket tonight, in the middle of this," Luis remarked.

"There will be a little noise," Gomez admitted, "but you will rest well."

"We will rest very well," said Pepe.

"Tomorrow at noon you can see the procession from here," said Cofino, "when they take Santa Barbara out, and parade her around the square."

Tacho spoke. He was interested. "Senor, will you tell the reason for this celebration of the Saint?"

"She saved the town once," Eladio Gomez offered. "She stopped an earthquake when they paraded her. That's what they say, anyway. The trembling stopped and she saved the town. Long ago. God knows how long. The town celebrates it."

Cofino said, "I don't know how much of the fiestas you care for, Luis, but I would be glad to take you around. This afternoon are cockfights, rodeo, five hundred vara horse races. Carnival tonight with dancing at the Casino and all the rest of it. The Indians dance on the street with torches. Whatever you like, we are at your orders."

"I am grateful, senor. We take it easy. We face bulls tomorrow. But those races, for example. I used to work horses like that when I was a kid — "

"Certainly," Cofino said. "We'll see them, and everything you like."

"I'd like to see the Las Astas," Pepe said. "I'm going over to the ring. The cuadrillas will probably be over there. I want to see those bulls."

"Luis," Gomez put in, "and Pepe — we have arranged a little dinner of aficionados at the Plaza Club tonight. Very simple. Just to wish you well. The radio will be there, for you to say a few words to the fans of Cuenca. Just a few words. It will stir them. May we have the honor?"

"How not, Senor Gomez? But we can leave early? Because of tomorrow — "

"Exactly, diestro," Gomez said. "Plenty of rest. I will go now. The plaza keeps me busy. Senor Cofino will see that you lack nothing, I am sure. The dinner is at nine."

"I must leave now myself," said Cofino. "Wait for me here at three o'clock. We will see the fiestas."

"Until then," Luis said.

"Say," Paco Saya said when their callers had gone, "this Cuenca is not so bad!"

"Eehah!" Pepe grinned, looking at the crowd down in the square. "In fact — "

"Gala." Luis spit over the balcony. "So merry."

"Let's eat," Pepe said, "and then go see the bulls! Eehoh! I want to see them. How about you, Luis?"

"I'll see them tomorrow. They'll be there."

"At four o'clock sharp, in the afternoon," Paco quoted, brightly. "The most beautiful festival of all."

Callers began to knock on the door, to see the Swordsman of Guerreras, to shake his famous hand and to talk about tomorrow.

FIFTEEN

IN THE BRIGHT Saturday afternoon sun, the city of Cuenca partook of the fiestas of its patron Santa Barbara. Dwellers in the hard world of daily bread shut the doors of toil behind them that afternoon, according to custom, and walked out into the light. The ropers and riders raised a great dust over the wooden stands and corrals on the charro grounds where rodeo unfolded with music. Horses unlimbered for the five o'clock races along the quarter-mile track in the mesquite at the edge of town. The sun filtered pale through the white canvas cover of the Cuenca cockpit where bettors screamed their odds and handlers petted their baleful fowls, blowing down their throats, in the thick smell of damp dust and sweat and stale beer. The carrousel and Ferris wheel made their turns to the sounds of their whiffing musics in the swarming plaza where the urchins squealed and citizens promenaded in holiday noise and carnival smell by the street stalls where food was frying. The pink lemonade, the popcorn, the brown sugar and quince candy, the bright balloons, the ribboned toy canes were selling. And the bars of Cuenca crammed full and loud, tuned up like strings on the mariachis' guitars, for an evening. Fiesta was in the air over Cuenca as the shadows grew longer and the sunlight turned yellow above the violet western sierra.

Eladio Gomez, with fiesta all around him, was busy as a man tending bar. At his bullring he watched the completion of a thousand details, giving orders. Chon and Miguel finished dragging the plaza, leveling up the low place with new sand in front of the cuadrilla gate. They got out the hoses then, and began wetting down the wide tan circle to make the footing firm and smooth for tomorrow. The sweepers with Vicente finished cleaning the stands; Sanchez's new paint looked fine and bright. Jacinto had the little flags fixed, sixty of them for around the top of the plaza, and the red and yellow TOROS banner for the pole, clean and ready. Eladio Gomez checked over the list of memos he carried in his pocket, crossing them off one by one. The beer and cushions were all delivered, stacked in the storeroom by the plaza entrance. The block was installed in the hoist by the hooks, for the plaza butcher who would be busy tomorrow beyond the arrastre; the meat of the four Las Astas was contracted for. Gomez rehearsed the new head usher and his crew. He tested the blue neon light over the chapel altar; it pleased him, with all the new flowers. The infirmary was scrubbed, smelling of carbolic acid. Landeros delivered his flea-bitten nags for the picadors, and promised to bring the three rented mules to Chon Munoz in the morning. In the midst of the exertions around them, the bulls of Las Astas chewed quietly on their cuds. Gomez was proud when Pepe and five of the Bello cuadrillas arrived at the plaza pens to see those bulls. The impresario stood listening curiously while the toreros and Policarpo Cana argued the points of each animal, in preparation for the sorting and the drawing of lots for each matador, in the morning. When Gomez went back to his office on Hidalgo Street, he found it neither dim nor lonely. The line of ticket buyers in front of Lara's box office window brought the fiesta feeling almost into Gomez's heart. It warmed him. If only the weather held. If only the sun were strong. If only the wind did not blow. O Sainted Christ of the Conversion of the Good Robber, Eladio Gomez, you might fill your plaza! A full house to watch Luis Bello work with Las Astas. He picked up the phone on his desk and called to be sure about the sound truck with the loud-speaker. It was ready, with the signs. It would play bullfight music by the carnival square for an hour tonight, and through the streets of Cuenca for three hours before the corrida tomorrow.

"Tune it loud," said Eladio Gomez.

Up the street at the Plaza Club aficionados gathered. For them there was one theme worthy of consideration in the fiestas of Santa Barbara. They drank over it, savoring it in advance.

"The mob does not understand what it sees in a plaza," said the Engineer Vilar. "Much less those gringo tourists, leaving after the second bull in the *Mexico*."

"No fiesta for tourists and neurotic girls," Zeferino Ramos stated. "The flavor is strong."

"Aficionados of the true red bone are often ignorant of the meaning of our festival," the Engineer said, sipping his manzanilla. "It is true that all the arts are surrounded by cults and loose tongues embroidering upon meanings far removed from the impulses that give birth to those arts. It is nevertheless necessary to have philosophy to view an art with understanding."

"Let me remind you, Engineer," Santana said, "that most of the human race are far from considering bullfighting an art. To them it is a bloody sport, a debased and useless violence."

"A good point, Santana," old Alberto Iriarte said. "Let us go farther into this inquiry of the Engineer's philosophy."

"For that matter," the Engineer said, "none of the great arts originally came into being as art. Art grows from what is first a utility or a pastime. The festival of the bulls, for instance, grew from both. First it was a hunt for meat in the mountains of Spain, and then later a sporting pastime for horsemen armed with lances, before spectators. But it developed. In the beginning, music was perhaps no more than grunting while beating two sticks together, and painting was the daubing of dots on cave walls and jugs. They are more than that now. And a corrida de toros is more than a sport."

"It is of course necessary," old Iriarte put in, "to understand our festival is not a sport but a spectacle. It is a form of drama as certainly as the works of Sophocles. But what a difference between the happenings on a stage or in a poem, and the happenings in a plaza!"

"Exactly," the Engineer said. "The festival of the bulls is the only art form in which violence, bloodshed and death are palpable and unfeigned. It is the only art in which the artist deals actual death and risks actual death, as if a poet were called upon to scan his lines with his life. It is the contemplation of this visible violence and actual death that gives the art its peculiar power, gentlemen."

"It is also that actuality which confuses the art with sport and confounds foreigners who find real blood a revulsion — or a morbid thrill," Santana said.

"All arts, even the most abstract," Don Alberto broke in again, "are essentially creations to thrill. To allow man to participate in God's designs at one step removed from the anguish of living them. Sitting safely in a chair."

"The heart of the matter is this," said the Engineer. "There is enormous difference between the thrill given by art and the thrill given by watching merely exciting forms of peril. The difference, let us say, between a corrida de toros and a motorcycle race. Peril moves us simply as witnesses to a gripping body sensation. Violence, or peril, made significant by art amplifies the sensation beyond the body, distills it, lifts it above the realm of mere incident. A corrida de toros, by that token of art, presents us with a moving image and symbol of our own hearts grappling with violence and death. Can this be a sport? Unless, indeed, man facing his destiny is sport, combat between equals. No! In the plaza the man lives, by his bravery, and the bull dies. Sometimes it is another case, but that is not the plan of our festival which is designed to show the glory of courage over the power of death. Each of us reads into this theme our private response. It is that meaning of man face to face with the inner and outer brute force of living, and man's tragedy in dealing death while subject to it himself, which has gripped the mind and emotion of the Latin race."

"Do you know what Juan Belmonte said in his memoirs?" asked Don Alberto. "He said, 'And at the end of a faena, when my enemy was exhausted and caring no longer for the trouble of the muleta, and I had to mount the sword, then it gave me compassion, then I felt pity, feeling pain and remorse that I must kill my bull, such a noble beast, that many times pardoned my life and in return for that pardon I only sent him away forever from his green and happy pastures.' "

"It explains our feelings when we leave a plaza," Zeferino Ramos said. "We have seen it, the tragic brave festival."

"Who speaks of brave festival?" Meliton Esparza asked, walking up to their table in his ranch clothes, a tequila in his thick hand. "I like to sit there in the sun with a bottle and hear that bugle blow! I like to see a freight train come out of the door and scare the Sainted Jesus out of those frilling dolls waving their pretty rags! I like to see the horns at work. I like to whistle when the devil gets unchained. Ole for the festival!" He slapped his pistol. "Is it going to be a good one tomorrow, Zeferino?"

"How not?"

"I just got to town. Are the bulls big?"

"Big enough."

"Who are these Bellos with the pretty name?" He drained his tequila and called Carlos for another. "Are the Bellos any good, Don Alberto? Or are they some more of those dolls in the gold panties?"

Old Iriarte frowned. "Meliton, you get brutish in the sierras. You ought to come to town more often."

"About the panties?" Meliton grinned. "That's why I came! But without the gold. Just pink. Eeehoh! It's dead in this tomb with your festival." He banged down his glass and swaggered out the door.

"That son of a whore should bait bears," Benito Bombach said, watching Esparza go. "But what do you really think of the Bellos, Don Alberto? I just saw Luis, out at the races with Salvador Cofino."

"There has been no killer of bulls like him since Luis Freg. On a good afternoon, Luis Bello is ample with the cape, immense with the muleta, enormous with the sword. At the Hour of Truth, when he goes in to kill, there is no one like him."

"He gives the tragedy. All alone, out there. Nobody can work closer to the horns."

"But he has been lacking lately. He was frankly bad at Guadalajara."

"He has been sluggish since the leg wound in September. That benefit performance at Irapuato. I saw it."

"And did you hear about the girl, the one killed with Fuentes? She absolutely was, they say."

"I know. A double blow. Has Cofino ever told you about Fuentes and Bello? They were very close. Bello is from the humble, of course. Fuentes was the one that made him person of decency. Taught him how to read, how to dress; he even taught him how to eat at table. And took care of his money. What a blow!"

"The bulls punish Luis Bello. My God, but they punish him. They will get him someday."

"What about the kid brother? How do you like Pepe?"

"You remember him here, the summer before last. I saw him in Mexico too. Regular. A nice boy, but only regular. It's rare to have two good ones in a family."

"Don Alberto, what do you think of Pepe Bello?"

"I think some words of Sanchez de Neira in his classic dictionary of bulls. He wrote of 'a young man just beginning of whom there is yet little to say. He has gained a certain name for courage, but those valiant among men are not always so among bulls.' We will judge tomorrow."

The hours toward tomorrow unwound to the sound of fiesta. The stars were bright and many in the sky above it, but the Bello cuadrillas were guided by nearer lights when they left the San Andres to find their suppers and sample the celebrations before they went to bed. Tomorrow was a constraint upon them. It held them together like a group of tourists from another world. They only stood upon the edges of the festivities, like wry inspectors, eating in a crowded cafe, hearing music, eyeing the girls on promenade, watching the Indians dance by torchlight to the squeaking of fiddles and thumping of drums, and milling in the aimless crowd around the lighted booths draped in bunting by the entrance to the Casino.

"What is the use of it?" the Jank asked Goyo Salinas. "For me, the spark ain't working. The engine's dead tonight."

"My sad life is just bread and bulls. Let's find a bar and have a few beers and then go to bed. Come on, Pancho."

"Eehah, did you see that one?" Monkey Garcia smoothed his hair and smiled. "A front like a plaza de toros! Did you say go to bed, Goyo?"

"Reminds me of a girl back home," said the young banderillero Enrique, sadly. "In Cusi."

"There he goes with Cusi," the Little White said. "Give us the name of your town again, Enrique. It illuminates the soul and puts musicians to work."

"Cusi, Cusihuiriachic."

"I been there. It's nothing," the Jackdaw said.

"It's a name," said the Little White. "They call it Cusi to save time and not be late for dinner."

"It don't matter," said the Jackdaw. "They don't eat much in Cusi. I didn't."

"Let's get the hell out of Cusi and into a saloon," the Jank said.

They found a bar where there were chairs to sit on, and musicians singing in the smoky light. They had dark beer from Orizaba.

When the musicians changed the tune, Goyo banged his fist down on the table. "There goes that frilling funeral again! Enrique! Go tell them to play something else or

I'll stick a puntilla down their throats." The musicians were singing that new ballad, "The Tragedy of Juan Salazar."

Pancho Perez knocked on wood. "A dead bull has no horns," he mumbled.

"Big mosquitoes with long stingers tomorrow," Enrique said.

"Have you seen the racks of sorrow we ride here?" the Soup asked, rubbing his head. "I spit in the milk."

"The picador's complaint. They ought to write a song about that."

They drank their beer quietly in all the noise, and ordered again.

"Goyo," said Pancho Perez, looking down in his glass, "you and I know that sometimes in the plaza the bull is the one that knows the most. When the bull knows he is going to get us, and we know it too, what a pity! The public up in the stands don't hear what the bull is saying. They don't know his bad intentions. So they whistle. Now between a whistle the wind carries away, and a horn wound you carry away, which is the most acceptable? The boo passes, the wound remains. I am glad we are peons and do not make the choice. I am getting old."

"The hell with bulls at night, like this," said the Soup. "They're enough when the sun is shining."

"Jackdaw," the Jank said, "how does it feel in Cuenca, away from the pearl of Mesones Street? You think she misses you?"

"She is probably having fiestas of her own tonight," said Monkey Garcia.

"To fight bulls or stay married to a pearl, you got to stand close," the Little White remarked.

"Bulls are safer," the Jackdaw stated.

"He has angels in the mouth," spoke the Soup. "A woman, she is the most problem of the complete creation."

"I could solve a problem tonight," Monkey Garcia said. "I wish I had a complete problem in my lap. Listen to that complete music!"

"The girls and the bulls," the Little White said. "They hook."

"What an age for toreros," the Jank said. "With the Father and Senor Penicillin!"

"That's the name of the stuff I was telling you!" Goyo said. "For the hookings."

"There's no future in this saloon," Monkey said. "Shall we have another round? Or go?"

They saw Luis Bello out on the street.

"Where's Pepe and the Flower of Seville?" the Jank asked.

Luis looked the cuadrillas over, estimating their condition. He was very sober. "You on your way?" he asked.

"Yes," Goyo said.

"I'm giving a little circuit, to the Casino with the Senor Cofino here, and then I'm making myself some sleep," Luis told them. "We just finished the dinner. Pepe and Paco are giving their own little turn."

Back in his room at the Europa, Luis Bello told Tacho to keep the rooms quiet, by God, in the morning; to keep the crowd out; he wanted rest. Tacho and Abundio left him then, and he undressed and turned off the light and got in bed. The glow and the sound of the carnival penetrated the shutters on the balcony doors and came into his room. He heard the bells jangle on the church tower of Santa Barbara, announcing midnight. The mechanical music from the carrousel and Ferris wheel stopped; but there were flurries of song and he heard laughter and voices passing in the streets.

The carnival came to him from far away, from the other side of the moon, and stopped on the edge of his mind. Looking up at the slits of light reflected on the high dark ceiling he felt as calm as if he were someone else, as if from up there Luis Bello stood looking down untroubled upon himself. Stretched out flat upon the bed, he felt the soundness of his body, somehow proud of this care he gave it, this rest, this complete sobriety. It pleased him as if he were fulfilling some honorable obligation.

He closed his eyes but sleep would not come.

The fiestas in the gardens of San Marcos. It was long ago. He saw the blue flowers on the jacaranda trees against the blue sky. He smelled the springtime and felt the new green leaves in the garden where the music played. He saw the blue dusk settling upon the streets of Aguascalientes during carnival time in the spring, and the people all walking and laughing to the gardens where the colored lanterns began to glow beneath the darkening trees while the music played. He saw the girls again, walking arm in arm and smiling, with the fiestas in their eyes and confetti caught in their hair, in the lantern light with the music playing in the hubbub of the crowd. Oh, those were the fiestas in the spring at the gardens of San Marcos! He saw the slender girl again walking in the light and he heard her say her name was Barbara and he felt her move and sway when they danced. He could see her smile when the guitars played "Maria Elena." In the spring of the year.

The bullring in the fall that year, there at San Marcos by the fiesta grounds. How he dedicated the first bull. The first pertaining to Luis Bello, Matador de Toros. "To thee, Barbara, I dedicate this bull." How many hundred bulls and dedications since then! How he killed that first one for her and how they carried him from the ring on their shoulders, and he saw her smile at him that night.

The days when I was thirsty. When I drank it all and my throat was never full. Oh I was thirsty.

Thirsty for the bulls in those times. I killed a seventh bull in my head after every corrida and when I went to bed at night I had fought two whole corridas more, complete. I kept on fighting bulls in dreams and when the morning came I wished I could put on my suit of lights! Luis Bello, Matador de Toros. Thirsty for the bulls. The fame, the shouts, the smiles, the money, the drinks, the girl. And I had them. I had them, every one. In the days and nights before I made mysteries in my head. In the times before I cared about the horns.

He heard the door open in the next room, Pepe and the Spanish kid coming in from the fiestas. Coming to their hotel room in a town named Cuenca, on the night before they might get killed, coming in laughing, late, in the times before they ever cared about the horns.

Luis Bello shifted his body on the bed. Standing up there outside of himself so strangely, he looked down at himself so full of care.

Jesus and Mary, when I was a kid! There were some things I hadn't done and I was going to do them. And sometimes I did. I never wondered then if I could do as good as I did before. In those days what I done before wasn't enough, and when it ever gets to be enough, I'm finished.

That's the way to say it, what there is about the bulls! I tried to tell Linda there was something about it and she called me proud when it wasn't that. I didn't know the words to say it then, exactly what it was about the bulls. It's knowing what you can do out there alone. It's feeling what you got inside and doing it the best you can, regardless. I didn't get to tell her that, but I know it, here in this frilling Cuenca. And the only way to fight bulls is not in bed alone in the dark, but by God in a plaza at four o'clock in the afternoon, when the horns are not so big.

SIXTEEN

THE BELLS OF the Church of Santa Barbara across the plaza awoke Luis Bello. They were answered by church bells in the distance. The sound of bells came to his room from many directions, from all over the city of Cuenca, answering the bells of Santa Barbara. Luis Bello awoke

in the strange room sharply aware. The light that came
past the shutters now was not the colored lantern light of
carnival; it was the light of the sun in the sky. It came
through the closed lids of his eyes to rob him of the secur-
ity of dark sleep so that he lay in a waking grayness
tinged with the redness of his blood. The pale ghost red
behind his lids was alive and impatient, now that the day
was here.

He opened his eyes and looked at his watch. Eight
hours and twenty minutes. Then the red door would open.
He stared at the ceiling high above his head, feeling four
o'clock coming. Slow, and yet fast too. With the package.
He lay in bed waiting, with his eyes open, rubbing his
bad leg.

At nine he heard a knock, a tentative, padded, familiar
knock on the door. It was Tacho.

"Hola! How about a little tea, Luis? Something warm to
start the day. How's that leg?"

"It caught a knot when I first woke up, but it's all right."

Tacho came into the room with the tea.

"Have it, Luis, and then let me rub the leg. We'll limber
it. Three letters for you this morning. I have a kid posted
outside your door. I told him I would kill him if he let
anybody disturb you while I'm in here and can't watch."

Luis drank the tea, sitting on the side of the bed, while
he opened the letters. Two of them were the kind he got
in every town; the paper of one was pink and scented,
the other pale violet. It was so enormous to have Luis
Bello in Cuenca. There would be prayers and applause
for him all afternoon as he deserved and should he care
to celebrate the triumph afterward, of course it was too

much to hope for, but at the Casino after ten o'clock to
the right of the entrance door inside, with a red carnation
in the hair . . . Luis Bello had to smile while he opened
the third letter, typewritten on white paper, unscented. The
writer begged only a moment of the diestro's time, a moment of great portent and fortune. The writer had discov-
ered a gold mine. If Luis Bello cared to . . .

"Here's a gold mine if you want to get rich," Luis said.
"The others are probably pure gold too."

"On the front teeth," Tacho said. He had the liniment
in his hand. "Let's work with the leg."

The door opened from the adjoining room.

"How goes the big Luis?" It was Pepe, grinning. He
and Paco were in their undershirts. "We join you for tea?"
He crooked his finger with elegance. Abundio de la O
followed them with a teapot and more cups. They drank
sitting around Luis's bed, while Tacho rubbed the leg.

"The wind," Paco mentioned, relaxed, looking out the
balcony doors. "Have you noticed the filthy wind? It's
blowing."

"It will stop," Pepe said. "It isn't allowed."

Luis pointed to the colored letters on the bed. "There's
some literature for you boys. Faenas after the plaza
closes."

"I got one," Pepe said. "In green ink."

At ten-thirty there was another knock on the door from
the hall. Tacho answered; it was Goyo and Pancho, the
peons of confidence.

Goyo looked at his matador, sampling the spirit of the
day. "How goes, Luis?"

"Not bad. Cuadrillas bright?"

"Innocent and strong as boys. Pancho and I came to ask you and Pepe about sorting, and drawing the lots. You want to leave it in our judgment? You want a real drawing like you were unfriendly, or you want us to set it up? We seen the bulls."

"The show is for Pepe," Luis said. "Give him the cream."

"They are paying to see you, Luis," his brother said. "You ought to work the top stuff. You take them. They are all because of you."

"A bull is a bull," Luis said. "Are they fairly even?"

"There's one son of a phenomenon that got out of a zoo. The others are even."

"Well," Luis said, "let's run it on the level. What you say, Pepe? Pair them even and really draw. How's that?"

"Suits me. They all got horns."

"And none are children," Pancho Perez said. "The pics are going over with us to try the horses. There will be some knots on the heads of picadors tonight, after falling from great heights."

At eleven the matadors had their breakfasts brought to the room. They each had more tea, a fried egg with chili, a slice of bread, and an orange to finish. They ate very slowly. It was all the food they could have until after the corrida.

Tacho opened the balcony doors and the noise of the crowd in the square filled the room with babble and murmur of holiday and expectation. A gust of wind slammed one of the doors shut suddenly while the matadors were eating. No one said a word; Tacho propped the door open again with a chair.

"They are going to have the Saint out at noon," remarked the Little O.

The boy on guard outside the door allowed another knock. It was the aficionado Cofino, carefully dressed in double-breasted tailoring with wide shoulders. He was smiling.

"I just came to see if I could do anything for you this morning. If you needed anything."

The matadors thanked him, chewing. Luis indicated a chair. "Please sit down. And excuse this room."

Tacho answered another knock, scowling, and stepped outside, closing the door.

"Eladio Gomez is going to fill his plaza this afternoon," Cofino said. "We have the sun in Cuenca, with the Bellos and Las Astas!"

"Can you do something about the breeze?"

Cofino laughed. "I'm having it stopped. I'm using influence."

They could hear angry voices outside the door. Tacho came back in, shaking his head.

"What's that?" Luis asked him.

"The same old stuff." Tacho grinned. "Two crazies. With two of the reliables. Barcelona to Cuenca, always the crazies! One with a love drink, guaranteed. The other with the rare powder. Dust it in the muleta, the bull is yours. No risk, no trouble. Scientific! God of my life! I had to insult them to get them to go away."

"You really should have bought some," Pepe said. "The love drink for the bulls and the rare powder for the girls. Eehah!"

"Imagine!" Cofino said. "I must go. It's time for the procession and I must find my family." They all stood and Cofino embraced each torero, saying, "Have luck!"

When he had gone, the bells began to ring. The three matadors walked out upon the balcony, into the sun. The whole plaza was jammed.

A cheer went up as the gilded palanquin of Santa Barbara, borne on the shoulders of a dozen bearers, came out of the church door, through the iron gate and into the crowd. A banging salute of guns joined the bells and the shouting. A band of mariachis took their places leading the litter of the Saint, with little girls in white dresses following, throwing flowers in the path of Santa Barbara. When the bells stopped their ringing, there were the shouts and the music of the mariachis, coming around the plaza, the *Viva la Santa! Viva Santa Barbara Patrona de Cuenca!* with sombreros sailing into the air, and the little girls throwing the flowers.

The Saint came around past the balcony where the toreros stood, and they saw her clearly. Santa Barbara was a framed painting of a solemn pretty girl with a great gold halo. She stood by a dark tower with three windows, and by a cannon, and behind her were storm clouds with a lightning flash. She was calm in the midst of her picture, in the midst of her storm, in the midst of the noise of Cuenca. The plinking, jigging, fiddling, thumping strings of the mariachis beat a solid swinging tempo in the shouting. It was the music of the Mexican heart pounding in the sunlight as the Saint went by.

"Making a circuit!" Pepe yelled. "Touring the ring! Taking an ovation!" It was a good sign, for a change.

"Que alegria!" the Spaniard Paco was shouting. "Viva la Patrona, la Santisima Barbara!"

When she came back to the door of her church, the bells all rang again, and Cuenca gave her another Viva, the loudest one of all, for another year.

As they watched the crowd dissolving from the plaza, the three toreros on the balcony heard bullfight music. A sound truck came around the corner, racking out a paso doble of the bulls. On the sides of the truck were gaudy big lithographs of Luis Bello.

"Ole!" said Paco Saya. "After the Saint, the Swordsman!"

"Christ in His pain!" Luis said. He went inside.

Focusing his eyes in the dimness, he saw that Tacho had been busy. There on a chair, laid out according to ritual and with formal care, he saw his suit of lights waiting for him, blue and gold. A black band of mourning was sewn upon the left sleeve of the jacket. Outside the bullfight music stopped abruptly and Luis Bello heard the rasping of his name. At the Plaza de Toros of Cuenca, at four o'clock sharp.

The chair with the glittering traje was placed by a table at the end of the room. Upon the table Tacho had opened a flat leather case and set up a colored image of La Virgen de Guadalupe and lighted a votive candle by it. At the side of the image he had placed the silver talismans of the Virgin and of Santa Barbara, strung on a thin gold chain. They were always placed so, by the traje, before every corrida; no one could touch anything there, no one but Luis Bello and Tacho his servant of swords, until after the matador was all dressed for the ring. No one. It was something Luis

Bello felt very strongly. It was one of his ways of dealing with the horns.

At a quarter to one a barber came to shave the matadors and trim their hair before they dressed. He had finished with Luis, and just lathered Pepe's face, when Goyo and Pancho came to report their sorting of the bulls and the results of drawing the lots from a hat. Luis was in a bathrobe ready to go down the hall for his shower when the peons came.

"We took the two that looked the best," Goyo explained, "and paired them each with one of less promise." The matadors were listening hard.

Pancho said, "The lots are about even."

"Who got which?"

"Luis got the big Number 74 and the ugly one with the whiskers. You got the pretty Number 37 and the one with the spread horns."

"Which one of mine comes out first?" Luis asked.

"I'm sorry about it, Luis," his peon said. "As the first and the third of the afternoon pertain to you, I wanted to get the ugly one out of the way so you could hit the summit with your final bull. But the dueno Gomez was afraid. He was scared to run the ugly first. He said the crowd would howl. He insisted on 74 to begin. So you got a freight train first and a buffalo last."

"A bull is a bull." Luis was dry, standing with his hands in his bathrobe pockets. "This is Pepe's show."

"How do mine come out?" Pepe asked. The barber had quit trying to shave him.

"The right way," Pancho said. "The wide horns first and the 37 to close plaza with a sweet taste."

"We have to hurry now and dress," Goyo said. "I hope we did good."

"Sure," Luis said. "Thanks." He went to take his shower while Pepe and Paco were barbered.

When Luis came back, Tacho had the room cleared, ready for the dressing. It was a careful ceremony and it took time. The matador first went over to the table, made the sign of the cross, then put the gold chain over his head and around his neck so that the medals were on his chest. They were cold for a moment.

The clean cotton underwear came to his elbows and knees, fitting snug, and it looked very white against his brown body when he sat down on the side of the rumpled bed. Tacho knelt on the floor and put white stockings on the matador's bare feet. The stockings met the underwear above the knees. Luis pulled them up and secured them with ring garters of white elastic. Over the white stockings went the outer pink ones — the color of "rosy times in our history long past," as a Spanish bull critic once wrote — and Tacho smoothed them up to the garters and Luis fastened them tight.

The swordhandler put his master's stockinged feet through the legs of the taleguilla, the skin-tight gold-embroidered breeches, and Luis stood while they tugged, working and smoothing the breeches up the legs. To accomplish the final "mounting of the taleguilla" Tacho called Abundio into the room. The two swordhandlers rolled a towel and Luis straddled it, with the helpers holding it tight at both ends.

"Don't touch him." Tacho warned the Little O. "Just hold the end of the towel."

Riding down hard on the towel between his legs, Luis finally worked the crotch of the breeches up snugly to where it belonged.

Leaving the waist unbuttoned, he sat down then and extended one leg at a time while Tacho fastened the breeches below the knees, pulling them shut and tying them with the machos, the gold-tasseled drawstrings that held the bottoms tight around the legs.

Standing again, Luis got into the white shirt with the embroidery down the front. Instead of tucking in the shirt-tail, Tacho folded it up evenly all around so that it came only a little below the waist. He held it in place while Luis buttoned his breeches over it.

"I'm thinner," Luis said. The waist was not as tight as usual.

Tacho did not answer. He got down and put the soft-soled heelless black slippers, the zapatillas, on Luis's double-stockinged feet.

Looking in the mirror, Luis tied his crimson necktie of narrow satin. Tacho put a sash of the same crimson about the matador's waist. It was a single tight turn of silk to cover the joining of the shirt and breeches.

When the sash was in place, Luis sat while Tacho carefully wound a lock of the hair on the back of Luis's head around a flat clip and fastened to it the anadido, the torero's artificial pigtail mounted on the black velvet button. Luis shook his head hard, to see if the anadido was secure. Satisfied, he stood up and put on the brocaded vest and buttoned it over the sash. Then Tacho held the dozen pounds of gold-embroidered, tasseled, epauletted jacket while Luis got into it, snugging it up to the back of his neck, and he was dressed for the plaza. On the chair there remained only the montera, the torero's black hat with the bulges at the sides, and the elaborate silk cape for the parade into the ring. Tacho did not touch them.

"I'm dry," Luis said. "Get me water. I'm very dry." When he had taken a swallow, he rinsed his mouth and squirted the water on the floor. Then he slapped his flat belly. "You got some limes to squeeze in the water jugs this afternoon? I'm dry."

Before a corrida, he was always dry; the more nervous he was, the drier. He must be very nervous, he decided, remembering a phrase. He could remember the dry way Manolete said it, sitting by him on the way to the plaza, "the battle of nerves we suffer." Luis walked to the mirror and looked at himself, straightening his tie. That the battle won't show! That I keep it hidden like the Cordoban.

"All right, Tacho."

The swordhandler crossed himself and left the room. In accordance with his ritual, Luis Bello was alone, in his suit of lights.

There was a physical way a man felt, trussed and weighted and strange in such dress, with all the lower body gripped in glistening tightness, with the arms and shoulders housed and burdened in stiff gold, with the feet queerly light and tender in the pliant slippers and the pigtail pulling at the back of the head. There was also the way a man felt in his heart. Luis Bello's heart was pounding too fast.

He heard the voices on the square outside, and the hum of the town on its way to the plaza de toros, and he stepped to the balcony door to see about the wind. There wasn't any. The trees were nearly still now, in the bright sun. It was five minutes to three, it was almost time. Beyond the bell tower of the church across the plaza, the sky was empty blue, the color of his traje, without the gold.

He turned back into the dim room and walked to the table where the wax burned in the red glass by the familiar image. He got down on his knees. Oh, he was dry! The words came dry in his mouth. Holy Virgin of Guadalupe. Queen of Mexico and my sweet Mother, he always began it. Give me the grace of thy protection and the good luck. Save me from the horns of the beasts. That I may venerate Thee to the end of life. Amen.

When he had said it, it did not seem enough but it was all that came. Amen. He got up, dusting his knees, and took the black montera from the chair. Holding it with both hands, he pressed it down firmly on his head, low and straight across his brow. Then he folded the parade cape across his left arm carefully, and walked out of the door without looking back.

Tacho was waiting in the hall, with the boy who watched the door.

"One moment, Luis, and we will go." Tacho went into the room and came out with the sword case, the towels, and the water jug. He had his old tweed cap on, for luck. "We are ready," he called to Abundio, opening the door to the next room, and Pepe and the Spaniard, both smiling, joined Luis. Pepe was dressed in his new traje of lilac and silver; the color made his face look ruddy brown and his teeth very white. He had the black band sewn on his arm. Paco Saya was smoothly rigged in bottle green and gold.

Tacho, with a sword case under his arm, led the procession down the worn stone steps and into the high glassed-over patio that formed the lobby of the Hotel Europa. Luis followed, then Pepe and Paco, with Abundio and his swords, and the boy who watched the door and was now promoted to carry water jugs and towels bringing up the rear. The toreros made a dazzling show of color in the gray stone lobby; there was a round of hand clapping and feminine sounds of admiration from the crowd gathered there, and out on the sidewalk, to watch the toreros depart for the ring. They got into the back seat of a car waiting for them at the curb. The swordhandlers and their assistant caught a taxi on the corner.

Now was the nervous time. The Bellos and Paco Saya had little to say, riding together through the Sunday streets to the plaza de toros.

"The wind is gone," the Spaniard observed.

"A day for the bulls," Pepe said. "The sun is the grand torero, at the top of every cartel."

The street leading to the ring was crowded. They sat silent driving up to the shadow of the curved wall, with the noise and the movement growing around them. They could hear the band playing. They could feel the sunlit crowd and the color, the hurry, the tension, and it entered into them as they got out of the car by the horse patio gate.

The cuadrillas were waiting for them inside, rigged in their trajes, ready.

"All set," Goyo reported to Luis. The picadors were adjusting saddles on three nags and tightening the heavy quilted pads slung under the horses' bellies.

"You think they can still stand up when you get on?" Paco laughed.

It irritated the Little White, who was sweating under his

wide beaver hat, and breathing hard. "You help the monos
prop them while we pic," he said. "They'll stand up. Christ
of the Good Death, they got to stand!"

Tacho and Abundio arrived with the sword cases and the
assistants carrying the cape baskets. They went down the
cuadrilla passageway that led from the patio under the
stands and beyond the gate into the ring, where they walked
around the callejon to the burladero on the other side of the
plaza, to lay out the capes and unfurl the muletas and ready
the swords. They left one of the gates partly open, and Luis
could see through the tunnel under the stands out to where
the sunlight shone on the empty sand in the ring, and the
stands on the other side where he saw the crowd packing
in. Eladio Gomez came through the open cuadrilla gate
and up the tunnel to where the matadors stood. He was
smiling.

"We're filling the plaza!" he said. He gave each matador
an abrazo and a "Have luck!" The impresario of Cuenca
looked well and smelled of tequila. He could feel that
paying crowd in the stands over his head and it went to his
heart.

Old Don Alberto Iriarte entered the patio with a companion and walked directly to the Bellos.

"See who honors us," said Don Alberto.

Luis turned. "Don Marcelo!"

The man with Iriarte was Marcelo Cadena, the eminent
critic of bulls for *La Lidia* of Mexico. He gave Luis an
abrazo and a cigar. Don Alberto introduced him to Eladio
Gomez, then to Pepe and to Paco Saya.

"An accident brought me," the portly critic said. "I had
to go to the North this week on private affairs. Coming back

I heard of the corrida and got off the train this morning to attend. I never miss Luis Bello!"

"Magnificent!" said Eladio Gomez, expanding. He saw visions of propaganda in *La Lidia*. "Will you be my guest in the callejon, or would you rather sit in the first row?"

"I will sit with Don Alberto, thank you," the critic said. "The plaza is yours, Don Marcelo."

"Don Marcelo," Luis Bello said, "I am glad you came. To see my brother Pepe with real bulls."

"I will be watching," the critic stated.

Eladio Gomez was hoping the matadors would use his plaza chapel. He was proud of it, and he pointed to its door at the end of the patio. "Perhaps now you would like to make devotions," he suggested to the toreros, looking at his watch. "Twenty-five until four."

"Thank you," Luis said. He turned to his brother. "I'd like to go last. If you and Paco now —"

Luis stood with his face set, trying to be cool, and easy, waiting for Pepe and Paco to come out of the chapel. Aficionados found their way into the patio, and there were hands to shake and faces to be pleasant to, while he waited for the chapel door to open. When Pepe and Paco reappeared, a photographer was waiting to line up the matadors. The flash bulbs blinked. Then Luis went in the chapel and closed the door.

He went in wanting to be alone, and as soon as he was alone he was sorry. The blue line of neon arching over the altar, and the candles burning at either side of the Guadalupe, were the only light. In a niche on a side wall he saw the image of Jesus del Gran Poder. The noise of the plaza was completely shut away. In the silence he put down his cape and the montera, and knelt at the rail before the altar. The words came to him.

Holy Virgin of Guadalupe, my Mother. Who remained brave seeing the suffering of Thy Son. By the sword of sorrow that went into your heart that day, and by the reward you now take in Heaven, look down from the Throne and hear my prayer. Shelter me in your blessed mantle. Give me courage in the moments of great peril. Amen.

When he had said Amen, he looked up at the image of the Gran Poder. More words came to Luis Bello. O Father Jesus of the Great Power, Saviour and Redeemer, who was also mocked by a mob. Grant that the evil of the crowd will not fall upon me today. Help me in this hour when I make a parade of vanity forgetting Your example. And do not permit, Senor, a fault of mine to bring injury to those I care for. Amen.

The words kept coming to Luis Bello kneeling in the silence. The most words he ever had. He touched the medal under his shirt. Santa Barbara, Blessed Saint whose name I guard well and do not speak because of thy purity and my evil. Santa Barbara, be with me on this thy day, and this the day of thy namesake, the Barbara dear to me. Santa Barbara who can stop storms and tremblings, help me today. Amen. Holy Mary, Mother of God, pray for our sins now in the hour of our — now in the hour of our death. Amen. With the finger tips of his right hand he touched his forehead, his breast, his left shoulder and his right. He asked it in the name of Father, of Son, of Holy Ghost, Amen. Crossing the thumb over the bent forefinger of his right hand to make the cross, he kissed it, and got up from the rail, taking his cape and montera. His shoes squeaked going toward the door; he heard himself plainly, walking out to the bulls. He knew he was afraid.

When he came out of the chapel he carefully pushed his montera down straight on his head and arranged his cape over his left shoulder, gathering it about his waist tightly and holding it there with his left hand. Then he decided he would light the cigar Marcelo Cadena had given him, to wet the dry taste in his mouth. Goyo borrowed a match and held a light for his matador. The toreros were all silent now, lined up in place for the procession. Luis stood at the head of the single file of his peons. At his right Paco Saya had taken the sobresaliente's position, alone in the center, a pace behind the two matadors of cartel. Pepe stood even with Luis at the far right. With the addition of the local union toreros, the cuadrillas were evenly lined behind the matadors.

The last five minutes before four o'clock were always the longest, always the hardest, for brave men or cowards regardless, who stood behind the cuadrilla gate in the shade under the stands, looking out into the sun, waiting. It always smelled the same there in the shade under the stands with the tobacco smoke and the horse manure and the nameless acridity where the sun never reached. It was the smell of the feeling of the bulls. Luis Bello smelled it, his mouth dry and his hands sweating.

He could see the bulls waiting now in the dim chiqueros behind the red door, waiting for Luis Bello. His mind built their blackness and their size high and massive waiting for him there in the dark place. He could hear the rattle of their horns hitting the wood and feel the terrible power leap into them with the jabbing bite from the barb of the divisa as they came out of the door, and the surge of the blackness heading for Luis Bello.

Sweat pricked out on his forehead. The cigar tasted bitter. He concentrated on the gray smoke wreathing from the ash, trying not to see the bulls waiting, feeling the seconds, the minutes, thin as smoke, and ticking like the clock on the mantel at San Angel. He felt the mystery in his head of four o'clock in the afternoon and how it always came. And how it always went away. How the sun went down and the plaza was empty then. Between now and the time the plaza is empty — not long — and whatever it is for Luis Bello — when the sun is down — when the plaza is empty —

The opening drumbeats of "La Virgen de la Macarena" abruptly pounded the air and brought a great shout. The gate in front of Luis Bello swung open. He saw the sand and the crowd before him and he straightened. He pulled his cape tighter around his waist, feeling the wet sweat in his hand on the silk, and he threw his cigar in the dirt.

He heard the brave steps in the drumbeats. He felt the dark shape the music made against the sky. He listened to the trumpet speak, looking into the sun, and when the drumbeats carried the brave steps away, it was four o'clock sharp in the afternoon.

In the cheering, the band began to play again. Luis Bello reached up and took off his montera with his right hand and brought it down to his side. Pepe and Paco uncovered, following suit, all three matadors signifying by this action their first appearance of the season in the plaza of Cuenca.

Then Luis stepped out in time to the music; Pepe and Paco caught the step, and then the toreros behind them, and the parade moved marching in the sunlight. The applause swelled in a clamoring roar. Luis Bello felt it, felt the need to respond to it. He felt it wryly, as if it could not belong to him. But he lifted his eyes from their levelness, he had to lift them. His lips made a smile in spite of themselves: the plaza stood cheering. Across the ring, in the shadow under the shady side, he halted at the barrera, the smile gone from him. He looked up at the Judge of the Plaza in his box, then gravely bowed. Tacho took the parade cape from him across the barrera; Luis turned to face the ring and the continuing applause. He called Pepe then, and brought him to his side, holding his arm. The two brothers stood together for a moment, taking the plaudits of the public of Cuenca.

They saw Eladio Gomez coming out of the cuadrilla gate across the ring. His brown hat was in his hand and a boy carrying a sign was with him. Stopping in the center of the plaza, unsmiling, Gomez held up his hand. He pointed to the sign with his hat. A MOMENT OF SILENCE. IN MEMORY OF THE VALIANT TORERO JUAN SALAZAR. With a rustling murmur the crowd stood and the men uncovered.

Luis Bello felt his jaws clench. He stood stiff, looking down at the sand, hearing the small sounds in the moment of silence. The dirt of the filth of the dirt of the moment of silence. Looking down, his eyes wandered from the ground and he saw the black band on his left arm. He saw how black it was. The uncle. Salazar. Raul. Linda. And Barbara so long ago. Everybody in the world. Everybody finally. The color of the coffins, of the bulls, of the nights.

When the moment of silence was over, Luis Bello put his montera tight on his head. He walked behind the barrera and asked for the water jug. He rinsed his mouth, tasting the lime, and spewed the water. It rolled along the dust in little pellets. He watched them. Then he took up his fighting cape, letting it fall unfolded in front of his chest, and leaned against it behind the red plank shield, looking out across the sand. The huge, empty, wide, lonesome desert of sand, rimmed with voices, waiting.

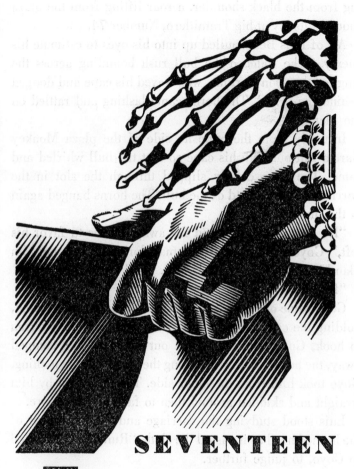

SEVENTEEN

THE BUGLE BLEW and the waiting was finished. Luis saw the toril door open, saw Chon Munoz peering into the darkness, poised with the divisa ribbons in his hand. He saw the horns come from the darkness; Chon's hand swept down. The bull plunged into the sun, ribbons flutter-

ing from the black shoulder, a roar lifting from the plaza
shouting its joy at big Tramillero, Number 74.

All of Luis Bello pulled up into his eyes to estimate his
enemy as he watched the bull rush bounding across the
ring for the peon Enrique, who waved his cape and dodged
behind the shield. The horns came lashing and rattled on
the planks.

Instantly from the opposite side of the plaza Monkey
Garcia ran out with his cape so that the bull whirled and
came. The peon calmly slipped through the slot in the
barrier one step ahead of the bull. The horns banged again
at the timbers.

"He sees good, near and far away. Seems to favor his
left," Goyo said, close to his matador's ear, helping him
plan his campaign. "Lots of bull. Shall I take him?"

"Run him."

Goyo came out fast. Ten paces from the barrera he cited,
holding the cape before him. As the bull rushed, lowering
to hook, Goyo swung the cape out sideward and stepped
away, the horns sliding fast along the cloth, finding nothing.
Goyo took him from the other side. The bull went by him
straight and skidded around then to face him for more.

Luis stood studying the carriage and the movement of
the horned head as it passed the cloth. "Run him," he called
to Goyo, to judge further.

The peon of confidence took a few steps backward, tacking around, glancing at his terrain. As the bull started for
him, he held the cape in one hand with the cloth dragging
while he ran for Enrique's burladero, zigzagging in front
of the bull with the horns chopping after the veering cloth.
Goyo controlled his twisting run so precisely that he flung

himself into the shelter a split second before the pursuing horns hit wood. The bull turned from the planks, baffled and breathing hard. Goyo looked inquiringly toward his matador.

It was time. Luis heard the cheer as the crowd saw him step out with his cape. He felt as if his feet did not meet the ground, as if his hands had no sense of the cloth they gripped so hard. Here it comes. The size of a house. He saw the lunge with the head going down, with the eyes glaring at the cloth, and he flipped it outward and stepped back as the black mass hurtled by, pounding the sand.

Holding the cape with both hands low, he turned profiling, citing for the dangerous thing, the beautiful thing the crowd waited for. He saw the horns scoop down, he felt his wrists send the cape in a proper tiny flick outward to take the horns — and something happened in his feet, in his arms. He jerked the cloth high and away, stepping back, choked with a surge of dread he could not control.

I got to make one. I got to glue it down. Jesus and Mary, I want to, I want to stand still and get that rag swinging low and slow, O help me Jesus, I got to.

The bull came back and Luis Bello tried. With all the dread in him he tried, and he jerked away like a frightened amateur when the horns arrived. The stunned plaza reacted with a shrill jeer.

In the corner of his eye he saw the horsemen enter, jogging close to the barrera. He took the bull again, stepping back, spinning the cape in a tight fast curve that wrenched the bull around short, stumbling and skidding on the sand. When he tried to walk away, the bull came after him; he tossed his cape one-handed, deflecting the charge,

and let Enrique worry the bull away while the crowd
hooted.

Luis Bello's voice was hoarse. "Set it up for the ponies,
Goyo. Tell them to plant a ton of iron."

The Jackdaw saw the big bull start. He braced himself
in his iron stirrup, gripping the lance under his right arm,
aiming, to take the shock. Overanxious, he reached out
jabbing too soon, before he could set the vara high in the
crest. The iron ripped into the bull's left shoulder, with the
crowd howling at the crippling placement. The picador
leaned hard against the lance but the horns shoved on,
striking, the great neck muscle tossing, the horse and the
Jackdaw and the lance all rising up and slamming down
sideward on the sand. A lump of wadding flew from the
belly pad as the left horn tore and the black nose bumped
trying for the kicking horse's entrails, while the capes came
flapping.

As senior matador it was Luis Bello's duty to take the
bull away, work him through a set of figures in a quite,
and leave him facing the next horseman for the second
pic. Luis ran up from the right, automatically, flipping his
cape over the bull's face to blind it, while a mono and the
peons pulled the Jackdaw from the other side of the fallen
horse. The horns jerked the cape from Luis's hand. He
stepped back, the bull tossing to lose the blinding cloth.
When it fell, the bull swiveled for Luis.

Goyo cut across flashing his cape, swerving, turning the
bull, holding him. Luis picked up his torn cloth and gripped
it for citing. When the horns came for him, he could not
plant his feet. He ran like a peon, veering the charge away
with a cape toss as the bull went by, headed for the Little

White, ready on his horse. The crowd howled, cheated of the quite they expected of the Swordsman of Guerreras. *Yai* the coward of a filth from Guerreras! Luis heard it, with the sweat on his face.

He saw the Little White nail the bull's withers with the lance, and stay mounted, pushing hard, delivering the iron. Plenty of iron. He saw Pepe Bello dance out, taking the bull away, flashing his quite with swirling cape, wheeling the bull to a stop facing the Jackdaw again, remounted on his shaken nag. Luis heard the applause like a probe twisting in him. He watched the Jackdaw strike the vara into the pushing shoulder, with the horse standing stiff at an angle, the bull feeling the iron now and stopping, with the blood glistening red on the blackness.

He heard the bugle signaling the horsemen to leave plaza, and saw the cape of Paco Saya take the bull away. Walking toward the burladero of the matadors, Luis heard applause and brought his eyes around to see Paco swinging with the cloth gathered and held at his hip, wringing the bull around sharp and fixing him to the spot by the twist of his cape. Seeing Paco smiling up at the stands, Luis turned away and walked behind the planks. The horses were through the gate. Goyo trotted up to his master.

"You and Monkey nail sticks," Luis ordered. "Nail hard and see if you can hook four pairs on that mountain before the frilling bugle."

He heard the catcalls and the whistling as he stood behind the barrier while his peons served the banderillas. He was conscious of the tense good humor of Pepe and Paco standing by him, fresh from applause. They said nothing. He felt it like a stone, watching Goyo and Monkey as they in turn cited and ran quartering toward the bull, barbing the pairs of bright sticks into the bloody shoulders, fast.

Too fast, too fast, for Luis Bello now in the last moments before he must take his sword and go alone. His eyes were fastened to the horns. He could feel them. He could feel everything about them. Horns still high as a bandstand. He heard the bugle. Tacho handed him a muleta.

Luis Bello stepped out of the shelter. Tacho offered him the red sword handle over the top of the planks. He drew it, seeing the steel slide out with the emptying leather going limp in Tacho's hand. Holding the furled muleta and the sword in his left as he had held it hundreds of times, he lifted his montera with his right and looked up at the Judge, asking the routine permission to kill. He saw the Judge nod.

Like it was easy. Like it was nothing at all.

He handed Tacho the hat over the planks, seeing his servant's gray frightened face. He wondered if he looked as gray as Tacho, and turned, taking the sword and cloth into his right hand, letting the muleta fall unfurled, walking out to the horns.

All of Luis Bello, the breath he took, the blood that pumped through him, the hands and wrists that held his knowledge, the eyes he saw with, the feet that felt the sand under him, all of Luis Bello, all of him cried out the sentience of being alive as he stepped toward being alive no longer.

Step by step he came to where he stood ready before the horns. There at the cruel place his mind groped away from its task for a wry instant. It tried to tell him he had done the hardest part now, the hardest part. Walking out to it, knowing it. The crowd hooted because he was afraid.

He shook the muleta, luring the horns to him.

The cloth in his right hand led them past. His mind was of no use against the horns. He did not elude them by any process of thought: the years he had spent in the plazas were his servants now, rushing up to guard him while his eyes and his wrist and his feet took desperate command to lead the horns safely by.

The bull turned and came back; he led it, jerking the cloth to stop it sliding, twisting. Then he stayed close. He gave no distance for a charge, smothering the assault with the flapping muleta as he backed away side-stepping, keeping the horns from passing, chopping the cloth from side to side in front of them, with the bull heaving after it a raging step at a time. He held the cloth at arm's length, reaching out, and when the horns gained and chopped closer, he doubled back fast around them, along the harmless flank.

In the onslaught of the horns all feeling left him but the value of his life. His yet living eyes, his wrist, his feet commanded him. Keep chopping, backing, jerking. Stay with it. Stay alive, stay alive, Luis Bello. Wrench the monster neck. Tire it. The horns will come down. Then you can kill it. You can walk away if you kill it. It's your chance. Keep wrenching the cloth.

His right wrist went numb with the twisting weight. He could feel his hand slipping and he stepped back leading the horns out and away. The beast wheeled to face him and stopped, racked for breath. Watching the horns, he changed the muleta to the other hand.

A cushion from the stands hit near his feet and skidded along the sand with a puff of dust. The bull snorted and lunged. He saw the left horn coming, coming too far. He stepped back hard, feeling the horn strike his leg and the whirl in terror with the sand in his face, the bestial breath over him, the horns hacking, grooving the ground. Now, O Christ, it's now. Yet he heard Goyo's strident *Yah-hi Toro!* with the cape's whish and the feet led away. His brother Pepe picked him up.

"You all right, Mano? You all right? It was the flat of the horn! It's dry! You all right?"

Luis tried to brush the sand from his wet face. There were grains of it in his eyes. He pushed his hair back. Pepe picked up the sword and muleta and handed them to him.

"The left horn, Luis! He's learning. Come on. Wash your face with a towel before you go back."

Luis pushed away. He walked toward where Goyo and Enrique had fixed the bull. He came up shaken, spitting sand from his mouth, arranging the sword and muleta in his right hand, pricking the sword point into the cloth to spread it.

"Keep on his right, Luis! He's getting heavy. Chop him a little more and then let him have it."

Luis motioned Goyo away.

The frilling children, then the peons, telling me. I'll do it. I'll take it. I'll get it. Father Christ, let me do it soon.

"Huh Toro!"

Let me do it before I fold.

"Huh Toro!"

Let me do it.

The bull was blurred but he saw it gather. He saw the ear twitch and the tail bobble and the whole thing lunge, coming. A man in a sick dream of thrusting horns, he felt the heat, the cud smell, of the crushing blackness he swerved and warped with the scarlet flashing cloth. He grappled swiveling against its lashing closeness, seeing the ruby-red lights in the bulging eyes, seeing between them, coming at him, the whorl of dusty coarse curls flecked with blood drops from the streaming shoulders where the spattered stick shafts jounced and clattered at him, rattling like bones.

The crowd banked up around the rim of his lonely place looked down and jeered him. He heard the shrilling as the horns tossed and thrust. He heard the sound of the crowd seeing the man they paid to be brave writhing for his life, as if the pay were not enough.

It was no faena. It was nothing. It was a dirt of a coward ruining a bull. He heard it, with the stick shafts rattling and the breath hacking at him from the flaring wet nostrils, coming, and his right hand slipping from the cloth.

The horn wrenched. He felt the notched stick under the wool, and the sword handle, leaving his hand. He saw the sword glitter falling and the cloth hanging crazy on the horn. Luis Bello ran. He ran away and jumped the barrera.

A raving clamor pierced at him. Luis Bello ran from a bull. He jumped the barrera. He quit. He beat it for the planks. O the sorry son of a whore, he did it. He took the olive. O that bigshot bastard, jumping the boards. The yellow chickenshit, waving the olive! O the fine beautiful torero. Beautiful like his name, the beautiful pimp of the olive!

The cushions thudded when they hit. They hurt. He was conscious of Tacho and Pepe standing by him yelling, batting at the cushions as they sailed down from the stands at his back. He looked out at the bull standing heavy with the red cloth at its feet, the red the color of blood, the color of the slow pumping rivulets spilling from the shoulders.

"Are you going to kill him, dolly? Or are you going to stand there and cry? What's the matter, dolly? You're not scared, are you, dolly boy?"

Luis turned. He saw the heavy red face that roared it. He saw the thick hand slam the cushion whirling. It grazed his head, raking his ear.

"A pillow for you, dolly boy!"

He touched his ear. It left blood on his hand. Soldiers and policemen were closing around him in the callejon.

Mute, grasping the top of the barrera tight with both hands, he pulled himself up suddenly and flung himself over into the ring and stood on the sand.

"The stuff, Tacho. Gimme. Another sword. Gimme a rag."

He felt nothing, walking out to the bull. He had nothing. Nothing but sand-scratched eyeballs looking at the blurred black bull. Nothing but the sword and the muleta. Nothing but the hands to hold them and the feet to carry him to the place.

Goyo spoke as he went by. "Square him, kid. Line him up, and lay it in. We'll finish him."

The horns came. Luis jerked them, crisscrossing with his cloth, holding tight, tight, swerving, wrenching the neck that reached for him. Doubling back along the flank, he swept the cloth up and outward and backed away, leaving the bull standing fixed, facing him.

"Now!" Goyo called. The bull's forefeet stood evenly together.

Luis backed a half step, taking the cloth in his left, firming the grip on the sword in his right. He turned profiling, looking across his left shoulder at the bull, furling a twist of cloth over the stick of the muleta. Watching to be certain the glowering eyes were fastened upon his cloth, he raised his sword, then aimed along the blade.

His left arm swept the muleta rightward across his body as he ran forward — not straight, but veering to the left — aiming along the sword. The bull's head went down to hook, following the cloth. The horns flashed by to the right as he thrust, feeling the sword enter, turning loose of the handle as the bull jerked it past.

He saw it halfway in, on the forward edge of the right shoulder, crooked. He saw the bull stop, the blood splashing from the mouth, as Goyo ran in flinging his cape to spin the bull around, and Enrique coming in fast from the other side to spin the bull back, wringing the bull from side to side, dizzying the stricken thing to make it fall, to hasten the bright frothing hemorrhage from the sword-pierced lung, while the crowd screamed the cowardice of the sword thrust and the illegality of the dizzying capes.

The brave bull of Las Astas, Tramillero, Number 74, bleeding to death, folded its legs slowly and got down patiently on the sand to die. The union torero of Cuenca, Jose Prado, in his faded traje with the black braid, ran up from behind, with the puntilla dagger. He placed it cautiously at the back of the bull's neck, to sever the spinal cord behind the horns, and he jabbed hard. The bull dropped stiff and sudden on its side, lifeless in a wink.

The instant it was still, shame came sick and fevered into Luis Bello. He walked with it, trembling, toward his shelter behind the planks. He walked by the bull, hearing the mule chains jingle coming to drag his enemy away. As he passed, he looked down at the horns on the sand.

They weren't the ones. They were dead.

An empty tequila bottle skittered across the cushion-spotted sand in front of him.

"O dolly boy!" He heard it. "Is that a spot on your panties? Are you crying, dolly boy?"

Tacho ran out to him.

"Come on, Luis. Let's go. Let's go to the infirmary. Stay away from the planks. Let's get your eyes washed. Come on, Luis. Come on." Tacho took him by the arm to hurry him. The swordhandler's voice was unsteady. "That sack of yelling pus in the rancher's hat! They got him now, Luis. O that bag of shit! The cops have got him. He threw that bottle, too. They're taking him out."

Police met them and flanked them as they went through the cuadrilla gate and under the stands, away from the bleating din. They walked in the infirmary door.

"Bring a senor doctor, please," Tacho asked one of the police. He closed the door. "Sit down, twin. Let me clean off your face. Your ear's bleeding."

Luis said nothing. His eyes were closed when the doctor came.

"What's the trouble?" said the doctor.

Tacho answered. "Can you wash out the eyes? The sand. He couldn't see. He can't see." Tacho was dabbing with a wet towel.

The doctor found boric acid, dumped some in a glass, and poured water in it by the sink.

"No eye cup," he said. "Come over here, diestro. Let me pour this in the eyes."

"Inflamed," the doctor said, holding back a lid, pouring.

Luis felt the stinging watering cool on his eyeball.

Muffled by the infirmary walls, a sudden shouting came in to them. They felt it from all around them, from over their heads. As if the plaza had only one throat, they heard a great Ole! They heard another, cracking sharp Ole! and another, Ole! The sound raveled out into a dim rattle and a roar. In it they could hear the beats of the bass drum. They heard no tune but they knew the tempo of those drum-beats. It was the "Diana," the honor music played in the roaring of a plaza when it was pleased.

"Hold this wet gauze over them for a while," the doctor said. He daubed merthiolate on the bleeding ear. It burned. "You need anything else? I seem to be missing something out there — "

Neither Luis nor Tacho spoke. The doctor slammed the door as he went.

Tacho's feet scraped on the bare wooden floor. "Eyes better?"

"The eyes are all right." He held the wads of wet gauze over them. He did not have to look at Tacho, look at any-body, anything.

The plaza cheered again. Muffled, coming from all around him, he heard it. The sound came to him behind the gauze, there in the grayness tinged with his blood, still pumping, still alive.

"Well," Tacho said. He hesitated. "Must be hooking on the twigs by now."

Go back. Not finished with me, oh no. Not finished until I get it. Until I get it. Walk out to it again. Get it. Really get it now.

He lowered the cool wet wads and blinked, seeing the white, metal-fitted table born unfocused into his eyes, too bright after the grayness, after the nothingness, behind the gauze. He tossed the wads at the sink and stood up.

"The towel, Tacho. You got a comb?"

The swordhandler served him with both. Setting his mouth tight shut so he could feel the muscles clamped at the sides of his jaws, he walked out the infirmary door, down the shady tunnel, through the gate into the noise, into the ring, behind the red planks again.

The plaza did not notice Luis Bello coming back, walking with his swordhandler around the callejon. The plaza's eyes were fastened on a figure dressed in lilac and silver standing light-footed on the sand, a pair of green banderillas held high, poised and pointed at a black bull.

Luis looked out and saw the bull start. He saw his brother Pepe start too, his gay fast tiptoe steps perfectly timed in his quartering run across the curving course of the bull's charge, pausing a fluid instant, pivoting, as the green sticks flashed down into the driving black shoulders and went away. He heard the applause rattle, seeing Pepe walking toward him, toward the burladero of the matadors, coming for his sword. He heard the "Diana" as Pepe walked. When he stepped up grinning to the planks, Luis saw the bursting sweat of elation on his brother's face, his eyes glassed with combat as if he saw visions, and not the world.

Pepe swallowed, still grinning. "You all right, Luis?"

Luis nodded.

The Little O handed Pepe a muleta, and he drew his sword. He stepped out, turned, and looked up at the Judge, for permission. Pepe Bello had practiced the ceremony standing straight and solemn before a mirror, a hundred times. He saw the Judge incline his head, a real Judge of flesh and blood, smiling.

Pepe turned back to the burladero, with his hat in his hand. He stood before his brother. "Luis," he said. He handed him the montera. "I dedicate this bull to thee, Luis. Because thou art my teacher. Because I owe thee everything."

The brothers heard the cruel shrill whistling of the crowd.

"Thank you, Manito. Have luck. Have luck, Pepillo. Have luck."

The lilac and silver blurred in Luis Bello's eyes. He watched his brother walk out to the bull.

He saw him spread the red cloth with his sword and seat himself on the stirrup, the white-painted plank shelf built around the face of the barrera a foot from the ground. He saw his brother citing the bull as a dare, from that position, cornered, seated, his back to the wall. He saw Pepe lead the bull past him with the red cloth sweeping, the crowd on its feet, roaring, and the bull coming back and the red cloth sweeping the horns away.

Pepe danced out from the barrera, adjusting the sword and cloth, holding them out before him with both hands, glancing around fast at his terrain, correcting with a half turn, stopping, standing straight, quiet, citing. The bull came. As the horns touched the extended muleta, Pepe lifted it. The blackness rushed under going up, forefeet leaving the ground, horns heaving for the dramatic skyward billow of the cloth, going by.

Pepe had to run following then, to where the bull stopped and turned, close to the toril door, to face the maddening cloth again.

"Pepe'll have to pull him out of there," Goyo said, by Luis's ear. "That's where he goes for defense."

"The kid's rabid."

"Feeling fever."

"And the horns sticking sideways. Wide."

"Pancho keeps telling him."

"Too frilling wide."

"He's hot. He don't see it."

They watched him work the bull away from querencia, a step at a time, chopping the cloth, leading.

"The kid's keeping his head. Now — "

"Jesus and Mary."

They watched him plant his feet, saw him bring the bull by his belly, the cloth held low, going slow, pulling the horns around like a magnet, pivoting, pulling them by again. Ole! cracked sharp each time the horn grazed and came back and passed once more. When the bull turned away and stopped, winded and heavy, the "Diana" rollicked in the shouting. Pepe stepped to the barrera, calling Abundio for a change of swords.

Luis saw the tension in Pancho Perez's face as his lips moved speaking to Pepe drawing the new sword. He saw

Pepe turn smiling, fixing his cloth in his left hand, going out to the bull.

He saw Pepe standing straight and the beautiful sweep of the cloth molding the man to the lunging bull with a smooth red slow-motion line in the sunlight.

"Look at the kid, Goyo. Torero! We got a torero, Goyo, O Jesus, look at him!" Luis Bello shouted Ole! with the plaza. He shouted it.

The horns went by again, and turned, and came back for the lilac and silver and he saw it happen.

He heard it, seeing it, the quick razzling rip of the silk and Pepe in the air, the red cloth whirling and the smash on the sand, and himself with every cape in the plaza running without thought, croaking dry-mouthed, coming to the place. Running, he saw old Pancho whip a cape blinding over the horns. He saw Monkey at the flank yanking the tail. He saw Ramon Delgado come jumping from nowhere, barehanded, grabbing at Pepe's ankles, pulling him out, out from under, away, through the sand.

Luis knelt down over his brother. He saw the taleguilla ripped half the length of the front of the leg, with the white drawers torn, hanging out, and the blood beginning. Pepe was unconscious.

"Take him. Get him to the table quick in the name of Christ!"

The Jank and the Little O lifted Pepe, with two red-shirted monos holding his legs. Luis saw them running, jogging their burden across the sand, through the gate. He stood there, seeing them go.

They got Pepe. O they got him. The horns of the bulls. He turned his eyes and saw Paco Saya standing calm with a ready cape, holding the bull fixed while the ring cleared. Luis Bello's mind gathered itself in that image. It brought everything together fast, for the first time, since the sound of the ripping silk. The impact hit him like a blow.

All the horns, all the bulls, all the afternoon. I do it all.

He walked toward the planks; Paco Saya came with him. The bull stood waiting. Through the fog of his agony, Luis heard the outcry from the crowd. It yelled at the Judge. Let the sobresaliente! Let anybody kill it. But not that son of the dirt of a coward Luis Bello. Cobarde! Not that friller. Give the Spaniard a sword!

Luis turned, looking up at the Judge. The Judge peered down with a face made of stone.

"Paco." Luis grated it. "Don't fret yourself. When they move Pepe over to lay me on the oilcloth, the plaza's all yours. Luck to you."

Saya's eyes flashed wide for an instant of resentment. He knocked on the wood of the barrera and crossed himself, saying nothing.

Luis took a muleta and unsheathed a blade. He threw his hat on the dirt. The plaza railed at him as he started toward the horns.

No sentience possessed him now, no mind, no body, no hate or love or pride. Death possessed him. The shouters were silent suddenly in the watching plaza.

Nothing reveals so much of what a man has carried within himself, nothing strips him down so bare, nothing probes so sharp into his yet living heart, as the true expectation of violent death in the moment of its approach. It came to Luis Bello now, revealing what his life had planted

strongest and left waiting in him to save him when everything else had been stripped away. It was the molding
smooth red slow-motion line in the sunlight, and when
the horns came for Luis Bello he made it. Death held his
hand as he described it. It curved taut, full and lovely,
and its power like some great current flowing from beyond
fear pulled the plaza to its feet.

Death held to the notched stick under the scarlet cloth
as the line curved out again growing smooth and beautiful
and breaking as the horns went by, and came back, to tempt
the line to its slow swinging tautness once more, Luis Bello
untouched, standing straight and still, a blue golden hinge
for the curve of the cloth and the blood.

Heedless of the horns now as death held his hand, Luis
Bello mounted the sword. He aimed, lunging in crossing
the cloth, seeing, feeling the blur of the circling blackness
of the black band on his left arm as it crossed his heart
below his eyes, feeling the blade sink, feeling the handle
gone, feeling death slip from his hand, from his heart,
to go grip at the horns that lurched away, falling, in the
noise from the high curving verge of the lonely sand.

EIGHTEEN

THE LIFE LUIS BELLO carried with him back to the barrera stirred in him like a stranger whose responses he could not yet measure. As he approached the planks and the crowd banked up beyond, he realized only vaguely that the noise he heard was applause, a scattered clapping rattle as if the plaza had no use now for its throat but only its nervous hands. He walked in the sound as if he were alone and unwatched, carrying a bloody sword. He saw the Jank's face before him suddenly; Luis Bello was a stranger to his life no longer. He made a word aloud.

"Pepe?"

"Not grave. I came to tell you."

Luis wet his lips with his tongue, teaching them to talk again. "God I thank, I thank Him."

The toreros stood around with their capes.

"Father mine, how you sworded! You made my beard grow."

"Shut up. What about Pepe?"

"Bleeding. The leg. But not deep. Not bad, Luis. Saw stars and heard birds, landing on his head. He's rabid again already. Says you had to kill the bug he toasted to you."

"I killed it."

"I told him. Jesus!"

"Go tell him again. Tell him not to be crazy. They got to sew him up."

In the midst of his toreros, Luis Bello took a cape and turned away, finished with words.

The blue shadow had traveled across the sand to its edge; the sunlight's yellow rim touched the toril door. Luis Bello saw the lettering bright on the redness of the door. 23 BRUJO. The bugle blew.

His mind had neither time nor skill to make into utterable thought what he felt, but he felt it strong now: he had never been afraid of death, he had only gotten afraid of the act of dying.

There was a great difference. Death was an abstraction beyond him; dying was a personal violence. Not to have fear was actually not to fear any rending physical act. It seemed such an obvious thing. Yet the only way a man ever learned its meaning and felt it lift him beyond fear was in the doom of combat feeling the grip of death's hand.

As the red door came open again, Luis Bello's mind jumped past the unworded discovery of his heart, to try to frame the feeling fast, with words he already knew. *It comes as God wants it.* He had heard it and said it all his life in the plazas. But in the flash of his mind gathering again toward the violence, it was different: he believed it. It left him free to fight his enemy instead of his fear. Luis Bello was ready.

The package came hurtling from the door. In the center of the plaza it stopped, head up, searching. It stood trembling, lusting to kill. With all the power of the piston drive in the black haunches and tight swelling crested neck, with all the pride in the reaching curves of the high horns, the bull Brujo, the Wizard, the ugly beast the crowd came to scorn for ugliness, challenged the plaza, challenged the world.

The crowd did not scorn it. The crowd saw neither the whiskers nor the hook of the nose; it did not miss the tassel on the tail. It saw the blackness, the primal wrath, and in its deepest heart the crowd was glad it sat in seats high and safe above the beast.

When the peon Enrique stepped out to tempt it, the wrath pointed and came like a shot. Luis Bello watched it wordless. His servant Goyo stood silent, waiting at his side. They felt each other's tenseness growing, saying nothing.

their eyes glued tight to the rushing of the beast. The peons in the side burladeros ran and re-ran it across the width of the sand, making pink moving billows of their eluding capes to test, to slow, the flinging rage.

"Now," Luis said.

Goyo stepped out and the bull came straight like a rocket. It whished as Goyo tossed his cape wide out and stepped back, measuring the charge, turning, receiving it fast and straight again from the other side, and yet again, swinging the rustling cloth.

Luis Bello watched the driving weaponed head. He read it. He felt his instinct and his knowledge rise up, taking hold of what he read with his eyes, filling his heart, so full he could not wait. He shouted.

"Goyo! Lead out toward Monkey! I'm coming!"

The horns raked the emptiness of Goyo's cape and he danced back light-toed into the slot, breathing hard.

"You got one, Luis!" He couldn't help saying it. He had to, fast. "A flag bull sure as Jesus! Torazo! Whiskers on wheels, Luis!" He had to say it.

No one who saw it ever forgot it. Writing a week later in the journal of bulls *La Lidia,* Don Marcelo Cadena called it "a combat without adornment, all tragedy, all truth." A queer thing happened in the course of that combat. The fear that drained away from Luis Bello's heart, leaving him free, neither dried nor disappeared. It seeped strangely outward through the sand, past its rim, up through the stands of the plaza, into the heart of the crowd.

The mob felt the burden of what it had reviled.

The bullring of Cuenca possessed suddenly a quickened life of its own torn by the violence penned and pent within it. It was afraid as it shouted, seeing the blue-gold symbol of its life taunting the darkness and about to be destroyed.

Luis Bello came out with his cape like the music in the "Macarena." When the bull turned and saw him and he could judge the angle of its course, Luis stopped, his body profiled, and he planted his feet, hard. One. Two. Nailed down. The whole plaza heard him nail them. Holding the cape low before his legs, his arms unbent and straight as his back, his wrists feeling the life they sent coursing into the folds of the cloth, he received the assault.

His body turned like some solemn sculpture swaying with glittering arms, sweeping the cloth low, fastening the horns into a long pink swing that pulled the plunging blackness past, and, when it was gone, settled to rest around the immobile slippers on the sand. Weightless and poised, divorced from time in its magic slow lightness, the rosy arc of the veronica flared out, curving and carrying away the rush of the beast as it returned and returned again.

The noise, the crowd, the bullring of Cuenca, melted away from Luis Bello, leaving him alone with his wrists and his cloth and the slashing great blackness.

When it came again, he felt his hands at his right hip holding the gathered folds of the cloth as he spun sharp whirling, wrapping the blackness coiling close. He heard the whuff, the grunt of the bull hurt as he wrenched it hard around; he knew he had it nailed, and he walked away, his back turned taunting to the baffled horns. A cracking burst of applause hit him like a blast as he turned. There was music. He neither looked up nor smiled. Horsemen rode into the plaza.

The Little White was too late with his lance against the

speed of the charge, too late with the iron that tore blood from the terrible neck. He felt the jolt smash, lifting, and he went up, high, hearing the iron stirrup bang the planks and scrape; and down, feeling the wrench, jabbing pain, dive sick bright into him. It flung him over the barrera.

Luis saw the bull grind in, chopping the nag against the planks. He saw the heads bobbing up and down in the callejon where his picador had fallen. He skipped forward veering, his cape unfolded before his chest. He saw the bull gouging into the pool of red under the sprangled thin forelegs, avid, and he ran whirling by the flank, flapping his cape, "Eeee *hah*, Toro!" The horse was dead.

The wet horns came up turning, reaching. One-handed he swept them out and away with the margin of his cloth, and ran three steps following, cutting around, seeing the bull, the terrain, the Jackdaw, seeing everything, screaming, "Yai *eeee!*"

He gave the crowd its quite. He shoved it down the crowd's dry throat. His cape took the horns four times rushing. Each time the cloth went flowing an instant with them and then spun abruptly whirling opposite, furling around the blue-gold hinge, wrapping it fast in rosy folds, then falling away, the hinge turned, revealed, ready again for the onset of the horns.

As the monos carried the Little White to the infirmary, the bull ripped at the Jackdaw. The picador shot the stick hard and lucky into the charging crest and bore down, bringing applause, all his body against the grip of his huge hand on the angled shaft, leaning out shoving, the blood welling, the horns lashing; and he held it and stayed, pushing, reining, to ease away. When the iron lost its hold and came free, the bull thrust, recharging, blind to the flapping capes, raging for the horse. It was too quick and too close under for the Jackdaw to fend it. The vara slipped, fumbling, the bull struck, the horse sprawled.

In the shrill cry of the plaza, Luis heard the foghorn anguish of his picador pinned by the leg under his mount.

"Mother of God get this cathedral off, O Mother of God this cathedral — "

Three whipping capes got the bumping nose, the grooving horns away. Goyo and the monos lifted the Jackdaw groaning and helped him through the slot in the planks. The horse was done; it could not gain its feet. The dagger of a mono, acting on orders, with reluctance sent the broken thing beyond pain and terror.

The union pic of Cuenca, Gonzalo Olanda, rode in, yellow with his fear. Goyo bellowed at him above the shouting.

"Get moving! Move up and plant one! Do it!"

The bull came without prompting; in self-defense Olanda put up his vara, and hoped. He held the iron too high. It only scraped sliding off the lunging back. The horns hit. Horse and rider went down with the plaza roaring, the capes flailing, the bull swerving out of the tumbled melee in a wild quite by Luis Bello that brought Oles.

Goyo was shouting. "Yai! We're running out of cavalry!" He danced toward the one remaining horseman, mounted by the planks. "*Soup!* Deliver it! You better deliver it!"

The Soup delivered. A puyazo. The iron struck into the withers and held, while the Soup pushed praying, and the bugle blew.

"Take it, Saya!" Luis grunted, out of breath. "Don't

twist hard! I want him. I'm going for darts." He walked
fast for the fence, calling over his shoulder. "Set up for
sticks, Goyo, I'm hooking them. Watch! He'll take them
al quiebro!"

Paco brought the bull out and turned him with a snaking whirl of his cape swinging around like a dancer's
skirt, while the Soup and the union labor got their horses
from the ring.

The bull stopped still, alert, taking breath. The long
hairy whiskers along the brisket were caked damp against
the glistening hide. Wet red pumped rich on the shoulders
by the tinged green and gold of Las Astas.

Tacho handed a pair of banderillas over the top plank.
His voice shook. "Remember the leg, Luis! Watch it, O
watch it when you run!"

"I'm not running." Luis turned away with a stick in
each hand.

He walked out very slow, the sticks pointed down, his
eyes checking the positions of his peons with their capes,
and then turning intently to the horns. Twenty paces from
the bull he stopped still, feet together, body straight.
Slowly, with grace, as if he commanded some great music,
he brought the sticks up pointing, holding them high,
higher yet, rising on his toes, lowering slowly, arms out-
spreading, in the silence, pointing at the beast. He saw the
bull's eyes fix, the hoofs gather. Suddenly he hit the stick
shafts together with a clack and called "Toro!"

The crowd rose, sucked to its feet by the hurl of the
bull toward the unmoving, pointing arrogance of the man.
At some split perfect instant before the horns scooped
down, the blue-gold figure swayed on its rooted feet. It

flashed the sticks out sideward, luring, and swayed back, lifting, then flashed the sticks down, the horns grazing by, the empty-handed figure standing still, the sticks carried away like magic high in the rushing shoulders, the plaza finding its voice tearing its throat, seeing Luis Bello walk untouched toward the barrera, for another pair. Lured away by the capes, the bull plunged, pitching its head with the pain of the barbs.

When the great stained crest lunged by him again, carrying the second pair clattering in the wild cry of the crowd, Luis Bello stood too close. The bull's flank bumped him and he stumbled, wringing a scream from the stands as the peon Enrique's cape flared, taking the threat away. Goyo ran to his matador as he headed for the planks.

"Luis! No! You put Jesus in my mouth!"

"I'll hook the last ones running."

He felt the twinge as he came cutting across the face and straightened, in the instant as the horns passed and he darted the sticks down. The leg twisted as he pivoted; he felt it go, falling, his hands hitting the sand, his eyes jerking around seeing the bull skid turning and Monkey Garcia snaking his cape, holding the bull in the turn, taking it pounding away. He heard the bugle. He felt Goyo's hand helping him up.

"The leg," Luis said. "It folded." He hit it with his fist.

He came to his burladero hearing the "Diana," and rinsed his mouth from the jug and wiped his face, before he took his hat and the cloth, and drew a sword. Turning from the planks he looked out for a moment upon the ring.

He saw the bull waiting with the tight cluster of the sticks flowering from the dark shoulders. He saw the two quiet mounds, the dead horses covered with gray raveled canvas on the sand by the planks. He saw the crowd, the lines of many faces, and the colors sloping high to the pennants on the rim, and beyond, the empty blue. He heard the living hum of the plaza de toros. He felt it.

He stepped out and stood very straight, raising the montera high above his head, holding it, looking up, turning slowly right and left, saluting the circling plaza. In his hand at his side he held the unsheathed steel and the cloth the color of the final violence, the red shuttle to weave the darkness about him. In the shout of the plaza he could not hear the sound of the words he spoke. He neither heard them nor understood them exactly, but they came to him. He said them: "I dedicate this bull to all of it. All. Knowing bravery has grace." He tossed his hat over his shoulder, and went to the bull.

He led it past him, raising it as if its threat soared weightless with the scarlet lift of the cloth. Pass of the Death, toreros named it, opening a faena, like a wide waving of a banner before furling death closer about.

Luis Bello entered the terrain of his enemy feeling his toes reach out holding to the earth. Then he swung a low scarlet line of his cloth, pulling the horns past the parcel of life hot in his belly, drawing them around and tempting them again, flat-footed, feeling that life working like a hinge on a door of dying, opening, and closing and opening again.

The bull came ravening with his blood-lined nostrils centered in the cloth and when he left it he turned and came back straight unasked, like bulls of triumph in toreros' dreams.

Dizzy with the spin of the scarlet line, with the horns, with the death he pulled close about him curving in the sharp crack of the Ole each time death came surging, Luis Bello felt without thought how the bull began to falter, winded, how he must repair the steps of his terrain and the grip on his cloth; as the horns came again he led them past and spun the tight whirl of the molinete to stop the bull's charges and pause a moment, before he began again. His leg failed him as he spun it.

He felt the flashing wrench of the blow on his back, ripping silk jerking as he slammed down seeing the shape loom gugging, hearing the bumping scrape of the horns. He felt the queer jerk at his foot, stinging numb, the capes flapping like big curtains in the noise, the hands under his armpits pulling, the rim of the plaza tilting gray down.

Twisting, he saw the Jank's face over his shoulder, feeling the Jank's solid hands holding; he struggled from them, coming to his feet shaking the gray blur from his head, feeling the hang of his heavy jacket ripped up the side. He looked at his left sleeve torn open, and the red on the whiteness of his shirt under his arm. He saw the black band. It was half torn away from the golden sleeve, ripped loose by the horns.

He took hold of the hanging blackness, gripping his fist tight around it, and he jerked it off. It seemed important. He threw it on the ground.

"That thing," he said. "Now — "

"The infirmary," Tacho said.

"Frill that."

"You're bleeding!"

"Not me. That's from the bull. Gimme a towel."

"The foot, Luis! You're barefooted. With the slipper gone and the stocking destroyed."

"The foot's still there." He looked down at it to be sure. "Shut up and gimme that red rag and a hatpin."

He grabbed the muleta and sword and shoved away. The plaza stood up screaming, seeing him come, with his bare foot, with his jacket riding crazy across his back and the shirt hanging with the red on it. He heard the voices, "No, Luis! No!"

He came holding the sword pointing downward in his right hand, and the red cloth in his left. He cited, talking.

"Now. Toro, Torazo. Great bull. I'm tired of waiting. Let's take the package. *Harrhh Toro!*"

The plaza never sat down again. It stood as the red line flowed out and took the horns, carrying them now so that death wove and braided tight with the gold and blue and magic scarlet. Luis Bello's lips pulled back, baring the unfleshed grin of his skull. The pumping darkness of the blood flowing from the shoulders of the beast brushed him, staining his belly, his breast.

Now he saw the horns and not his fear of them. He saw everything about them sharp and clear at last as they came to kill him and he led them away and led them back, closer. He saw the milky mottled amber of their curved shafts. He saw the pale parallel lines of gray in the hazed milkiness melt rich into black at the lustrous points as they came reaching. He saw the ridged scratches, the stain of rust and slime yellow from the guts of horses, the newer smear of blood-shine near the tip of the farther horn. He saw all there was to see about the horns as they rushed him. Suddenly sure of his knowledge of them, he lifted his eyes as they came again. With his face tilted up at the frightened plaza, he led the horns blind across his belly.

Santana in a newspaper account of the corrida wrote that Luis Bello made nineteen linked pases naturales. But he did not really know how many there were; he stood screaming with the rest of the plaza, in the Oles, losing count at the end. Luis Bello did not know. He and the bull Brujo were both drunk with the whirling red-lined turns of terrible battle.

He ended them moving his left foot back to brace himself, citing, leading the bull from his left. The emotion of the plaza sliced at the air with a high hysterical cry as he swept the cloth up rightward across his chest, leading death grazing past his heart, sending it out from him and away.

The bull slowed wheeling to face him again, and stopped. The wild driving power was spent, gone from the massive blackness. The horns were no longer high. Yet the wrath glittered red in the watching eyes, ready.

Luis Bello stood still. His naked foot, dirty and bleeding on the sand, stood precise and unfavored at the side of his one black slipper. Unmoving, chin drawn in so that his head brooded downward, the back of his neck straight up from his straight back where the torn gold hung, he looked at his enemy.

His voice came in a whisper unheard in the shouting. "I love thee, Toro. Torazo. I love every whisker."

In that moment he knew with the sudden instinct and flame of art what he must do. In all his life he had not done it. The plaza of Cuenca in all its life had never seen it.

He whispered again. The technical detail gathered clear

and sure in his heart without need of mind, of thought.

"You can do it, Toro, you're the one! I can do it! We know. Only us. Together."

The shouting caught in the throat of the plaza of Cuenca.

"What's in my soul," he whispered to the bull. "What was born in yours."

Luis Bello turned the torn blue-gold hinge a quarter turn. The soaking, widening red on the whiteness showed under his arm as he furled a twist of the scarlet serge over the stick of the muleta. With a slowness like a dream he raised his sword in the hush, and aimed. His left knee bent from its straightness then, bringing up the heel of his naked foot so that only the bleeding toes gripped arching to the ground.

He flicked the red cloth calling death to him, standing still. The plaza heard him as the cloth moved.

"Brujo!"

The blue gold bent in over the final plunge of the blackness as it came, melted with it, joined it. Slow time slid with the steel, with the red-shrouded horns, and paused; the package opening, breaking, emptying at last, the red line flowing out bearing the horns falling away to earth, carrying the buried sword, leaving the blue gold standing where it stood, straightening, standing free.

The hushed plaza of Cuenca saw all the brave festival in that figure standing free. It felt the flame of it reveal-ing for an instant the secret empty heart of the blackness. It felt the somber magnificence of life lending to death the only majesty death has. And then, alive, sure of its blue-gold hope, the plaza moved. It moved, all of it, in a cry, a roar, a pealing thunder.

Luis Bello, unbelieving, stood motionless. Then he

swayed, with the red cloth hanging in his hand. He walked to the dead bull. He looked at it, and suddenly bent down, reaching out his sword hand, seeing it stained red. With that hand he patted the bull between the dead eyes.

"Toro." He was crying. "Senor Toro."

In the blur he felt them put a slipper on his foot and wipe his face with a wet towel. They hugged him. It made him dizzy, looking up, seeing the plaza whirling white with the whirling handkerchiefs, the people all standing in their seats whirling, jumping up and down, waving their arms, bawling.

He felt the two hairy black ears they put in his hands. He felt the cry pierce him in the din and turned, seeing Goyo running to him with a length of limp black cylinder like a piece of hose. He heard them laughing as he took into his hand the untasseled tail of the brave bull Brujo, and then stood with it, unlaughing.

The mules galloped, dragging out the dead sorrowful bodies of the horses.

And then Goyo came trotting in the rising din, in the dizziness, handing Luis Bello the dusty foot the Judge ordered cut from the leg of the bull.

Goyo grinned. His eyes were moist. "Forgive the hacksaw, kid. I don't know how to cut feet! No practice."

Lacking its ears, its tail, its right hind foot, lacking its noble life, the bull was dragged by mules with flags in their collars, three circuits of the ring and out the arrastre gate, while the stands stood, saluting.

In the unceasing sound Luis walked circling the sand. He held his black trophies high and he tried to hide his limp and the hurt under his arm as he went. Flash bulbs winked bright. Hats sailed down thick. Coats, scarves, handbags, high-heeled shoes, shirts, flowers, cigars. His peons followed along dragging their capes according to the ritual of triumphs, stuffing cigars in their pockets, holding flowers in their hands, tossing the rest back into the stands.

Eladio Gomez piled through the opened gate in front of the toril door. His brown hat fell off and rolled in the sand. He embraced Luis Bello.

"A bath, a bath, Luis, never have I seen it, felt it, but for God get to the infirmary!" His voice jerked. He almost blubbered. "Here is the representative of Las Astas!" Gomez pulled Policarpo Cana into the ring. "Take him."

Luis took him, linking his arm. He came bashful, walking spindle-legged in his tight charro pants, gripping his crimped straw sombrero in both hands.

"I'm the humble," he kept saying. Nobody heard him. "Not for me. Ovations for duenos, not for me!"

"Ole Las Astas, vaquero! Ole the guardian of the casta!"

Luis Bello tossed the trophies up into the weaving rows of faces and flapping arms, hearing the girls scream. He saw the respectables in the expensive seats as wild as the sunny-side hoodlums. They all stood waving their arms, howling. It made him very dizzy. He saw Cofino, his hair mussed, pounding a man on the back, his mouth forming words nobody could hear. The first-row regulars yammered at him, wringing their hands. As he looked up in the blur he saw one still figure. It stood stiff, face upturned, calling heaven to witness. Tears rolled down the cheeks and caught in the white mustachios. The old Spaniard Iriarte. He looked down from his ecstasy suddenly and bellowed.

"Recibiendo! Receiving, he killed it! His feet planted

on the mother rock, Ai God of my life! Recibiendo!"

Don Marcelo Cadena, the portly critic of bulls, stood jerking his double chins up and down, beating his hands together.

There was a final thundering roar when Luis Bello stood with his arms raised hurting, in the center of the sand. As he came toward the planks to enter the burladero again, his peon Goyo Salinas stepped out with a sudden flourish and inspiration. He whirled out the rosy fullness of a fighting cape upon the ground for his matador to tread on leaving the sand of the ring.

"Que tio!" Goyo said. "Que tio mio!"

"*Yeeeee Luis!*" Paco Saya's eyes were shiny wide. He almost sang what he said. "The faena with four kidneys! Ole tu gracia, bello Luis!"

The bugle blew.

Luis Bello felt his face creasing into a grin at last. He slapped Paco on the back. "We got another one coming out, kid!"

"Christ of the Misery, Ai Luis!" It was Tacho with a towel. "In your condition?"

"Fight a bull? It's what I do, swordhandler."

NINETEEN

REGALON, NUMBER 37, came jumping.
"Take him, Paco! I'll be there in a minute." Luis stood
behind the planks while Tacho tried to fasten the side of

his jacket together. The swordhandler's hands trembled, feeling the wet red. He bit his lips.

"You shouldn't, Luis. You — "

"When you finish the needlework, get the trash out of my left shoe. And shut up." Goyo and Pancho Perez were running the bull. "Delgado, what's new from the oilcloth?"

"The White's ribs are not good from raking the planks. And Father Jesus, the knot on his head! Jackdaw suffers where the pony sat in his lap." The Jank spit. "For a business, the hell with picing bulls! Here comes the Soup. And that son of a local whore on a horse. I hope he gets a horn in his windpipe."

"The oilcloth took a load today," said Monkey, dry.

"Delgado," Luis said. "Thanks for pulling Pepe out. You pulled me out too. A regular Red Cross wagon with the siren blowing. What you trying to do?"

"Don Luis. I will tell you. I want to manage a couple of bullfighters. I want to sign contracts for Bellos and smoke Havana cigars."

"Bandit! *Eehoh!* Get going, Tacho. For Christ's sake you're not Madam Morena of Valencia. I got a bull waiting."

The plaza was dulled by long expense of spirit. It was tired. The day itself seemed spent. Only the pennants on the rim caught the lowering sun. A chill crept into the shadowed cup, below the deepening empty blue.

Out on the sand Paco Saya felt the dullness, the lateness. It entered his wrists. He tried hard, leading the horns and swinging; the crowd was not impressed. Its mind wandered. It was listless watching picadors serve iron, cautiously, into another black bull's shoulders.

Holding to the planks while Tacho sewed, Luis felt the dullness, the lateness, grow. Winding out now to its end, the corrida lost its pace.

"Delgado! Get out there and stir that Spaniard up. Shove those horns under the Soup and tell that friller to lay one on!"

Nobody watched the last vara. A rattle of applause by the cuadrilla gate turned the crowd's eyes. The rattle grew into a cheer. Luis looked up, and jerked away from Tacho's needle. He saw Pepe walking around in back of the planks, coming. Pepe was grinning, waving at the crowd.

"What the hell are you doing?" Luis grinned too.

"I got business."

"Is that so? The Little O bring you a chair?"

"Watch me, Mano. I owe you one, you know."

"Like hell. Like hell you get in that ring."

"Like hell I don't."

The horsemen were out. The bull was waiting.

"You don't look like Sunday on the Paseo yourself."

"Frill that stuff, sonny. Goyo! You and Monkey get busy with the darts."

Paco ran in from the ring. He reached over the planks and patted Pepe on the back. "Hola, Pepillo! How about letting me hook on the twigs? You can't run with that leg — "

"He can't do anything."

"Sure, Paco," Pepe said. "Hang some stickers on *my* bull."

He took the banderillas from Goyo's hands, and gave a pair to the Spaniard. "With pleasure," Pepe said, looking at Luis. The plaza was interested. It applauded.

Paco nailed the banderillas with a high Sevillian flourish and danced back to the burladero.

"The salt and cinnamon, Pepe! Gimme some more. The alegria!"

He laid on another pair, high and perfectly placed in the withers, and ran back in the applause.

"Just a minute, goats." Luis stepped out on the sand and bowed to his brother so the crowd would see it. "Petitioning a pair of sticks from the diestro." He lowered his voice. "Gimme, goddammit."

"Eh Luis! In the name of God!"

"Gimme those things."

"Jesus Christ, let me break off the thread!" Tacho wailed, coming out of the slot. "The needle's hanging!"

Luis drew up his knee and broke the two banderillas in half. He threw the handle ends on the ground, wet his thumb, and ran it along the barbed tips of the halves he held, looking up at the stands.

"I'll show you boys how to play with toothpicks." He ran out from the planks. The crowd rose to its feet.

"Ho, Torillo!" he called, stopping in the center. The bull's eyes fixed on him. The bull started.

Holding the two sticks in his right fist out before him, he ran curving in from an angle, across the black nose, as if he gracefully fended the horns with only the colored uprights in his outstretched fist. Safely past, he doubled back around the swerving flank, winding a slow light-toed maze with his steps like an arrogant dance as he took the sticks ready into both of his hands, curving, swaying a final taunt and turning in, quartering across the charge, paus-

ing, feet together, darting his arms down deep over the
grazing horns, pushing back clean, the bull gone with the
stubby sticks in the withers.

He heard the "Diana" in the shouting. He felt a new
stickiness under the arm, hurting, as he ran to the planks.

"Okay, kid. The plaza's awake." He grinned at Pepe.
"You be careful out there."

"Be careful he says." Pepe drew a sword. "Watch me,
Mano."

Luis watched him. He picked up a cape and walked outside of the slot, ready.

He felt the effort of his brother's desire as Pepe Bello
walked out to the horns trying not to limp, trying to pre-
tend there was no makeshift adhesive taped over the
stained rip, over the surgical clamps in his flesh. Luis
Bello read all his own desire in his brother's walk, felt
all his own strength, all his own will gathering, as Pepe
planted his feet and stood straight.

He felt all his own pride in his throat as the red line
curved out smooth and slow, and curved again. He watched
it with his heart and his eyes, hearing the Oles build rolling, feeling the plaza alive again with the pull of the line
flowing slow and red and sure from his brother's wrist,
from his brother's heart.

"The flavor of the Fiesta Brava," Paco Saya shouted.
"Ai Luis, we have a merry trade!"

He saw the color gone from Pepe's face strained suddenly, and the falter pivoting and the fall, feeling himself
running in a dream with his cape, running. He heard
himself holding to his brother's arm, saying *No* with the
crowd as it shouted *No! Don't, don't do it!* — holding.

When his brother shoved away from him, there by the planks with the crowd yelling *No*, Luis Bello saw himself in the dream. He let his brother Pepe go to the horns. He let him go, seeing the red streaming new from the lilac and silver, soaking down dark on the rosy stocking.

Feeling the grip of his hands on his unfolded cape, feeling fire reach down into his feet ready to jump with the flame in his throat, he saw Pepe profile, aiming, and lunge. In, in, far over in, the weight on the good leg, pushing. Leading out, O Jesus and Mary, with it done. Down to the knuckles, a matador de toros Pepe Bello, raising his hand, seeing his bull stumble pitching down as the peons ran in.

Luis caught his brother before he fell, and held him.

"Wake up, Pepe! Wake up and hold this ear! See it? A big black one! It looks good in your hand."

The band was playing "Guerreras, the Place Where I Was Born."

Eladio Gomez was out on the sand bareheaded, shouting drunk with the drama he had made. "Pepe! Luis! Ole the casta of Bellos! Luis! Luis! I'm saving the head of the Brujo, too! I'm having it stuffed. The cost means nothing to me! Nothing!"

The rabble from the sunny side were jumping down swarming in the roar.

"Like hell we're leaving on shoulders! Turn loose, *goddamn you! Don't touch him!* Don't touch me neither! *Frill that!* We're leaking ink. O look at the babes up there smiling, Pepe, look at them. Pepe. Let's walk to the oilcloth. Get away! Bastards! Can you make it, Pepillo? Come on, kid. We'll live forever and both get rich."